ILL-FAME
a novel
Erik Rivenes

ISBN: 978-0-9773471-5-5

Published by
Trampoose Press
P.O. Box 587
Beaverton, OR 97075

Cover design by James T. Egan, Bookfly Design

ILL-FAME

a novel

ERIK RIVENES

CHAPTER 1

May 30, 1901

The rains had come hard in April, and while their showers were meant to bring May flowers, Detective Harm Queen wasn't in a position to stop and appreciate them. The rough path leading down the bluff was soft and slick, and he concentrated hard on maintaining his balance. His expensive shoes and trouser cuffs were spattered with mud, and he cursed unrepeatable words with deft skill as he half-walked, half-slipped after the boy in front of him. Not actually a boy. A man instead, probably, although he had difficulty seriously considering a hobo as anything other than a boy. *These shiftless bastards,* he thought with disdain. Bouncing through life without a care or responsibility. Spending a Friday, a working day, fishing.

And what had caused all this steam in his boiler? Only that he'd been shaken out of his chair in the midst of a damned busy afternoon. Roused by the kid because of a washed-up body.

Your fits of temper have eased, he reminded himself. It had been a hell of a lot worse a few months ago. He knew, now, to take a slow breath when he felt the urge to slam his knuckles into whatever wastrel slowed his stride. He wasn't drinking now, either, a promise he'd made to his betrothed, Karoline Ulland, the calmest, sweetest, most common-sensical woman he'd ever met. He knew he was lucky to have her. It was a high price to pay, ending his decades-old love affair with his whiskey flask, but it had to end. She was too good, too pure, to pollute with his inebriated self. He'd given the flask to his sister, and asked her to dispose of it. That had been difficult, for the flask was a gift from

Doc Ames, the mayor of Minneapolis. A gift from their first days together, when the old man had hired him as a detective during his first term, almost twenty years prior. Doc had lost, and won, and lost again, various political seats since then, but they'd always remained close. Now ol' Doc was mayor again, and Queen was busier than he'd ever been before. So it wasn't that Queen didn't find the boy's claim important. It was only that he didn't want to go climbing down embankments himself. At age forty, and with bad knees made worse in recent months, he preferred the easy, gentle slope of a city street to a muddy river bank. And despite his being chief of detectives, he didn't have any detectives to chief today. They were all out on various pieces of business, and that left him to brave this sloppy late spring day alone.

Yankie reached bottom, and looked back up at him eagerly. A weathered old wheel cap perched atop his head to block the mild sun. He strummed the suspenders that covered his thin white shirt, with sleeves rolled to the elbows. Any respectable citizen would be wearing a jacket, at least, Queen thought. A jacket and a proper hat. But a young vagrant such as this could do damn well what he pleased.

"It ain't more'n ankle deep here, Mr. Queen. T'aint no trouble." The kid's pimples disappeared behind his beaming smile. "Want I should pass you a stick for you to hold on to?"

Queen waved his hand and felt his body tighten as he skidded the last two feet to where Yankie stood, almost falling before his stop.

"Ya made it! Good fer you!"

The detective refused to acknowledge the boy's enthusiasm with a return smile. He didn't feel he owned the kid a kind word as his shoes were soaked with water and probably ruined. And while recent city business had been generous to his pocket book, spending extra cush just because of this dirty traipse made his brow almost touch his nose.

"Let's just be done with this," Queen said. "Where to?"

They were standing on a narrow bank along the swollen Mississippi. About a quarter mile north, the Lake Street Bridge, with its mesh of wrought-iron trestles, lifted and fell in two broad arcs across the water. They were on the Minneapolis side, of course, but the bridge led to enemy territory. Saint Paul. He wanted nothing to do with *that* city, with its rotten Irish mobsters and deceiving whores. Let 'em stay there to stink and quarrel and stab each other in the backs.

"Foller me," Yankie said. They trudged along the bluff, his shoes sucking and popping in the mud. Yankie had removed his shabby brogans and tied them together with their laces. They hung around his neck, allowing him to move more nimbly than Queen, whose own left shoe had twice been lost and found in the muck. Queen clung to budding saplings and tramped forward carefully, grumbling as mud flecked his tie and even his mustache. He wiped it with his sleeve and then sneezed. Hell, he thought. Have I caught a cold now?

A tall, bald man with a bristly brown beard leaned out from a rock and motioned to them with a dirty finger. Queen recognized him from around town. His name was Slim, and he was one of the hobo elders. Queen gave him a curt nod.

"Hullo, detective," Slim said, returning the nod with his own. He wore a baggy brown sack coat. A rope cinched up his trousers. "Sorry to drag you down here like this. I know'd you bulls are busier 'an bees on a rotten apple. But there's somethin' we figgered you'd wanna see."

"Let's make this quick, Slim." Queen lifted his derby and wiped the sweat from his brow with his sleeve. It wasn't a scorcher, but the descent to the river had worn him a little. "Where's the body?"

"Body?" Slim's eyebrows raised to arcs that almost matched the Lake Street bridge's trestles. "Well . . . er . . . I guess you mean this." The hobo held out something silver and yellow in both hands. Queen stepped forward and sighed when he saw it. A northern pike, by the looks of it, with its head cut off and opened wide in a messy massacre of a perfectly good fillet.

"It's a goddamn fish, Slim. Your chum told me there was a body down here."

"A body?" Slim looked at Yankie disapprovingly. "Ain't no body, Yank."

"What's going on here?" Queen asked, anger rising. If this was some kind of jest or mistake he would march these chuckle-heads down to Central station with the toe of his shoe to mark the time.

The kid looked flummoxed. "I figured we found a finger, Slim. That means there'd be a body somewhere."

"Aw, Yank. The fish swallered the finger. That's all we knowed." Slim bowed, just barely, to Queen in deference. "I told you to tell 'em it was only a finger."

"You found a finger in a fish?" Queen asked, disbelieving.

"Here, look, see?" Slim held the fish up by the tail, and pushed his own dirty finger inside the white flesh. "I found it when I was gettin' ready to clean it. Our lunch, as it were."

"So where is the goddamn finger?" Queen's voice strained with the question, and he looked from Slim to Yankie and back to Slim in growing irritation.

Slim patted his coat pocket confidently. "Got it wrapped in my hanky." He pulled a thin, soiled rag from the back pocket of his trousers.

How long has that gone without a wash? Queen wondered in disgust. Slim delicately tugged on the handkerchief's corners, as if peeling a banana, to reveal his prize. Queen leaned in. It was a finger, all right. He took out his own handkerchief, a silk beauty that he'd gotten as a gift from a saloon keeper who'd appreciated his patronage—and protection. Yankie and Slim let out gasps of wonder at its sight.

"Lovely stitching," Slim said.

"Just roll it into mine."

The finger plopped into Queen's handkerchief, and the detective held it close to examine. A man's finger, he concluded. Bits of brown stubble were growing from the wrinkly skin. The bone, he noticed, had been broken and the flesh torn. It didn't appear to have been cut with any knife. Well-groomed too, he decided, from the looks of the trimmed nail. And there was something else, too. Something missing.

Stolen, more likely.

"Give it to me," he snapped, eying Slim with distaste. Generally speaking, he disliked hobos, especially thieving ones.

"I don't understand." Slim ran his hand over his dome of a head. "Give you what, Detective?"

"The ring you snatched." Queen pinched the top of the finger with the hanky and swung it in Slim's startled face. "Can't you see the discoloration? There was a ring on this finger and now it's gone. A ring of substance, it seems, from the width of the band. Don't tell me you didn't find it." Queen felt his anger begin to boil. *Keep it in,* he told himself. *Keep it goddamn in.*

But hell. If he didn't hate people who tried to do one up on him.

Slim shook his head and smiled. "Don't know what you mean, sir."

"Take off your shoes."

The tramp's eyes lit, and his smile got wider. "Whatever for?" he asked.

"Because you keep your booty in your shoes. I didn't fall out of my mother yesterday."

"Come on, Slim," Yankie pleaded, with a look of wild concern on his face. "He's a smart ol' bull and knowed what we . . ."

"I'll put the shoe in yer mouth, Yankie, if you don't stop yappin'," Slim said, his voice sinking.

Queen had had enough with this failed little vaudeville act.

He pulled back his coat to reveal a Smith and Wesson revolver in a shoulder holster. "Take them off," he repeated.

The hobo took one look at the pistol and immediately got to work, tugging off his hole-infested shoe in a clumsy dance. He tried to keep his dangling foot from touching the mud as he tipped the shoe over into his hand. Out came two nickels, three pennies, and a gold ring.

"F-for you, detective," he stammered, hopping forward to deliver the contents.

Queen snapped up the ring and examined it. It was a handsome piece of jewelry, inscribed "1900." He recognized it as a class ring, probably from a high school.

It could be from a dead body. Someone might have leaped from the river bridge in some terrible state of melancholia. Or a murder, perhaps? But the ring was solid gold, which meant some level of influence. There had been no reports of a well-to-do young man disappearing or committing suicide, to his knowledge. And of all people in the city, the detective would be privy to that.

He had a hunch, but a calculated one. The University of Minnesota campus was up river, and he suspected he might find a student there who wanted his ring back. A young freshman, whose father could support the tuition, most likely.

But why would he squander his time searching for the owner of a missing finger? Anyone who wanted his ring back could come to the police station himself and ask for it. He was up to his eyebrows in work at the moment. Colonel Ames, the police superintendent and Doc's brother, had him managing the ten or so detectives on the police force. That was a full time duty, and one of many *legitimate* matters.

The Ames brothers were also taking full advantage of their two year term in power. Other sources of income were flowing in, under the table, and the money was absolutely staggering in volume. Doc was busy having slot machines installed in every saloon and brothel he could arm-twist, with much of the profit swelling his bank account. Brothel owners were shaken down every month, forced to cough up "fines" to stay in business. Instead of the money going to the city, however, it was greasing Doc's palms.

And the biggest graft of all was the big mitt game. This is where Queen was raking in most of his chink. He was in charge of the entire scheme, and it was finally chugging along at full force, after some hiccups months prior. He had two professional steerers working every evening of the week: Billy Edwards and "Cheerful" Charlie Howard. They were like slick, shiny lighthouses, luring in wayward businessmen looking for a good time. Except there was no safe shore. Only the crush of ragged rock. Or more literally, the crush of bones from uncooperative rubes.

And to add to the pressure of work, Karoline Ulland was planning an enormous wedding at the end of the summer.

His schedule was full.

To hell with a finger and a class ring. Right?

He held the ring and the finger next to each other, measuring the match. It had been a while since a mystery had presented itself to him, and the old tug of curiosity began to pique his interest. This should be easy to solve in an afternoon, he decided. And a good story to relay to Doc, who would about fall off his chair in laughter at the thought of a couple of hobos discovering a wrinkled finger in their precious lunch. And Doc would want to know where it came from. And he cared about pleasing the old man.

The finger secured in his pocket, he fished out two dimes and flipped them to the hobos.

"I wouldn't eat that fish if I were you," he said. His mood had suddenly brightened, as radiantly as the turquoise sky above.

CHAPTER 2

The University of Minnesota campus felt like a completely different world from the big city. It stood in grand glory atop the river bluff, upwind from the stench of Minneapolis proper. Here were expansive green lawns instead of dingy, clanging, smoky streets. A dozen solemn brick buildings stood, formally spread amongst the greenery, a statement of the state's noble intent to grant its elite sons and daughters a chance at higher education. Shade trees, now just beginning their burst of buds, dotted the wide spaces. Absent were the crowded, smelly markets, the shanty-filled slums, and the gigantic hotels and department stores that blocked the sun from shining in the detective's usual environment. Queen couldn't grasp this kind of life, but he couldn't help but feeling awe whenever he came here. He himself had only finished high school, and instead of dreaming of college, he'd instead worked his way across the Great Lakes as a deck hand on a Michigan schooner. While he had a natural head for numbers, it'd been his fists and his quick thinking that had developed the fastest in his years after primary school. College had never been an option. His father would have laughed at the very notion.

This was a peaceful place, and he could appreciate its tranquil beauty. Students were taking advantage of the warm afternoon breeze, and sitting in circles in the grass, talking and laughing. More chatted as they walked in twos and threes on the sidewalk that followed the road. Queen pulled his gig to the side of Pillsbury Drive and stepped down. He brushed at the dried mud on his clothes. A couple of young, smartly dressed women wearing wide hats and skirts, clinging to books in their arms, walked past, surprising him with their giggles. One pointed at his face and covered a smirk with her hand.

For a moment he thought to take out his handkerchief and wipe the mud from his mug, but then he remembered what was wrapped inside, and used his sleeve instead.

"Are you a professor here, sir? I haven't seen you before." He turned to see a boy standing behind him. He was a broad-shouldered, well-cut young man, dressed in a tailored gray suit and matching derby, with a satchel strapped to his side. Queen sized him up immediately from the costly clothes and the gold watch that hung from his pocket. Rich parents, he guessed. The kid was good-looking, but with a babyish face, and his chubby cheeks didn't quite match his solidly-built physique.

"Do I look like a professor?" Queen asked.

"Well, you parked your buggy right in front of Old Main," the boy replied with a lopsided grin. "I figured you to be a pretentious teacher running late for class. Who else would have the gall to leave their ride directly across from the front door of the most important building here?"

Queen couldn't help but crack a smile. He liked the boy's quick thinking. This was as good a person as any to start his investigation with, and he extended his hand.

"I'm Detective Queen, of the Minneapolis Police Department."

The kid gave a look of surprise, and then stuck out his hand and they shook. He gave his goofy grin again.

"Pleased to meet you. My name is Richard Darling. But everyone calls me Moonlight."

Moonlight Darling? *The* Moonlight Darling? Queen knew who he was. Everyone who followed the Minnesota Gophers football team in the newspapers did. He was the team's star half-back, who had run with reckless joy over the backs of opposing defenses for the last four years. Of course Queen had cracked jokes about the kid's name like everyone had, when he'd first heard it. It was sappier than the title of one of those romantic pieces of sheet music. The ones with the girl on a swing under the stars and the boy kneeling down beside her. Sentimental gush. But after the kid had broken school records the fun-making stopped. The kid was a bona fide sports hero of the North Star state. For a moment, Queen found himself happily amazed, but quickly regained himself. He still had work to do, and the small talk needed to be brief.

"You fellows really played a fast game this year," Queen said. "Pummeled Northwestern, by how many points?"

"Not a pummel. Twenty-one to zero," said Moonlight with slight embarrassment in his voice. "It was a slow-moving affair."

"But you had dash in the second half," the detective remembered.

"Yes, sir, I did my best." The boy cocked his head a little, and looked at Queen intently. "Can I ask you what your business is here? Not that it's any of mine, of course. I am asking out of curiosity's sake, more than anything."

This was a smart lad, Queen thought. A lot of hard drive, just like himself. If anyone has his ear to the ground at this school, it's probably him. He held out the class ring to Moonlight. The boy took it and his mouth fell open. Queen had been right in his guess. Moonlight Darling knew whose ring it was.

"Was there a finger attached to it?" The kid flashed a wide smile as he asked, unable to hide the dark humor of the situation.

"Here in my pocket," Queen said, and he patted it securely.

"I know the owner. Moonlight pointed to a distant set of figures, lounging on the grass near another building. "Follow me and I'll introduce you to the pup."

"Do you know much about the history here, Mr. Queen?" Moonlight asked as they walked together.

"I don't."

"Dear Old Main." He pointed to the light-colored, four-story, stone behemoth as they walked by. "The first building at the University. Here since the 1850s. It was the only college building for thirty years, in fact. The rest of these," he said, sweeping his arm to the other dignified-appearing structures spread along the road, "didn't come until the last twenty years. It's a school with a crack reputation. I'd always wanted to attend."

"Did you come for the football program?" Queen asked.

The boy reddened, and turned his head away, slightly. "I came to get away from my father."

"Who is your father? A mucky-muck, I'd imagine."

He shook his head with force, and grimaced. "No offense, but not a subject I want to talk about. Mathematics, physics, and Latin. These are the subjects I'm bothered with. And history. I especially love history." He broke another cheery grin. "Finals are around the corner, and I graduate soon."

"Good luck."

"I'll need it. I struggled a bit during the football season. I'm trying to catch up."

They approached a group of boys, smoking what smelled like cheap cigars and lying on their sides in the sunshine. They hopped up, staring at Moonlight like he was some glowing god from the heavens. Queen understood their admiration. The boy had a magnetism to him. A confidence and charm that was hard to resist.

"Going to the dance on Saturday night?" asked one, patting Moonlight on the back good-naturedly.

"Which one?"

"The Senior Promenade of course!"

"I don't waltz and I can't two-step. And there are more important things afoot. That's why Detective Queen is here. He needs to speak to Herbert."

One of the boys' eyes shot wide open. That must be Herbert, thought Queen. He was lumpy-shaped kid, with a sprinkle of whiskers where a man's mustache would normally be. A maroon sweater with a giant golden M tightened around his rotund frame. Queen's eyes went to the boy's bandaged hand.

"You bet your sweet life, Moonlight. Whatever you say." Herbert followed them as they walked to a nearby tree.

"Mr. Queen's got something of yours."

Queen showed him the class ring, and the boy nodded furiously at its sight.

"I've got your finger too," the detective said.

Herbert looked at the bandaged stump where his finger had been, and then to the lump in Queen's pocket. Blood drained from his face and he started to wobble. Moonlight put his big arm around the boy's shoulder and shook him gently.

"You don't have to see it if you don't want to."

"Where'd ya find it?" Herbert asked, looking sick.

"In a fish's gut, just south of the Lake Street Bridge. Any idea how it got there?"

The boy just stared, disbelief in his eyes.

"I'll tell you," said Moonlight, with a glint of excitement. "It's been the talk of the campus. Even made the *Minnesota Daily*."

"I don't subscribe," Queen said. "What happened?"

"Herbert and a couple of others were strolling along the cliff, about there." He pointed to River Road to the west. Queen could see the outline of the city on the opposite bluff; the brown-bricked skyline cut against the bright blue sky.

"When?"

"Two days ago," Moonlight said. He pulled a piece of orange peel from his pocket, and put it in his mouth, slowly chewing.

Probably to freshen up his breath for the multitude of young women drawn to him like mosquitoes to a plump arm, thought the detective.

"And, what then?" he asked.

"I'll say," said Herbert, stepping forward. Agitation wracked his face. "It was one of those low-lifes, doncha know. Preaching their revolutionary drivel."

"An anarchist?" Queen was surprised. Anarchists harassing students on their way to class? Really? It wasn't completely shocking, he decided. Anyone bent on changing the world would most likely find some sympathetic ears on a university campus. But this was first he'd heard of it. "Was it reported?"

"Immediately," said Herbert. "A detective came down and questioned me already."

"Who?" Queen demanded, that familiar fury rising to his chest. He should have been made aware of an incident involving one of his detectives.

"A queer fellow," said Moonlight. "His nose looked like a limp balloon, and not to offend his position, sir, but he reeked of the cheap variety."

Queen knew immediately that Moonlight was referring to Chris Norbeck, Queen's longtime partner, and a man who guzzled more spirit than an Irishman at a funeral. His excessive drinking was the cause of his cauliflower nose, and a rash on his face that looked like someone had poured a boiling pot of water between his eyes.

Despite Norbeck's love affair with Duffy's Pure Malt, however, he was a trustworthy detective, and wasn't the kind to bury an investigation. *So why hadn't the goddamn ass told him about this?*

It had Queen flummoxed.

"He took lots of notes," Moonlight explained.

"And then gave a smile when I told him about the finger," Herbert said with a shudder. "Like he found the whole thing a barrel of laughs."

"I still don't know what happened. About this so-called anarchist," Queen said.

"The little ghoul jumped out from behind a tree. The girl I was with fell down, she was so petrified."

"What did he say?"

"Babbling about the proletariats being suffocated by Carnegie and Hill and Morgan, doncha know. He was waving his hands and screaming. Spit flying from his mouth like we were strolling in the rain."

"What did he look like?"

"He had a thick, dirty black beard. His face was covered in grime. And he was short. Short and rail-skinny."

"And then what? After he'd finished his diatribe?"

"I turned away," Herbert said. "Turned to run, but he leapt at me, doncha know. Like a jack-in-the-box, it was so fast. He grabbed my arm, and I tried to pull it away. Then he did it."

Queen gave a nod, cuing Herbert to continue. The boy took a gulp and looked around anxiously. "As I took my hand back, he latched onto it with his teeth. My finger. Tore it off like a wild animal!"

"And then he ran to the edge of the bluff and spit it out," said Moonlight. "Herbert's blood dripped from his lips . . ."

"Stop, please!" Herbert shouted, covering his ears with his hands.

Moonlight leaned in and whispered. "I can't believe there are anarchists in Minneapolis, Mr. Queen." The detective could smell the bitter orange from the boy's breath.

Me neither, Queen thought. But these were unpredictable times. Who ever would have imagined the old fox, Doc, would make it to the mayor's seat again, either? If the hens in the coop could be so damn oblivious, then anything could happen in this city. "Where did he go once he spit out your digit?"

"He ran in circles, like a raving lunatic, and then made for the trees," Herbert replied.

"Did anyone follow him?"

"A couple of fellows did. He went north to the railroad bridge. His feet were on fire he was so fast, doncha know."

Queen lifted an eyebrow at the football star. "Faster than you?"

"Me?" Moonlight gave a little laugh. "I doubt it. I didn't see any of it, though. I was in class."

So a black-whiskered anarchist was stalking the city's citizens. Queen was uneasy about the news, and he knew Police Superintendent Fred Ames would be, too. And Norbeck needed a good tongue-lashing for sweeping this between the floor cracks.

There was always talk like this. Men sitting around in saloons and coffeehouses with nothing better to do than to spout off against the well-to-do. But this was something more, an unhinged finger-chomping crazy man a few cards short of a deck. If it was the work of an anarchist with a bone to pick, he needed to find out. He wasn't familiar with the dark world of revolutionaries, but he knew someone who might be able to help.

"You want the ring and the finger both?" he asked Herbert. Herbert looked queasy again, so he pulled out the handkerchief and the ring and handed it to Moonlight. "Give it to him when he's feeling better. I don't know what he'd want the finger for, but I sure as hell don't. Maybe you can put it in vinegar or something."

"A pickled finger?" Moonlight asked, with a horrified little smile, as he wrapped it in his own hanky, and passed back Queen's silk one.

"I suppose so. I need to go, boys."

Moonlight put out his hand for a final shake. "A pleasure meeting you, Mr. Queen. I've considered going into police work myself when I graduate."

"Wouldn't your rich father protest that line of work?"

"The hell if I care," he said with a smirk. "In fact, I'd do it just to spite him."

"Well, find me if you do. Mayor Ames would love to bring you aboard. The press would go wild, with a Gopher star in the ranks. And you seem to be a kid with a good head on your shoulders."

Herbert piped up. "Detective. You'll find the rotten fiend, won't you?"

Queen couldn't resist. "Whoever the bastard was that did this, I'll finger him."

Herbert was slow on the jest, his mouth finally dropping.

Moonlight just chuckled.

It had just started lightly sprinkling as Queen got back to his gig. He gave the horse, whose name was Arthur, a friendly pat. He'd bought the horse and buggy with some of the extra cush he'd been earning. His frequent trips to the Ulland house in south Minneapolis required regular transportation, and he also knew Karoline had some hopes for a normal life. Life with him would be far from normal, they both knew. But he figured a trim little two-wheeled gig with a proper high-stepping bay horse might melt her heart a little. It was open-air, and not so useful in the elements, but he anticipated some romantic rides around Lake Harriet with his love this summer, and that was more than worth the upkeep of his new toy.

He wiped the rain-spattered seat with his elbow and began to lift himself up when he spotted a familiar black carriage pull up behind him.

Fred Connor was at the reins. Queen gave him a friendly nod and a wink, and Connor touched his hat with his finger.

"Hello, Fred," said the detective, walking over. "Is the mayor behind those dark windows?"

Connor shook his head. "They're inside the building. Both the mayor and the colonel, in a meeting with President Northrop."

"Sounds devious. What about?"

"Mayor Ames is to give the commencement speech for this year's graduation. They're discussing the details, I think."

That didn't surprise Queen. The Ames brothers were busy solidifying their camp from every angle. Cozying up to students, parents and faculty was part of the job. It didn't hurt either that Doc loved being the center of attention, and the chance to give a speech in front of hundreds would be an opportunity he was too vain to pass on.

"How are you doing, Fred?" They went back together almost fifteen years, he and Connor. Connor was about as trustworthy a man as Queen knew on the police force. There weren't many colored officers in Minneapolis, but Connor, handpicked by Ames to be his personal bodyguard, was not only well-respected, but one of the best pugilists from here to Chicago. A cyclone of hooks and jabs, if called upon to be.

"Well, you know," he replied. "These are busy times, and Mayor Ames thrives on 'em."

"I do know," Queen said.

"What brings you out here, Harm? I thought you were permanently holed up in your office, buried in work."

Queen rubbed a drop of rain from his eye. "I decided to get an education."

Connor laughed. "You've got more of an education than anyone I know. You could teach the graduate class, I'd reckon."

"I'd also like to know why you're here," someone said.

Queen turned to see Colonel Ames, in his dress blue police uniform, stalking towards the carriage. Connor straightened, and Queen felt his body tense. The man approaching, a former army officer, carried himself like a clenched-up, joy-deprived puritan, but he was about as puritan as Jack the Ripper. Colonel Ames was an arrogant son-of-a-bitch on whose good side Queen had managed to land recently, but he knew it was a precarious perch. He was always ready for the other shoe to drop.

"I'd imagine your schedule is full, Detective," Colonel Ames said. His pointed nose gave a long sniff, as he stood, waiting for an answer.

"There was no one else to take the call, sir. It's been a busy couple of days."

"And what was the call, Queen?"

"A student had an ugly confrontation with what appeared to be a man with anarchist leanings." Queen lifted his hand, and bent one of his fingers down. "The boy got it tore off by the teeth two days ago."

"Active anarchists in Minneapolis? Why wasn't I apprised?" Ames pinched his eyes and gave a savage glare. "When did you hear about this?"

"Twenty minutes ago. "

"This needs to be taken care of, Detective. I refuse to allow any infiltration of filthy foreigners into our city."

"I don't know if he's a foreigner, sir."

"Of course he is! What respectable American would attempt such despicable acts as these anarchists do? I don't want a Haymarket riot in Minneapolis, for Christ's sake!

"And they kill kings."

Queen recognized Mayor Ames's gravelly voice instantly. He turned to watch Doc come down the steps, his handsome, graying features furrowed in worry as he approached.

"Good afternoon, sir. I know that this is nothing to take lightly."

"We just can't have this, Harm," the mayor said, putting his hand on Queen's arm. "Anarchists are assassins. They've killed countless officials and members of royalty in Europe. The king of Italy was killed by one last year!" The crow's feet that cornered his eyes deepened. "You can't let this happen!"

And there was the difference between the two men who stood before him and held power in Minneapolis, Queen realized. One was worried about conspiracies and uprisings, and the other feared for his own untimely end. Not that Queen didn't believe a ring of terrorists could be circling the Ames brothers. Anything was possible here. It was just that he felt confident that his own finger firmly felt the city's pulse. He would have heard something before now. If it existed in this town, it was in its infancy.

"If someone is planning a revolution from some dank gutter around us, Mayor, I promise I'll be quick to stamp it out. Right now, though, it's only hearsay."

The burnished buttons on Colonel Ames' collar glistened in the rain as he drew close to Queen. "I don't care if it is or not. I'm not going to take a chance. From now until your investigation's conclusion, Detective, this is your sole concern."

His attention turned from the desperation on Doc's face to the steely expression on the colonel's. Evidently little time for small talk, he thought. Whatever the threat of real anarchists was, it was multiplied a hundred-fold in their minds. And every moment spent chasing what were likely only ghosts took him from the city's real business. Best for all concerned to nip this in the bud.

"I'll make it my priority, sir."

The rain began a gentle increase, sprinkling the greenery and sending the lounging students scurrying for shelter in Old Main.

Fred Connor helped Doc into the carriage, and then waited until his passengers were settled. Connor gave Queen a wry smile and a quick salute as the horses pulled the carriage away from the curb and clopped off. As they left, Queen watched the Colonel stare from the dark window. The stare went past him, and into some far-off, deep place.

The police superintendent was far more concerned than Queen had expected. Perhaps something else was going on in the city. Something he hadn't been made privy to yet.

Best to make haste to the Ulland home and figure this out.

CHAPTER 3

She sat in her half-lit room and closed her eyes, listening to the patter on the window. The rain brought welcome relief. She was tired, and did not relish the thought of another grunting client pushing away on her this afternoon. Even one smelling of expensive French cologne, of whom there were many.

It was a well-earned moment of mental escape, and opportunities such as these were few and far between. Business was brisk, especially for her, here in Madame Nina Clifford's elegant but efficient house of ill-fame. Some of the most esteemed and moneyed men of St. Paul frequented this brothel exclusively, and many of them asked for her name specifically. Nellie Boyce.

That wasn't her real name, of course. She'd never met an inmate who used her real name in this place. That was too intimate. Too much a reflection of her past, and she had tried to put that behind her.

She lifted herself from the plush chair, and walked across the soft oriental carpet that graced her bedroom floor. Finery surrounded her. Enveloped her. From the exquisitely decorated parlor on the main floor, where she'd meet her clients, to the hallways with lush wallpaper and expensive lamps, to her own bedroom, dripping with the finest furnishings: she was surrounded by material beauty. She had a gold-trimmed box in the bottom drawer of her bureau filled with gifts from love-struck men, all of whom promised that in another life they would have married her and stolen her away in a heartbeat. But she didn't want that. Men toyed with women. Told them only what they wanted to hear, to achieve their own sordid agendas.

Love wasn't real. Only lust.

The girls that she worked with didn't seem to understand it like she did. They talked about romance, and dreams, and of being swept away to genteel and respectable lives. But that wasn't how the world worked. She'd learned that lesson in the hardest of ways over the last two years. It had been the bitterest of lessons, filled with wrenching heartbreak and wild, blind fear. And throughout it all, a deep, aching shame. Shame over having been lured off that train platform. For having been kidnapped and raped by brutal men. For having fallen for her captor, a man named Emil Dander. And the worst, most soul-sucking shame of all?

After finally getting her freedom, letting her grandparents think she was dead.

She'd read in the newspapers back in January that her grandfather had come looking for her. Her beloved grandfather, with his stooped back and his grizzled face, who was the best man she'd ever known. He'd been her protector and champion, and the only man who had ever loved her without question. When the article mentioned the name of Dix Anderson, it had first sent her heart leaping, and then plummeting. The joy that came with knowing that he was in Minneapolis, so very close to her, had been ripped to pieces when the shame settled in. She was a prostitute. A sport. An inmate.

And that news would have reduced him to dust.

But then he'd died.

Dust, anyway.

The papers had claimed it was an accident. He'd been in the woods, and a hunter's stray bullet had felled him. Her tears were uncontrollable after that. Buried tears that came out in a rushing, sobbing rage.

She had been devastated. It was a downpour of guilt and loneliness like she'd never felt in her life. Even worse than when she'd been broken in by her captor. At least then she'd known that Grandpa Dix was still out there, loving her and praying for her.

That had happened in January, and now it was May. Her senses had dulled since she'd heard the news. The shame was still there, but it had lessened now that her grandfather was gone. It was slowly and steadily being replaced with dispassion. She grew fonder of material things. She found herself enjoying the world's luxuries. She'd seen the other side of her profession in all of its cruel clarity, the slums and the filth and the beatings and the degradation. Now she was in another world. Well, the same world, but the opposite end of it. She had freedom to come and go. To choose her house and her madam. To go to restaurants and concert halls or sun-bathing at the river. The pain and loneliness still consumed her in moments that she dropped her guard and let herself remember, but she countered those feelings with expensive clothing, fine wine, and all the frills she could collect. The frills of a fleeting, meaningless existence. The more her senses deadened, the more she focused on immediate gratification. And that gratification included a few moments of peace, which she relished.

It was better just to continue on. To hoard as much green as she could, and set herself up independently. She thought about starting a store, perhaps. A ladies' millinery? She fancied hats, and thought she could design and sell them. She understood fashion, and it seemed a natural direction. Perhaps then, if she was legitimately successful, she might present herself to her grandmother. It had been so long since she'd seen her. She missed her plump open arms, and the smell of apple cake on her apron. Her grandmother would take her in, without anger or judgment or disappointment.

That was the only way it could be.

Her chance at a university degree had passed, but she was sure she could run a business.

A soft knock at her door stirred her from her thoughts. "Who is it?" she asked, as she put on a silk robe and went to the door.

"It's Maple, Miss Boyce."

She opened the door and the chambermaid appeared, hands crossed at her waist. She curtsied with a slight stumble, and looked up deferentially. "Madame Clifford would like to see you in her office," she said.

"Now?"

"As quickly as you are able to look presentable, is what the madam says," replied the girl. "An important visitor is here to see you."

"Can you help me, please?" She walked to her wardrobe, Maple following. It could be any of a half dozen men, she thought. She counted as her regular clients two state senators, the owner of a large department store, and a Ramsey County judge, among others. She glanced at her collection of dresses, shirtwaists and gowns. Mostly gowns for work. Nothing too revealing, not like some of the whores in the downtown brothels who left little to the imagination. These were constructed to accentuate the shape, and please the eye. She had more formal clothing, also. An occasional date in a courtroom required respectable wear. She thought for a moment and chose one of her more stylish, elegant dresses, a wool one with blue and black stripes, high collar and fashionable balloon sleeves.

"Help me take off this gown, and then the dress."

"Miss Boyce? Don't you need a corset, first, for a dress like that?"

"No, Maple. Just help me fasten it from the back. And when you're finished, give me a spray of the perfume in the white bottle."

There was no point in a corset, when it most likely would be off in twenty minutes. After a moment's thought, however, she picked out a black silk one and handed it to Maple. She didn't feel quite herself, as her grandfather was on her mind. The idea of a grind with a client suddenly made her stomach turn.

Whichever man waited for her below wasn't going to get a purring vixen today. *I want to look like a lady,* she decided, and took a deep breath as Maple pulled the corset's laces tight. The dress went on next. It fit well. Finally, Maple fetched a pair of lace-up boots, and helped her with the slow process of tying them up.

She went to her dressing table. Putting on cosmetics was taboo in normal ladies' circles, but she didn't belong to any of those. She arched her eyebrows with a pencil, darkened her lashes, applied some liquid rouge with a bit of cotton, and made her lips with her grenadine stick. She knew the age-old insinuation. Painted ladies ruled the night. Depravity, wickedness and other nonsense. She didn't care, however. She enjoyed the way the makeup made her look, and how it highlighted her facial features. She examined herself in the mirror; at her button-shaped, slightly turned nose. Her cheeks were full and her eyes large and blue. She had the look of a Scandinavian; even the yellow hair, which Maple was putting up in a bun. She had been blessed with good looks, and while they financed her fineries now, she also knew that they had been to blame for her abduction. That made her think of her grandfather again, and she felt more nausea. Whoever was downstairs, she thought, had better not expect a roll with her today. It would anger Madame Clifford, but she was resolved. Just like her grandfather, she thought: stubborn, once she'd made her mind up at something. That thought sent a rush of happy warmth through her body, and strengthened her determination.

You can withstand the reprimand.

She stood up, ready to face her employer and whoever else demanded her attention.

CHAPTER 4

His little bay was deceptively fast. It gave him a mild startle when he took the corner too quickly and felt the gig rise up a little on one wheel. Queen yanked on the rein to slow, and bounced down the dirt lane until he reached a squat frame house. The perfect-sized home, he thought with tenderness, for a bachelor and his sister. Peder Ulland was Queen's best friend, and quite possibly his only real one. They'd met years back when the detective had done some work for Peder, who made his living as an advocate for the masses of Scandinavian immigrants who were pouring into Minnesota. Many of them had settled in the working areas of Minneapolis, and needed employment, certainly, but in many cases their needs were much more immediate: shelter, clothing, food and medical care. This meant lots of contacts amongst the meager and disregarded. Queen figured his friend might be able to stretch out his feelers for murmurs of men with the whiff of revolution about them.

He hopped off the gig and immediately swore. Pain in his knee. *You're not a young man anymore,* he chided himself. He shook out his leg but before he could take a step, Peder was already at the door, waving and smiling. His thinning blond hair sat high on his head, whipping about from a breeze that crossed the yard.

"Vell, vat do ve haff here?" he asked, as he pointed to Queen's horse. "You've giffin up stealing police vagons to get around?"

"And about time, right?" Queen walked to the door, shook Peder's hand fondly, and followed him inside. It was a cozy interior, with a wicker settee, a rocking chair and a stuffed corduroy armchair filling the room. A parlor stove stood in the corner, and a kerosene lamp swung from a hook in the ceiling. A rag carpet lay on the floor, striped with red and blue, where a tabby cat stretched out lazily in the warmth.

Queen smiled when a waft of sour cream pie caught his nose, and he heard light footsteps in the kitchen. Karoline was here.

"I'd like to speak to you, Peder, while we're alone," he said, his voice dropping to a whisper. "I need your help."

"Vit vat?"

Queen told him the mad account of the chewed-off finger, and when the detective asked him for his favor, Peder nodded, concern rumpling his brow.

"Ya, ya. I can send some men to ask around. Dere's a saloon near de river. A rowdy place, vit a lot of dat kind of talk. I'll send Egeberg."

Egeberg was a cunning fellow, and Queen approved of his choice. However, while the man's English was perfect, his ability to use his fists left much to be desired. Queen didn't want to take any chances.

"Could you send Big Snorre as well? I think Egeberg might need some clout behind him."

Peder thought for a moment, and then nodded. "Ya, dat is a good idea, Harm."

"And as quickly as you can," he said, just as his future bride stepped in from the kitchen. Beaming, she ran to him and threw her arms around his back. He laughed; she pulled his head down to match hers, and after they exchanged a kiss, he glanced over at his brother-in-law-to-be with a sheepish half-smile.

"I don't care," Peder said, amused. "Ve don't have pretensions in dis house."

"Sit down," Karoline said, eyes sparkling. "I've missed you ever so much."

"And I you," he replied, putting himself in the rocker. It creaked under his weight, but not as much as it would have four months ago, before he'd stopped drinking. Since he'd halted his daily intake of whiskey, he felt more vigorous. More on edge, certainly, but not as depressed as before. Of course Karoline was the main reason for his sprightly cast. She wasn't a classic beauty, but he saw nothing but loveliness in her world-wise eyes, working hands, and unwaveringly positive spirit. She still had an air that would turn the heads of envious men, but it was naturally there. Nothing was hollow or contrived with her.

"Have you been staying to the straight and narrow?" she asked with a laugh, knowing the answer already.

He held back a smile and looked down, shaking his head. "That old chestnut, dearest? My job isn't peril-free."

"But you're not putting yourself in danger's way, are you? Not purposely?"

"No, Karoline."

"You were almost killed. Once in Saint Paul, and then near Hastings."

"I'm not going to either of those places anytime soon."

"Promise me, then," she said.

"Unless I'm invited to Saint Paul for lunch with the mayor, I've no business there."

"Good," she pronounced happily. Her smile broke wide.

Queen decided there that he was completely helpless against Karoline. He had no resistance when it came to her affection.

"I've got wonderful news, Harm!" she exclaimed, her cheeks glowing pink with elation. She sat on the settee near him, and then motioned Peder away with her hand. Her brother chuckled and slipped into the kitchen.

"Are the alterations on your wedding gown going well?"

"No," she laughed, "not that. Not something so insignificant as that."

"What, then?"

"Well, the wedding has been overwhelming."

"And I've warned you not to overdo yourself. I try and help when I can. I've arranged the finest private room at the West Hotel for July Fourth. We've got patriotic bunting and other decorations purchased, as you desire, not only to celebrate our union, but to celebrate your becoming an American citizen."

"I know, I know," she said, patting his hand. "And I love you for giving me everything I've wanted in this."

"What then?" Recently their days together had been occupied by a whirlwind of wedding plans. Details he honestly cared nothing about, but pretended to with every ounce of concentration and enthusiasm he could muster. Now he heard her tone change slightly. It wasn't flippant, nor patronizing, exactly, but it had a slight edge he wasn't expecting.

"I love you, Harm. You know I do. I still want to get married. It's just that an opportunity has arisen, and it is a very rare opportunity."

His chest felt afire, as if a blast of lightning had struck him from above and skewered him through the heart. He'd counted on this wedding to set him straight. No. He'd required it. He didn't want to hear what was next.

"Don't look so despondent, Harm. Please, listen to what I have to say."

He nodded, not even able to look her in the eyes.

"I've been invited to Chicago for three months. Jane Addams has invited me, *personally*, Harm, to live within her Hull house. To directly assist her in the famous Nineteenth Ward."

Queen found his mind suddenly racing, searching for reasons to convince her not to go. "That is one of the most dangerous areas of the city. And *you're* worried about *me?*" he finally managed.

"But Miss Addams is there, and her organization is world-renowned. How could there be any danger?"

His head hung low, like a twenty-pound round shot had replaced his skull. He rubbed his neck, and slowly raised his eyes to hers. "So you want everything to stop? Cancellations? Forfeited deposits? Is that it, then?"

She looked at him with tears forming in her blue eyes, and gave a smile so sweet and warm that he wanted to melt right into the rocking chair. "I love you, Harm."

"But you want this? More . . . more than me?" The words sounded horrifying as they slipped from his lips, and he immediately wished he could suck them back in. Her expression took no offense, however. She still looked at him with such affection, that he knew he wouldn't be able to get angry. She was born with an altruistic impulse, and there was nothing he could do to change it.

"Miss Addams says that this life is a glorious span of experience through which the upward surge of the race impels ceaselessly to action, action reacting always upon ourselves."

"What does that mean, Karoline? We've got plenty of action in Minneapolis."

"People here," she replied, "are in such need. Families are desperate. We . . . I have an obligation."

"But what will going to Chicago solve? You're already helping your brother's charities, and volunteering at the hospital almost every day."

"I'll *learn* better, under Miss Addams. She is the premiere social worker in the country, Harm. And she knows me by name and by reputation. It's such an honor. I have to go."

He felt guilty even asking, but it was nagging at his heart, so he did. "Is it something I've done? *My* reputation? Does it embarrass you?"

"No," she said, emphatically shaking her head. "It is about kindly human service. You understand that it is what gives me passion, don't you? You understand that?" Her eyes were pleading, and she was wringing her hands. He could tell she was concerned about his reaction, and hadn't anticipated that he would take the news the way he was. "You said you were drawn to me, to some degree, because of that. Please tell me that's true."

Queen loved her too much to question her feelings or motivations anymore. He felt sad, and he thought his expression likely showed it, because Karoline was crying now. He stood up, took his thumb, and gently dabbed at the corner of her eyes. She hugged him tightly around the waist. So tightly he felt his knees almost buckle. But he wasn't going to let her know that, because he was enjoying the embrace far too much.

CHAPTER 5

As the request for her presence had already grown stale, she bustled into the hallway. She passed the rooms of her fellow sports, and heard only some hard breathing from the room at the end. Otherwise, all was quiet. The other girls no doubt were in the reception room, waiting for business to pick up. Madame Clifford usually expected her there too, however Nellie still went to her own room when things weren't busy. She knew the madam was aware of her desire for quiet time, and allowed it as long as her generosity wasn't abused.

Nellie went down the stairs and the chambermaid followed, trying to keep the dress from catching on the corners or rails. Once below, she swept through the ballroom, and knocked on Madame Clifford's office door.

"Enter," came the reply.

When she walked in, she saw the madam sitting behind her French mahogany desk. An elaborate marble fireplace mantel stretched behind her. Next to that, a door led to the front parlor and the main entrance.

Madame Clifford was a graceful, taciturn creature in her early forties, both beautiful and wise. Her hair was black and her eyes equally dark, and she pursed her brow with mild disapproval at the tardiness. Nellie gave an apologetic curtsy, as trim and neat as the madam had taught her, and stood, waiting, for what was to come.

"Miss Nellie Boyce. Why are you dressed for tea?"

"Well . . . Madame Clifford. I felt . . . well . . . my intuition told me that formality was required."

"I see. Please, take a seat. This won't be long."

"Yes, Madame," she said, and sat on the red velvet sofa, folding her hands in her lap.

"I have someone waiting who requires a conversation with you."

"About what, if I may ask?"

Her eyes were sharp and puncturing. "My dear, have you benefited from your time in this place?"

Nellie was unsure of how to answer. Madame Clifford saw her discomfort and gave a restless sigh.

"Do you remember your time before coming here? Your situation was less than genteel, was it not?"

"It was very unpleasant, Madame. Yes."

"And the man who took you from that vile place, and brought you to me. Do you remember him?"

"Mr. Kilbane? Of course." She remembered her first and only encounter with the man very clearly. Five months and thirteen days into her captivity in that damnable hole, he had come.

Emil Dander had been swine-drunk that night. Drunk enough to hand out a beating, and she'd expected it from the moment he'd stumbled into the door, cursing and reeking and threatening whatever came into his vision. He'd been trying in vain to stick a fork with a piece of gray meat into his mouth when Mr. Kilbane came hurtling through the door, eyes blazing. She recollected his orange hair, as wild as the flames of a fire, and the way he searched the room, until he'd set his sights on her. She'd been unclothed, with her hands tied behind her back, lying on the floor. She'd watched with numb fascination as Kilbane's neck began to spasm and his hands tremble in outrage. Opium had dulled her senses, but not enough to not understand what was happening.

"I told you she wasn't to be hurt," he'd said, choking back his fury. "This was only 'spose to've been temporary." And the words he'd uttered in a low voice after that, she'd never forgotten. "This will cost you dearly, Dander."

Kilbane first cut her free with a thin dagger drawn from under his jacket. As she stood and tried to get her balance, she saw him suddenly fly at Dander like a coiled snake. She could see the flash of the iron knuckles that crowned Kilbane's fist, and watched Dander's face collapse into a mash of pounded meat and blood under the weight of the blows. Kilbane had been her raging, dancing, demonic savior.

She'd left with him that night, stabs of guilt in her gut for the other girls left behind. But she was too scared to ask for their rescue, as Mr. Kilbane wore an expression of absolute hatred on the ride back to St. Paul, seething in his seat and muttering under his breath. Without a word to her, she'd been left with her current employer, in the depth of the dark night. Madame Clifford had greeted her at the door with only a nod, and swooped her under her cloak like a headmistress at a private school.

And here, she was tutored. Educated in the art of seduction, desire, and fulfillment.

One day, she'd mustered the courage to ask Madame Clifford why it had been her, and not one of her friends, who had been chosen for tutelage. She'd expected a stern lecture about biting feeding hands, but surprisingly, the madam had answered her readily, without protest. She'd explained that Kilbane had seen some pluck and intellect in her. Some spark of life that would have been wasted, and probably extinguished, at Dander's low joint.

And now Mr. Kilbane was back, a year and a half after depositing her on the brothel's doorstep.

It was curious.

"You'd told me that Mr. Kilbane was a concerned gentleman, interested only in seeing me free from harm. Is he here to check on me?"

"I did tell you that, Nellie, and it is true. But not the entire truth. It is why I wanted to talk to you privately for a moment. Before you met him face to face."

Nellie had always taken the madam's words at face value. She was surprised and a little nervous at this admission of deception. She sat a little straighter in her chair.

"He is not a benefactor, Nellie. In fact, I've been paying him a percentage of the money you earn."

"So he's been profiting off of me?"

"Yes, Nellie, he has." Madame Clifford's face stayed calm, but her voice hardened. "It was the arrangement for you coming here. For your safety."

It dawned on her then. "But I could have left at any time, you said. I am free to go, you said. How could that be, if he had expectations of compensation?"

"We haven't had to address that situation, Nellie, because it has never happened. You've never left."

"What if I leave, though? What if I decided to go now?"

The madam gave a grim smile. "It has never been an issue."

"So I haven't, really, had my freedom?"

Madame Clifford looked away and stood up. "We cannot wait any longer. He's a busy man, Nellie. Please listen to his offer and consider carefully."

And as if the door had ears, it banged open, and in capered Jiggs Kilbane, tossing it shut again behind him. He was cut in garish green fabric, and he jounced when he walked, like he'd been caged for so long that he'd forgotten how to walk normally. Nellie stood up, startled at his sight.

Instead of the furious, twisted face she'd remembered, he wore a sneer. And the disturbing thing about the sneer was how comfortable he looked with it on. Nellie got the impression that this was the way his face looked when he wasn't smashing someone's skull in with a brick.

His eyes met hers, and she felt instantly like a block of meat at the butcher's shop. He was eating her with his stare, like a starving, bone-hungry animal. After an uncomfortable few seconds he blinked twice, and then put out his hand. She knew she had to take it, and did. His sneer widened into an ear-to-ear grin as he planted a whiskey-scented kiss on her fingers.

"Miss Boyce. It has been some time."

"It has, Mr. Kilbane."

"Please, call me Jiggs."

She was further unsettled by the drop of formality. Someone as powerful as this man doesn't relinquish the title of sir or mister, especially to a prostitute. She didn't know how to respond.

He stood, waiting, not comprehending her discomfort.

"Nice to see you again, *Jiggs*." She bit her lip to mute the embarrassment.

"Well, I'll be Injun skinned," he said. "You look like a goddamn proper lady." As soon as he cursed, he gave a sheepish laugh at the realization of his faux pas. "You'll have to excuse my language," he said, with a loose bow to Madame Clifford. "I'm used to communicatin' with buffoons for most of my working day. Hard to break the habit."

"Entirely fine," said Madame Clifford, forcing a gentle smile. "Would you like a chair, Mr. Kilbane?"

"Not on your tintype. I got business to run. Did the good madam tell you why I'm here?" he asked, turning to Nellie.

"I thought it would be best if you relayed the news to her," said Madame Clifford.

"Very good!" He lit a grin that threatened to decapitate his face. "Miss Clifford has taken very good care of you. A fine young lady with many talents, I've heard."

Nellie gave a simple curtsy.

"Without getting into the nuts and bolts of it, Minneapolis is a prime bit of real estate, currently, for establishments such as this. I've got plenty of my own places scattered about, but none in Minneapolis. Do you have any idea about what's goin' on over there?"

"None, sir."

"It's a goddamn free-for-all, is what it is. They've got a police superintendent practically begging people to come to the city and set up shop. They collect what they call fines, of course, like here. That's how they make their dirty money. Shakin' down madams. But even at a hundred dollars a month, it is still worth the fucking price of admission. And they want more!"

Nellie had lied to him. Of course she'd heard about the situation. There was plenty of scuttle amongst the girls over the opportunities in Minneapolis. She had no idea why he was telling her, however. Since when was she worthy of a conversation about business with someone like this? From Madame Clifford's deference, Kilbane had to be important. He'd had the power to bust into Dander's house and mangle him on the floor, without a single finger raised against him.

"So, here's the thing," he said with a gleeful smile. "I'm not exactly a welcome man in that city right now. And that's putting it goddamn mildly. I need someone I trust. Someone who owes me." He paused, waiting for the words to take their effect. "I want to give you the money for your own house. We'll be partners."

Her jaw went slack, and she looked immediately to Madame Clifford, who looked back at her without a hint of expression. She had no idea what to say. Her recent realization that this wasn't the kind of life she wanted to live anymore had given her thoughts of picking up and leaving. However, Madame Clifford had also just alluded that her ability to leave freely might be open to interpretation. That had certainly shocked her, and she hadn't had time yet to put her feelings all together. Now, however, Mr. Kilbane was here, in person, insisting that she was in his debt. It was all too much to properly digest.

Jiggs Kilbane looked pleased as punch at her awed expression. "I'll take that as a yes, then, Miss Boyce," he giggled and took her hand without waiting this time. He also lingered a moment longer in a kiss, leaving a strand of saliva on her painted nails.

"Wait, sir. I mean Mr. Kilbane. *Jiggs*. This isn't something I'm capable of doing, I don't think. First of all, I don't know anyone in Minneapolis. Why would you trust your money to me? You don't know my abilities . . . ."

"I do, Miss Boyce. Better than you." He folded his arms with assurance. "I may not have the manners of a prince, or the bearing of James J. Hill, but I'm a goddamn good businessman. I'm good at sizin' people up, and figurin' them out. And, you, Miss Boyce, have that elusive 'jer-ner-see kwa'."

"What about a building? Permits? A staff? Women to work? Where would I start?"

"Awww, hell," he said. "My lawyers'll take care of nailing down the location and other arrangements. And the fact that you know what a permit is already sets you a part from the other addle-headed titties in this joint. But I need you, as the face of the place, as front and center. I got someone to help you, too." He winked at her, and then suddenly turned. "I know yer listening behind the door!" he shouted.

Nellie's eyes grew wide in astonishment and recognition as the door creaked open. It was a girl she knew, intimately, from her months of confined hell.

Trilly Flick sauntered over, and stood next to Kilbane. Her pouty lips formed the barest of smiles, and she put her hands on her shapely hips, as if to emphasize her presence.

"Well, hello, Maisy Anderson," she purred.

Nellie's head swooned at the familiar sound of her name. Madame Clifford had insisted from the very moment she'd stepped inside that her real name should never be used again. But she was even more moved by the familiar voice that spoke it.

"You remember Trilly Flick, don't you?" Kilbane crowed. "She said she remembers you quite well."

"You made it out? I'm so happy you did!" Nellie's heart almost burst with relief. Her worst fears hadn't been realized after all.

Trilly nodded. "Jiggs got me out, just like he did for you, honey."

"So!" Kilbane exclaimed, with an impatient tap on his pocket watch. "We've had our little reunion. You've got a friend beside you. Everything is settled, then!"

This was all happening too fast. A madam? Could she do it? It would take her out from between the sheets, which she wanted. As far as she knew, she had no skills at running a business, although she'd planned to go to college to study mathematics. Balancing books would be easy for her. Her grandfather had been a taker of action. He'd made his way through the world living on principles and morals. Prostitution was not a moral institution, she understood. But it had to exist, she'd learned the hard way. She didn't know how yet, but perhaps she could use her grandfather's lessons, combined with Madame Clifford's, to create her own place, where women were respected and could call their own plays. Make their own decisions.

Could a brothel be democratic? Would a partner such as Jiggs Kilbane allow that?

Perhaps she might even reach out to Edna Pease and Ellie Van

Allen, wherever they were. If Trilly had found her freedom, might Edna and Ellie have discovered theirs as well?

In her heart she already knew that this offer wasn't one she'd be allowed to decline. But if there was a chance to rescue the other girls, she had to ask. She took a breath and did.

"There were two others in the house you took me from. I'd like them with me."

Kilbane's sneer turned to an uneasy frown, and he looked at Madame Clifford, who nodded and stepped forward.

"I should have told you earlier, my dear."

"Told me what?"

The madam shook her head solemnly. "There was an unfortunate incident at that house, Nellie. It led to the deaths of two of your friends, and of Emil Dander and his men. I'd meant to tell you when it happened, but didn't want to upset you."

Nellie looked at Trilly, who covered her mouth with the back of her hand and turned away. Grief swelled in Nellie's bosom, and she faltered back a step. Madame Clifford gently held her waist and Kilbane whipped out an embroidered purple handkerchief to offer her.

She put up her hands and steadied herself. "I'm fine. I'm fine."

Friends were hard to come by in this world. Two of them gone, now? And one left, here, in front of her. Trilly looked like an angel to her now. They'd been through so much together.

"Can we do this, Trilly? Can I really rely on you?"

"Hell, yeah, I would, Maisy. I'd do anything for ya."

She mustered her grandfather's courage.

"I'll do it."

"Good," Kilbane said, his chronic sneer set again on his face. "But one more thing."

A man emerged from the ballroom's door. She was surprised

at that, as the room had been empty when she'd walked through minutes before. He wore a fitted suit that was tied at the waist by a brightly colored wool sash. His hair and eyes were gray, and his shoulders were broad. He walked with a swagger, but his brow was low and his expression was cold and distant.

"My dear," said Kilbane to Nellie. "This is my guard. Allow me to introduce Henri."

Nellie felt her throat clench at the forbidding figure. The man stopped behind Kilbane and Trilly, with his hands behind his back, as if he meant to block escape.

And then she screamed when Jiggs Kilbane grabbed Trilly by the back of the head, and hurled it into the wall. Trilly crumpled to the floor, blood seeping from her forehead, bits of plaster sprinkling her dress.

The gangster reached down and grabbed Trilly by the hair. He dragged her up, until her wide, terrified eyes met his.

"Don't you ever fucking say the name Maisy Anderson again. Do you hear me?" She nodded weakly, and he dropped her back to the floor.

Then he turned to Nellie, spit hanging from his chin, and grinned. "I'm excited to work with you, Miss Boyce. Let's get this shit-cloud of a venture goin' at once. We'll be here tomorrow morning at eleven to get you." He leaned in to her ear, and she shuddered at the stink of his breath.

"Don't be late," he whispered. "Now shoo, fly. Shoo."

CHAPTER 6

Queen maneuvered his gig through the lively tumult and roaring trade of Cedar Avenue, hollering Arthur forward through the packed streets. The air buzzed with the wonderful din of competing immigrant languages. While he didn't speak Danish, Norwegian or Swedish, he still recognized and enjoyed the gentle roll of the "r," and the cadence that accented the first syllable of their words. Their speech sounded lilting and magical to him. Perhaps it was the Ullands' stories of the old country. The ravishing fjords, the ancient towering bridges, and the glistening blue ice were things he wanted to see one day, with his wife as his guide and escort, and the sound of their languages was a transient gateway to that dream.

He wedged the horse and gig between two lumbering work wagons, barely giving him room to step down. The street was filled with smells of potato sausage and sweat. Butcher shops, groceries and hardware stores wearing signs with names like Amonsen's, Larson's and Brastad's were scattered along the avenue, and rival newspapers like *Folkebladet,* the *Scandinavisk Farmer Journal,* and the *Lutheraneren* competed for the attention of the mushrooming population of Scandinavian immigrants moving into the city.

And the Scandinavians were political. Queen wasn't personally, which many might consider odd as he'd been involved in more political campaigns than most. But for him, it had all been for personal gain and prestige. It had nothing to do with his views on the conditions of the world, of which he thought little. He'd latched on to old Doc's coattails, not because of party affiliation, but because it had made him Minneapolis chief of detectives. He was where he wanted to be, and had no intention of letting go.

That is why he had to figure out where these anarchists were hiding out, assuming they were a real threat to begin with. The possibility of losing his promotion worried him every day, so long as the fickle Colonel Ames was running the show.

Peder Ulland, far unlike him, was like a human thermometer in Minnesota's political climate. He breathed, slept and ate the complexities of municipal and state government, and rallied his legions of immigrant workers with the deft hand of a seasoned organizer. He was in charge of the Norwegian Brotherhood, a group he had founded in the effort to smooth the immigrant families' transition into Minnesota society. It was an organization that kept him in rolled-up shirt sleeves most of his days, connecting his members to employers, making sure they were treated fairly and had the necessities for a good life.

Queen walked through the main door of Dania Hall, which sat at the corner of Cedar and Fifth. It was the most imposing building in the area, a four-story Victorian topped with a single tower at the front. The Danes had commissioned it, a Norwegian had designed it, and now the entire community used it. Queen headed through the lobby and up the stairs to the second floor, which was where the administrative offices lay. He walked past signs for the Society Fram, the Grieg Choral and Orchestral Association, and the Socialist Labor Party Club before finally reaching the door of the Norwegian Brotherhood. Queen knocked, and Big Snorre answered.

Big Snorre was one of the largest men Queen had ever seen in his life. His form not only blocked the frame, but went past it, over the sides and the top. Queen looked up, barely able to make out his bald head above, and a wisp of brown hair.

"Hullo Q-veen," he said, with a toothy smile. The detective had never heard English come out of the man's mouth before. He removed his derby.

"I'm here to see Peder."

"Ya, ya, ya." The man stepped to the side, and the light of the room's windows hit Queen's face. Peder's office was a flurry of activity. Typewriters rattled, men in working clothes stood in corners, animatedly discussing what Queen assumed to be politics, and volunteers busily dashed about. Old playbills plastered the walls announcing union meetings and musical concerts by Hardunger fiddlers.

Queen stood along the wall to get out of the way, just under a portrait of Knute Nelson. He didn't have to wait long, as Peder soon came out of his private office and strode over to the detective, looking troubled.

"I came as quickly as you called, Peder." He'd rushed over, in fact, when he'd received the telephone call.

"My men found him qvicker dan I tot dey vould."

Queen was anxious to see who Peder's men had rounded up, but had been equally anxious to ask about Karoline's preparations. It had been only yesterday that they'd seen each other, but the thought of her leaving had kept him up the whole night. Peder's flushed face, however, was a worry. Queen followed him into his office, and pulled the door shut.

Peder's desk, a couple of chairs, and an old lamp cluttered the tight little space. Queen looked past the plate of boiled potatoes and gravy on his friend's desk, to the man sitting in his chair. He was short and gaunt, and his hands were bound from behind. A thick, ratty black beard covered most of his face, and what little skin left exposed was covered in grime. Queen raised an eyebrow when he noticed the man's eyes. One darted about the room, while the other looked dead and glassy. And most ominously, a long scar ran diagonally across the socket of the lifeless eye.

"Peder, do you have a pair of scissors lying about?"

"Of course, Harm. In de drawer."

Queen reached over the desk, yanked open the drawer and pulled them out. He felt the edge of the blades, making a point of letting the little man in front of him watch and fidget.

"Vat are you doing?"

He turned to his friend. "Get Snorre in here. This might get unpleasant."

Peder nodded, an expression of mild horror on his face, and left. Queen twisted back to the bound man.

"So you're an anarchist, are you? I somehow doubt that."

He grabbed the man by the scruff of his filthy collar, and held the scissors up to his good eye. "Tell me who you really are."

The man shook his head wildly, and scoured the room for help.

Queen had had enough of this game.

"You're not an anarchist, and I know who the hell you are, you little rat."

The detective began to cut off thick, matted pieces of the beard. The man howled in protest, but Queen held him firmly to the chair, fighting against the squirming, wriggling body. More tufts of hair fell to the floor in greasy clumps. Peder and Big Snorre entered the room, and watched in fascination as the man's howls turned into whimpers.

Finally, Queen leaned back, and put the scissors down. He was satisfied with his work. The job wasn't perfect, but good enough for him to recognize the man's face.

It was Pock.

What a topsy-turvy goddamn world.

"I know you," Queen said. "Straight from the bottom of the Mississippi River, it seems."

Peder gasped. "Dis is de murderer of de girl on de fence at dat brotel? Ellie Van Allen?"

"Yes," said Queen. "Under his boss's orders, of course. Emil Dander, who'd been ordered by Jack Peach, who in turn had been ordered by Jiggs Kilbane. Quite a chain of command for such a cowardly crime."

"Christ, Queen," Pock sputtered. "How'd you know it was me?"

"Your eye gave you away. It was me who threw the bottle at it, remember? Just before you were about to shoot me? And just before you ran screaming into the Mississippi. I've got to give you credit, you goddamn little rat. I never ever thought you'd survive the undertow or the cold."

Pock closed his eye and shivered. Then he opened it and looked at Queen. Hard.

"What do you want from me?" he asked.

"What do I want from you?" Queen couldn't stifle a sarcastic laugh. "You killed a girl. Not to mention you terrorized a group of college students, and bit a boy's finger off, no less. I want to filet your carcass into strips and feed them to the catfish, for once and for all. You need to be put out of your misery."

"Then get a move on."

"Not before I find out why you waylaid that boy."

"He was the son of an industrialist. All of them that go to that university are. His father rapes the working class."

"And perhaps that rape you speak of will meet you in person. When I put you into Stillwater prison. In the form of a guy like him." The detective pointed at Big Snorre, who gave a pleasant, oblivious smile.

Pock drew in a wheezy breath. "Queen. I didn't want her to die. I had no choice. He'd have killed me if I hadn't pulled the trigger."

"Forget that for a moment." Queen sat on the edge of the desk, and looked down at Pock in his chair. "The only card you hold right now, and I'll admit it's an ace, is this anarchist nonsense. You're going to tell me now how you managed to get involved in this. Who are your chums? Who's calling the shots? It can't be you."

"There's nobody else!"

"Bullshit there's not. I'm on to your curves. You don't have the brains to organize a group of revolutionaries. Nobody would come close to you with the stench you're giving off."

Pock spit at the wall. "Anarchists don't need leaders. We're *anarchists!*"

"Tell me, you bedraggled little freak, who is in this with you?"

"You want to see what I'm up to, copper? There's a book in my jacket that will enlighten you about the crimes being committed against human kind."

Queen turned to Peder, who shrugged. He leaned over, patted Pock's pockets, and almost sneezed at the dust cloud that rose. After a moment of searching, he found the book, and pulled it out. He looked at the cover.

"Are you aware of this title, Peder? *What is Property?* By Pierre-Joseph Proudhon."

"Ya, sure. I've read it. De author challenges de right of property. It is qvite radical."

"Sounds like anarchy to me."

"I'm not denying that, Queen," Pock said with a sniffle. "I'm just sayin' that I read the book on my own. I got the ideas there."

Peder stepped forward, with a shake of his head. "I believe him. I vould have heard about dese revolutionaries if dey vere real."

"What are you gonna do with me?" Pock asked.

"I'm not going to do anything except throw you into a cell at Central Station," Queen said. "I'll let Fred Ames sort through the shit and he can question you himself. I've got other uses for my time besides you."

"I don't want prison, Queen," begged Pock.

"The hell if I care."

"What if I give you something?"

"Like who your friends are?"

"I already told you, I don't have none."

"Then what? Play ball, Pock."

Pock slid the corner of his mouth into a slight smile. "I know you're looking for someone."

"And how would you know that?"

"I still know everything. I know where she is at this very moment. I keep my ear to the ground, Queen. I can help you."

"Who?" Queen felt his face begin to burn, as he realized on his own who Pock was talking about. He thought for a moment about his promise to a sheriff named Dix Anderson, and then, suddenly, a rush of rage enveloped him. It took ahold of his hand, and his fist, and he felt it pull back in a wide arc, and then it came down on its own; down with furious force into the side of Pock's head. Pock and the chair fell over, and the little man scrambled backwards into the corner, shuffling as best he could without the use of his tied hands. Peder cried out behind him in objection, but Queen paid him no mind. He fell to his own knees and straddled the prone Pock, pulling his fist back again.

Pock pushed himself against the wall, terror and delight shining in his good eye.

"You need me, Queen. You need me to find Maisy Anderson."

CHAPTER 7

She couldn't free her mind of Jiggs Kilbane.

Her short time in Minneapolis had been filled with more horrors than a penny dreadful. However, she'd seen nothing in her short life more terrifying than the expression on that maniac's face. And even more queer was how easily he'd slipped back into his normal, empty-eyed, bughouse self. The random nature of his violent act was a thing of nightmares. Even in her worst moments with Emil Dander, she'd at least been able to guess his behavior.

And Trilly. Poor Trilly.

The fear in her eyes. The tears that burrowed into her cheeks. The blood that trickled from her nose. She hadn't deserved that.

Nellie's chest was tight with dread. She was about to walk to the precipice with an incredibly dangerous man. A hundred different ways to escape her fate flew through her head, and she shot each one down almost as quickly as it appeared. Every possible way out ended at the same dark corner.

And at that corner she was alone. Completely alone.

She had Trilly, but it wasn't enough. What were two women against a violent criminal enterprise? Jiggs Kilbane had access to some of the most vicious men in the country. The one Kilbane had called *Henri*, the one who had stood by while Trilly was brutalized, was simply the tip of the knife.

Kilbane had told her to pack her belongings and be ready. She'd be leaving tomorrow to God knows where. But she had to take measures to protect herself, and someone else as well.

With pen in delicate, trembling hand, she found her stationery and began to write. Two notes: one for her love, and one for a man she despised.

Once she had made arrangements with Kilbane for Nellie's departure, Nina Clifford had excused her from work. Nellie had been given the night to pack, and Maple to help with the hardest labor. Maple, however, had departed with the notes, and Nellie was left to fend for herself. Luckily she was her grandfather's girl, and tougher than most. While the luxuries around her had softened her, she could still reach down inside when required.

She had started packing the last of her clothes in a large steamer trunk she'd borrowed from Madame Clifford when she heard the noise outside her window. A pebble bounced off the glass, and she ran to it, unlatched the sash and pulled it up. The cool night air whisked in, giving her a shiver of anticipation.

"I'm already half-way," came the eager voice.

"Quiet," she shushed, looking down at the nimble shadow. When he got to the window he heaved himself up with his thick, muscular shoulders, and then made a magnificent leap inside. He landed with one knee on the carpet, and one behind him. He gripped a rose in his mouth, and stood up with a hammy, lopsided grin on his face. Her heart was racing a million miles a minute as she looked at his dashing figure.

"For you, milady," he snorted, and handed her the rose.

She smothered a laugh and pulled him towards her. They embraced, and he kissed her softly. She reached up and ran her hand through his oiled hair, pushing the strands that had fallen over his eyes.

"I came as soon as I got your note. The kitchen mechanic who brought it to me looked dead tired, too."

"Don't call her that," she scolded. "She's a chambermaid and her name is Maple. Did she stay long?"

"I offered to let her sleep in my flat, but she looked horrified when

I mentioned it. She said she had another place to go, anyway."

She'd hoped that Maple would make it safely. It had been a lot asking her for her help, but she'd given Maple a sapphire ring in payment for the risk. The poor girl had little in the way of money, and was eager for the chance to make such a score. Nellie had hoped beyond hope that the girl wouldn't abscond with the jewelry and leave her high and dry. But tonight's visitor was proof that good old Maple hadn't let her down.

"I'm glad you came, Dick. Really I am." She took his hand and walked him over to the bed. They sat together on its edge.

"I've missed you," he said.

She smelled the orange peel on his breath and relaxed with its familiarity. Her fears always melted away when he was near. He made her feel safe. Dick was a man who would gladly give his own life to protect her, she was sure.

"We said no notes," he reminded her, giving her another kiss on the forehead.

"I didn't know how else to get you a message."

"But notes, Nellie. They're too dangerous. If my father found any connection between us he'd kick up some dirt fast."

"You mean he'd be humiliated because his golden son is taking tumbles with a whore, right?"

"It's just none of his business."

He put his arm around her and they sat, in silence. They were such a mismatched pair, she understood with bitter clarity, as she ran her thumb over his. It was a wonder that they'd ever fallen in love to begin with. Madame Clifford had warned her about developing personal attachments with customers. All of the girls were told this. Any intimacy outside the bounds of business would be trouble, as sure and certainly as McKinley was president and the milk jars were delivered on the door step at 6:15 sharp. But he'd come with university friends one evening, as a lark. A night about the town, to blow off steam. Her mind had immediately cautioned her that a man who visited resorts could never be trusted, but they'd made an instant communion at first meeting. He was young, handsome, well-clothed and clean, and made her laugh, which she'd rarely done since arriving in the Twin Cities. She knew from his puppy-dog stares that he was smitten with her from the get-go as well.

He'd visited every night for a month after that, and she'd readily cleared her schedule to comply. It had helped that he'd liberally paid for that honor. Madame Clifford had disapproved, but not enough to turn down the cush and the pals that coasted on his coat tails and into the front door alongside him.

Even though he bought her time, there was a distinction in her mind between Dick and the other men she rolled with. She refused her portion when it came to him. It wasn't only about making goo-goo eyes with Dick, either. They'd talk, and joke and drink, often times so late into the night that they'd be too exhausted from each other's company to do anything else. He'd regale her with his exploits on the gridiron and adventures in the classroom, and transport her from the confines of her brothel bedroom to the campus she'd always wanted to call her home. On those nights she lived vicariously through this boy, and his company gave her momentary reprieve from her own loneliness.

Now that he was set to graduate, he came less frequently, but their bond was still strong. She knew he still held things back from her. She was sure that he dated university girls in his regular life. Although he didn't vocalize his displeasure with out-and-out anger, he was certainly bothered by the nature of her occupation, and jealous, she knew, of the other men who visited her chambers when he wasn't there. However he hadn't offered an alternative, to let them be together, so she assumed that they had reached their farthest point. It wasn't to say that the point was bad. It was what it was. But now her situation had changed. Changed for the worse, it seemed, now that she'd seen the terrible beating that Trilly had taken. She'd been a front-row witness to Killbane's true nature, and it shook her to her core.

"What's this?" Dick asked, breaking the quiet. He motioned with the tip of his shoe to the open trunk next to the bed.

And here was the moment, she thought. Faster than she'd have liked. But it was here, and he needed to know. *It was for his own good.*

"I've something to tell you. Something I hope you understand. I've been given an opportunity," she said.

The lie came out more smoothly than she'd anticipated.

"An opportunity for something better . . . than this."

"What do you mean? What kind of opportunity could be given to you?"

He hadn't meant it, she knew, but she still felt the sting of his question. She pulled away from him, stood up, and moved to the window. I can't let him see me cry, she thought, or this will be so much more difficult.

"I'm so sorry, Nellie. As soon as I said it, I realized it was wrong."

She heard his step behind her, and felt his hand on her shoulder. She wanted to push it away, but she couldn't.

Being around him tore up her emotions when he was said such things, but she also felt so at ease in his presence.

Love was confusing.

Assuming that this was love, which she wasn't sure it was. Whatever it was, though, both the moments of tenderness and the thoughtless comments made her feel alive. It was almost euphoric, this exploration of emotions she'd forgotten she could have. They cut through the dull ache that throbbed in her soul.

Even so, she still dreaded what she had to tell him. They'd grown so close. But she'd made up her mind.

"Dick. I'm to run my own place."

"A resort?"

"Yes. I've been approached by a wealthy individual . . . ."

Moonlight's face twitched with a look of panic and jealousy. "What? What does that mean?"

"It means that I'm going into business."

"With some man? How could you do something like that?"

"What am I supposed to do? Stay here all of my life? What happens in ten years, when I'm no longer young?"

He scrunched up his mouth in frustration. Rarely did Moonlight Darling have difficulty coming up with something to say, but he did now.

"I don't expect to stay here all my life, if that's what you mean," she continued, choking a little. "You're about to graduate. Move on to great things. Work for your father, probably . . . ."

"Never," he snarled, and turned away.

"Why wouldn't you? You're his heir, you've said. I don't know anything else about the man, except that you don't want him to know about me."

"That's because he's not worth mentioning."

"But you understand your position, and mine, don't you? I have to make my own way."

He looked back at her, perspiration soaking his brow. It was funny how he could bound across a football field, barely breaking a sweat, but a conversation such as this made his forehead slick and wet.

"I'll take you with me," he said, with a wild, determined look.

"You can't be serious," she replied. "That would never work. I know there are other women. What would your university steady say?"

"Those girls don't mean anything."

"And how do I know? You've also got your whole future to think about."

He shot her a hot glance. "Obviously you've been thinking about yours."

She slipped his handkerchief from his chest pocket and wiped his brow dry. "You worry too much, Dick."

"How could I not? You'll soon be in bed with a stranger."

He would be a dangerous one, too. Far too dangerous for Moonlight Darling's college sensibilities. She needed him away from her for his own good.

"I'll be fine, I promise," she told him.

"And I'll make sure of it."

She sighed. It was going as unpleasantly as she'd figured it would. But the worst was still to come.

"I can't continue on like this, Dick. I'll be very busy soon, and the distraction of you will be too great." She stroked his hair again, trying to let him down gently. "I care for you, but everything is changing, and our relationship, as it's been, is too much of a burden at this moment . . . ."

"A burden? A *burden?*"

She'd known this would be difficult for him, but she hadn't expected this level of despair. He wasn't accustomed to being told no, either.

God, this was hard. If there was a better way to cut ties with the one man she might actually love, she wished she knew.

He pulled a pint-bottle of something from his pocket, unscrewed the top, and took a deep swallow. Once it found its way down, he shuddered, but managed only an imitation of his usually impish grin.

"You seem to be taking your leave of me, Nellie," he finally said. "We're in such different positions, you and I."

And it could have been different, she thought. Perhaps if she'd made it off the station platform safely, and entered school like she was supposed to, they might have met, and loved, and it could have been different. But her lot had been cast in another direction, and that was that.

He rested his head on her shoulder, and they sat in silence. This would be their last night together, she'd decided. There was no other choice.

CHAPTER 8

He'd turned to Peder, as always, for the help he couldn't get from his own police force. Peder, as always, came through. The Norwegian had provided Queen with a coal wagon, and a driver, Big Snorre, along with the appropriate clothes: work shirts, overalls and boots.

The idea of a disguise was a sour one to Queen. Parading around in a silly costume bordered on cowardly, in his own opinion. He was a police detective, and proud of that fact. If he couldn't get the information he wanted by being himself, he had no business doing the job.

In this instance, however, a disguise made sense. Queen was not wanted in Saint Paul. The last time he'd been here, he'd irresponsibly raced a streetcar down the capital city's busiest avenue, crashing it in spectacular fashion. The police hated him, and a certain Irish gangster desired him dead.

But Pock insisted that Maisy was here.

Queen didn't trust Pock for a second. An ambush might easily be waiting ahead, or Pock might be looking for some perfect moment to escape into a city where he knew Queen wouldn't ever find him. But this seemed to be the only way forward, so he'd prepared in haste. He had tucked a small roll of money and his pistol into his pocket, along with a handful of extra bullets.

He'd also asked Peder not to tell Karoline where he was going. She can't be worried about me, he told himself. She needs to focus on her preparations.

Buck up and shoot straight with her, he told himself. *She asked you not to go to Saint Paul, yet you're still doing it. You've broken your promise already.*

But he'd made a promise to someone else, as well. It had been a promise to Sheriff Dix Anderson, one that followed him around like a maddening itch.

She would understand if she knew, and this might be my only chance.

The fact that Maisy Anderson was still missing bothered Queen to no end. Even as he worked his business in Minneapolis, he'd still kept his eye out for her. Asking questions. Looking for clues.

He might have looked harder, he knew. He might have asked more questions. He might have hunted through the city's brothels more thoroughly, or hired his own private detectives to continue the search on the sly. As far as he knew, no one else cared about the young lady, and that gnawed at him. A young girl, without a family, trying to survive under quite possibly barbaric conditions, made his normally gruff personality soften into warm butter. It just wasn't right, and as the old sheriff had died in his quest, Queen owed it to him to jump on any opportunity to finish it.

So when Pock mentioned her name, he knew he had to call the weasel's bluff. This was his chance to make amends, and to redeem his pledge to Anderson. No one in the police department would help him, he understood. Colonel Ames would have a conniption if he knew what Queen was up to. This had to be kept quiet.

And I'll be home in a few hours, to say goodbye to Karoline, with no one the wiser.

There. He felt rotten for the deception, but it was for a greater good, and she would understand. He wasn't alone either, and Karoline would certainly feel better knowing Big Snorre was by his side. He was grateful to have Snorre's muscle, despite their inability to verbally communicate with each other. He glanced up at the hulk, who filled up most of the seat with his wide girth. Snorre refused to carry a firearm, but chose to arm himself with a massive metal pipe wrench instead. While it wasn't a match for a gun, in close quarters Queen could only imagine what damage the bruising Norske could inflict with that weapon.

Pock, on the other hand, needed to be carefully watched. He sat in the wagon, across from Queen, with his arms around his knees, staring at the houses on the street. They'd crossed the Lake Street Bridge, which became Marshall Avenue once it hit reached the Saint Paul side. Then they made their way to Summit Avenue, clopping along broad crushed-slate streets as they headed towards the heart of the city. The sun was shining and birds were bountiful; singing and chirping from small trees lining the avenue. Scattered houses and wide fields began to condense as they moved east, and the houses became larger and more opulent.

Hammocks hung from stately front porches, and gardeners planted flowers to brighten the yards. Rich families wearing their Sunday church finery strolled down the sidewalk, along perfectly manicured and fenced lawns. Queen looked for men that he might recognize, and tried to match the names with their homes. Even Big Snorre smiled pleasantly as he sucked in the sunshine and the tranquil scene.

But something was wrong with Pock.

He fidgeted in his seat and mumbled under his breath. His eyes were digging daggers into the extravagance surrounding them.

It was then that Queen realized they shouldn't have come this route. Summit Avenue was the home to Saint Paul's elite, and Pock's latest little game was taking issue with the moneyed.

"Pigs," Pock muttered.

"Keep your mug shut," Queen shot back in a harsh whisper.

"Why should I?" Pock asked, turning to the detective. "Look at these buffoons, see?" He pointed to an elegantly dressed woman leisurely pushing a baby carriage on the wood plank sidewalk. "For the price of that lady's dress, you could buy brand-new stumps for a dozen gimps. Why does she deserve that and they don't deserve stumps?"

"Need I remind you that you shot a captive girl? I didn't bring you here to engage in discourse over goddamn social disparity or the price of wooden legs. You're here to help me. To redeem yourself, Pock. Save your hypocritical cheek for another time. You can actually do some good today. Make up for some of the pain and misery you've caused in your worthless life."

The words had some effect. Pock shut up, and stared sullenly down at his lap.

Much better, Queen thought.

Quiet.

Then Pock looked up, and he spoke in a low, scratchy voice.

"I'm trying, Queen."

"Trying what?"

"Trying to be good."

"So good that you bit someone's finger off?"

"I couldn't control myself. It got away from me. That boy, with his slick hair and his smug face, he ignored me. Didn't want to hear what I had to say."

Queen didn't know how to respond. He'd never expected that from Pock. He'd never expected anything at all.

"When we get there, stay in the wagon. Do you understand?" was all Queen could think of.

Pock nodded, and dropped his head.

CHAPTER 9

She awoke to a cool draft from the open window. She looked next to her in the bed. He was gone, as she'd asked. Already she felt his loss in the pit of her stomach. It had been a detestable way to end their relationship.

A quiet knock on the door interrupted her thoughts. When she answered and saw Maple, she felt horrible. The poor girl was dirty from head to toe, and swaying with exhaustion. Still, the young chambermaid managed a smile.

"I did it, Miss Boyce. I delivered them."

"Good girl, Maple. Did anyone see you go out or come in?"

"No, miss. I was careful like you said to be."

"Did you bring him?"

"Yes. He's exactly where you asked me to put him. And here." She handed Nellie a key. "You'll need this too."

"You'll have to stay awake a few more hours, Maple. I'm so sorry for that. Please go and wash your face and hands, and change your clothes. I don't think anyone has missed you yet."

Nellie slipped on a dress and a short jacket, and put on some shoes. She looked down the hallway, watching Maple as she disappeared down the stairs. Sunday morning was the quietest time of the week. The other girls were at breakfast most likely, and the brothel's staff was light. She tiptoed down the corridor, holding the jacket closed with her crossed arms. One of Madame Clifford's employees was a Scottish musician, who could tinkle out ragtime music when required, and she could hear him in the reception room below, playing "Fairest Lord Jesus" on the ivories.

She glided down the staircase into the entry room at the back door. The sunshine felt sweet on her face as she slipped outside.

The back yard was empty, and she fled past the alley to the adjacent house. She knew she was taking a big chance, breaking into Madame Clifford's personal residence, but it was a chance that might well save her life. She took out the key Maple had given her, and unlocked the door. She slowly pushed herself in, wincing as it creaked, and then pausled, listening for sounds from inside.

When none materialized, she moved to the basement door, only steps away. This one was already opened a crack, and she squeezed through, shutting it gently from behind.

Darkness enveloped her.

"Light your lamp," she demanded.

The light flickered on, and then grew bright enough for her to see the stairs. Down she went, following the source of the light with her eyes. The damp air tickled her throat, and she held back a cough.

As her eyes adjusted, she could make him out. He was fatter now, and even in the uneven glow she could tell that his clothes were patched and threadbare. She felt satisfaction, knowing he'd fallen on hard times.

"My dear," he pled, desperation ringing through his voice. "It is so wonderful to see you again."

As soon as he spoke, the memories came on like a muddy flood. It was all she could do not to scream at the top of her lungs, but she stopped herself from striking the alarm by biting her lip so hard that blood soaked her chin.

"You left me to them, you bastard," she hissed in a low, steaming rage.

"I was outnumbered!"

"You were a police sergeant! How could you let them take me?"

"There were too many," he moaned, stepping forward fully into the glare of the lamp. His face was paunchy and fallen, like a lump of wax left too long in the sun. He reeked of whiskey, and looked like death. This was her Uncle Martin Baum. Or the bloated shell of him, at least.

"I am so overjoyed that you are alive, Maisy. If Dix could only see you now."

"Shut your mouth," she snapped. "You've no right to say those things. You were never my blood. Only my grandfather's friend. And never mine."

"But I was, my dear. I've always been so fond of you . . . ."

"Did you not hear me?" She caught a sob in her throat, and then turned away wildly, not wanting him to see her.

Let me say what I have to say, and be done with it, she told herself. She wiped her eyes and turned back around.

"I remember that day with an accuracy so painfully sharp you can't even imagine. You promised my grandfather that you would escort me, yourself, to the university. You told me that my grandfather had wired you and asked that you meet me."

"Yes, that is true! And I had every intention . . ."

"I don't care what your intentions were. You drove the buggy to a neighborhood we never should have gone, and let those men take me. I'd been sitting right *next to you!*"

"They were heeled with guns and knives, and got to me before I could draw my revolver."

"I saw them," she snarled, "and I saw you see them. You recognized them."

"I-I didn't!"

"You did, I'm certain of it. And you let them take me, and you never came to get me."

Martin Baum burst into tears. He held his face in his hands, and wailed with all of the anguish of a tortured soul.

"*Shut it,*" she seethed. "Shut it. You're going to make it up to me now. Do you understand?"

He looked up, wet, bloodshot eyes blinking between his fingers.

"If you ever loved me, like you claim you do, and you truly didn't mean to leave me there with those jackals, then you'll do what I ask now."

"What is it?" He smeared his face with his sleeve and looked at her, quivering. "What? What do you want me to do? Anything, Maisy. I'll do anything!"

"You're going to kill Jiggs Kilbane."

"Wha . . . ? How? When? Where?"

She pulled a gun from inside her dress and pointed it towards a rusty orange door embedded into the stone wall.

"With this. In fifteen minutes. When he walks in through that door."

CHAPTER 10

It truly was a magnificent day, Queen admitted, as the wagon reached Summit Hill. It was a day he'd prefer spending with Karoline right now, in his new gig, leisurely enjoying the sights. On the right stood a masterpiece of Gilded Age architecture, the James J. Hill House, owned by one of America's most powerful men. The railroad magnate's massive red stone mansion perched on the edge of the Mississippi River bluff.

Snorre stopped the wagon and took out a snuff box. He stuffed some tobacco into his mouth, and then offered some to Queen, who shook his head.

The detective felt fortunate, actually, not to have to make small talk with his present company. He never felt like small talk with anyone. Action was his preference.

And they'd made it almost to their destination without things getting warm, which was a relief. The panorama of downtown Saint Paul opened to them as Snorre urged his team of horses forward, and he took the moment to savor the view. To the north was the polished white State Capitol. The dome was still under construction, but farther along now than it had been when Queen had raced past it in that streetcar in January.

The Church of the Assumption's twin spires burst through the skyline to the east. Saint Paul was a working-class Catholic town, and it made sense to Queen that the Assumption should have such prominence. This was a city he thought Doc might do well in, as he'd always been supported with vigor by the lunch-pail brigade. Too many Irish, though, for the old man to handle. The mayor had admitted to him his dislike for the Irish. Queen wondered how Doc felt about the new Police Chief of Saint Paul, John O'Connor.

He was a full-tempered Irishman, who he'd heard ruled his city like an ancient Celtic king.

Queen pushed his thoughts to something else, like the plan ahead. They were headed to Saint Paul's red-light district to find Maisy, once and for all. Pock would confirm the address, and their disguises would get them in the front door. After that, he honestly wasn't sure. He hoped the quiet morning would continue uneventfully, and they'd make their way unscathed across the river and back into the Minneapolis city limits.

The detective wasn't much for details when it came to the chase. In business, where money was involved, he tried to tread more carefully. Planning the mitt games, for instance, had been deliberate and thoughtful. But out in the open, when a woman was in the soup? He preferred, like now, to make his choices in the moment, with his gut.

These jumbled city streets must have been planned by someone either bughouse or three sheets to the wind, he thought, as they twisted and turned their way towards the river. Queen finally recognized Seven Corners, a large, confusing commercial intersection made up of West Third Street, West Fourth Street, West Seventh Street, Front Street and Eagle Street.

"Eagle," Pock said, and Snorre must have understood, as he veered down that street's gentle slope, crossing curving trolley rails.

It had been a while since Queen had frequented Saint Paul's lower levee, and the area known to locals as "below the hill." The Mississippi River lapped up against a community of ramshackle houses called Little Italy. It could be dangerous along the water at night, but this morning there were no screams of robbery, rape or murder. Only the melodic warble of songbirds and the faint hum of a distant train whistle. The Italians here worshipped the Mother

Mary, and as it was the Lord's Day, the streets were empty.

The wagon reached the intersection of Eagle and Washington. Most of downtown Saint Paul was now above them, sitting on the bluff to the northeast. The Wabasha and Robert Street bridges stretched across the river from the city center, and to the west, a criss-cross of iron beams made up the suitably named High Bridge, connecting to the towering heights of the opposite bank.

The notorious Bucket Of Blood saloon marked the entrance to the brothel district. Queen noticed a couple of men passed out in front of the door of the plain-looking one-story building. It was a saloon where knife fights and shootings were as a common as a piece of bread with a plate of spaghetti. The lonely bray of an accordion emanated from inside. The door was already open, beckoning the Italians who already were resigned to drinking their way to Hell instead of morning mass. While in the past Queen might have answered that call, he was beyond imbibing simply for the sake of it, despite the familiar tug of temptation. They continued on Washington, which turned northwest, towards Third Street. It rose steeply towards downtown. Snorre snapped on the reins to keep the team of horses moving against the incline. A series of a half dozen or so "boarding houses" hemmed the avenue's west side. All of these houses, he was aware, plied their feminine wares to the city's denizens. Farther down was Saint Paul's Central Police Station, which Queen had always thought was a laugh. Minneapolis had three major red-light districts, but never the nerve to put them a stone's throw away from the center of the city's law enforcement. Today, however, he was short on humor.

Pock motioned with his head toward the second-to-last place on the block, and Queen nodded. He climbed to the front of the wagon and pointed out a red-brick two-story building with a rounded arch door and adjacent matching window. Above that was a big bay window, topped by a pointed parapet. On either side of the door, long columns rose from the front steps to the top, jutting out above the roof line. Many joked that they looked like the ends of male members, and Queen was inclined to agree. Across the street from the brothel stood the county morgue and the Hill Street power station. Snorre turned their wagon right at the corner, onto Ontario, and pulled it over.

"You're sure she's in Clifford's place?"

Pock licked his lips. "I'm sure."

"Okay, then. Snorre and I will go in. This shouldn't take long. If you see anyone approach the door, like the police or Jiggs Kilbane, get to me first. Do you understand?"

"Yes." Pock moved to the driver's seat as Snorre lumbered down. The big man grabbed his pipe wrench and stuffed it inside his overalls, while whistling a cheery folk tune. Queen considered telling him to quit, but decided it was a normal thing to do. This was meant to be an average delivery on an average day. Peder had had someone paint *Pioneer Fuel Co. Coal — Coke — Wood* on the wagon's side, and he hoped it was generic enough to douse suspicion. The detective understood that they were not the brothel's usual delivery service, nor would coal be scheduled for delivery on a Sunday morning. But he was confident he could talk his way out of any line of questioning.

Queen stepped down from the wagon, with a sack he had specially filled himself. It was about two thirds coal, and a third coal dust. He heaved it over his shoulder, and headed to the front door, with Snorre close behind. He took a moment to glance to the right, where Clifford's personal residence stood, snug against the bluff. Next to that sat a little lunch shack, and behind it a staircase that ascended to Third Street and the civilized part of the city.

He knocked on the brothel's door, and a young woman dressed

as a maid answered. She looked at him with shock.

"You're supposed to bring that to the back! You can't come through the front door!"

"It ain't that busy, is it?" Queen asked with a wink, and pushed past her, stepping onto the velvet carpet of the bordello's reception room. He'd been in enough brothels in his life to understand what went on here. He looked around at the girls who lounged on upholstered chairs and settees, waiting to meet their prospective clients, and then to a man sitting at a baby grand piano.

"Where should I put this?" he shouted, to no one in particular. "I ain't never been here before, so I don't know!" Snorre laughed merrily behind him.

An elegant woman stepped out of an adjoining door and into his path, hands behind her back. He knew who she was.

"Madame Clifford, I'd imagine." He'd blackened one of his teeth for effect while in the wagon, and lit a grin to dazzle the room. If she was disgusted by Queen's appearance, however, she didn't let on. Instead, she looked at him like a stern teacher might react to a boy caught tramping through the classroom without first wiping his boots.

"You're at the wrong house," she said.

He looked at her quizzically, as he adjusted the coal sack on his shoulder. "Ain't this 147 Washington? I coulda sworn this is where my boss told me to go. He does this sometimes, giving me wrong addresses. Here, I got it written down on a piece of paper in my pocket. Reach in and grab it for me, would you?"

"I will not," she said, unmoved. The piano man, who he assumed was the chucker-outer, stood up and moved to her side.

Queen shrugged. "I'll do it, then."

He dropped the bag of coal on the floor and it burst on impact, sending coal skittering over the floor and a cloud of noxious black dust into the air. Madame Clifford put her hand over her mouth and backed away into her office, and Queen gave the bag a couple of kicks to increase the sooty haze.

"Make sure the bruiser doesn't follow me," Queen said, turning to Snorre, but Snorre had already moved forward, wrench in hand, to battle the musician.

Queen peered through the dust, trying to make out where the girls had gone, listening for their dainty coughs. They were running to their rooms, most likely, but he wasn't sure which way that was. One of them had to be Maisy Anderson, though, and he was determined to find her. Through the ballroom he ran, gun drawn. A staircase appeared through a second door, and he bounded up the steps. He could hear doors slamming and locking above him. When he reached the top, he started trying the knobs, and when they didn't cooperate, he used his shoulder to break them down.

He ignored the young prostitutes' cries of protest, and shouted over the hysterical ones. "Are you Maisy Anderson? Are you Maisy Anderson?"

A succession of shaking, sobbing heads were left behind him, until he'd checked every door but one.

The detective took a deep breath. This would be her, he just knew.

It was ajar, and he pushed it open cautiously. It creaked a little and then swung to expose the room.

A woman stood in front of him, with a man next to her. She blinked her eyes rapidly, a look of stunned surprise on her lovely face.

"Harm? Is that you?"

Queen's face went flush, and he felt his heart rip through his chest.

It was Karoline.

CHAPTER 11

It was damp here. Damp and cold and miserable beyond measure. He pulled on the edges of his coat, trying to make them meet his stomach in the middle, as he sat on the concrete floor. The gun shook in his hand, and he had to remind himself to point it forward. He'd never been fond of guns. Even as a Minneapolis police officer, he'd left his service revolver in the bureau drawer next to his long-johns more mornings than not.

Martin Baum had preferred a pencil, and had anchored a seat in various Minneapolis precinct stations for thirty years, doing his duty like a good soldier should. Mayor Ames hadn't seen fit to take him into his new term, though, and he'd been kicked like a beaten dog into the cold winter night. And that goddamn chief of detectives, Harm Queen, was to blame. He was sure of it.

How he'd managed to keep himself alive the last few months he didn't fully know. His wife had toed him to the gutter after he'd lost his job, and with no income, he could barely afford the rat-infested flophouse bed he slept in. His solace was in the dregs of a cup, but it only hid the pain for a while. When the whiskey inevitably ran out, he got even more desperate, and had even stolen kerosene from unguarded lamps to mix with water and sip until he couldn't stand. It was an excruciating existence. Every day when he awoke from sleep, he damned God that his eyes had opened once more.

When he'd received the message from Maisy he'd hoped for forgiveness. It was all he could think of as he and the chambermaid had ridden the trolley to meet her. He'd prayed for so long for someone to pay attention to him. After she'd disappeared from Hell's Half Acre, he'd lost track of her. What joy, to discover that she was alive and well, and asking to see him.

When they'd reunited she'd been furious, but he expected her anger would dissipate in time. There were too many happy memories for her to so cruelly sever their bonds. When she'd been younger, and she and her grandparents had visited Minneapolis, they'd stayed with him and his wife. He and Maisy had played together often, and when he'd teased her she'd gotten mad. She'd called him her bad Uncle Martin, and then skulked away for a few minutes, before cracking her sweet smile and jumping into his arms. He knew things were more serious now, and her accusations were cold, but she'd realize the error of her beliefs. His true character, in the end, would shine through.

Once he helped her, she'd realize it.

He could hear her faint breath as she crouched near the far wall of the black room. He wanted to go over to her, and to stroke her hair, and tell her not to be afraid. The problem, though, was that he was terrified himself.

They waited for a door to open in this darkened basement, a door that led to God knows where. A door that was about to produce a bona fide villain of terrible proportions. Jiggs Kilbane was not a man to surprise in this manner. There were stories, horrific stories, of the gruesome trail of blood that trickled in his wake. Beatings. Torture. Murder.

Baum was not cut out for this. He'd never taken a life in this way before. He'd never stood in wait for a man to appear, just to gun him down. But he had to. This was the only way to get forgiveness.

From a far distance, he heard church bells. Slowly they tolled, and he counted to eleven. He could tell Maisy was counting too, because she shifted in her seat when they ceased their knelling. He heard her suck in her breath, as if to draw the very last gasp of damp air from this cold hell.

And then the doorknob turned, and it groaned open. He saw Maisy's dim outline jump at the sound, and felt his own body jolt upright. A figure strode out, holding a lantern that spewed yellow light across the room.

Martin Baum rose, his arm extended, and pointed the gun at the man. His hand was so wet that he wasn't sure he could keep a grip, but he managed to pull the hammer back with his thumb. The man swung the lantern at the sound of the click, and suddenly Baum was blinded by the light. He fell back a step, and in a half a second the man was next to him. He wrenched the gun away from Baum with a quick twist, and tossed it across the room.

Baum's arm burst into pain as the man pushed him, and he stumbled into the wall.

"What is this?" the man demanded.

He had no answer. He was panicked. Panicked, he realized, not because of the man who threatened him, but because he was failing in his duty to Maisy. He had to know she didn't blame him for not pulling the trigger. There hadn't been enough time.

He had to see it in her face. The man followed Baum's head turn with his own, and saw her as he held up the lantern.

Oh, Christ, what have I done? Baum wondered. *I can't leave her again.* He reached out and grasped at the man, and his fingers tangled into some kind of string, and then something cold.

But a blow from the man's fist to Baum's gut made his legs crumple beneath him, and he went down onto the cold floor, rolling in agony. He looked up, trying to make out Maisy, but the lantern light was gone now, and it was black again. Only footsteps, and then her scream. He squeezed his wet eyes shut in humiliation.

"Karoline."

"Harm, what are you doing here?"

He curled his hands into fists, and moved towards the strange man, who had his back to him. The man turned, and Queen felt a rush of relief when he saw a stethoscope around his neck. Behind him, a girl lay on a bed. This wasn't what he thought it was, and then felt guilty for even thinking ill of his fiancée. He'd walked into some kind of medical examination, and it made sense, then, that Karoline would be here, although he'd thought she was at home, preparing to leave.

Queen lowered his gun, and then held up his hand. "I can explain, Karoline. I can. I'm looking for the girl. She's supposed to be here."

"But why are you dressed like that? And where are the others? Shouldn't there be Saint Paul police officers with you?"

He, of course, had no good answer for her, but the urgency of the search was too much ignore. He looked at the girl on the bed, who stared back, gape-mouthed.

"Is your name Maisy Anderson?"

She shook her head, eyes as wide as hens' eggs.

"You don't have to be afraid. I'm here because of your grandfather."

"Can't you see, Harm? It isn't her."

Karoline's face had tightened into a confused frown. Rarely had he ever seen her nettled, but at this moment, he felt that she might be. He also realized that he had no acceptable excuse for being here. She'd asked him not to risk himself by coming to Saint Paul alone and here he was. Big Snorre's presence would offer little consolation, and would most likely only implicate her brother Peder in this admittedly half-cocked plan. It was best to come clean.

"I'd agreed not to come, I know, but Karoline, I received a legitimate tip that she might be here. I didn't want to worry you."

"So instead, you went behind my back."

"Yes," was all he could muster.

She turned to the doctor. "I apologize for this. This is the man I am engaged to. His name is Harmon Queen, and he is a detective with the Minneapolis Police Department. He is here to rescue a girl from the clutches of slavers, although I'd never expected a brothel at this level to engage in such activities."

The doctor, a slender man with spectacles, gave an uncomfortable nod.

"I know nothing of such activities. But I appreciate you coming to my aid today, Miss Ulland, and at such short notice. I feel much more at ease having a lady by my side during exams to answer some of the more delicate questions."

"Certainly, doctor." She looked at Queen, her head cocked slightly. "Did you assume the worst of me?"

"I was shocked, a little . . . ."

"But I have an acceptable reason for being here, do I not?"

"Well, you've gone beyond your usual geographical range."

"I will ask again, Harm. Do you understand the nature of my presence?"

"Yes, dearest. Of course."

Pain shone from in her eyes. "Well, I can't say the same for you, Harm. Please go and find the girl."

"I'll come to see you this afternoon, Karoline, I promise."

She wiped her hands on her apron, and tried to look unaffected, but she was never one to be able to mask her hurt.

"If I see you today, Harm, we can talk. If not . . ." She choked back a tear.

Karoline didn't have to continue. Their relationship would be over if she left for Chicago before he could see her. And he needed to explain. To ask for absolution.

"I'll be at your house, Karoline. Of that, I swear. But I have to go, now, before things get out of hand."

She turned her head and shut the door, leaving him standing, staring at nothing. He desperately wanted a few minutes to absorb their conversation, this monumental shift in their relationship.

But if Maisy Anderson was really in this building, this was his only chance, and he had to act now.

Big Snorre had landed his blows, as the musician lay doubled up at the Norwegian's feet. He looked expectantly at Queen when the detective entered the reception room. Queen shook his head, and pointed upstairs.

"Karoline," was all he needed to say. Snorre's face broke into worry. "Take her home. Do you understand?"

"Ya, ya, Q-veen." The big man lumbered out, and Queen walked into Madame Clifford's office. She was on the telephone, receiver to her ear, when he pulled the cord from the wall.

"I apologize, Madame." He pulled out his wad, and counted out ten dollars. "That should cover the cleaning and repair costs."

"I know who you are," she said. "And your reputation is loathsome, Detective Queen."

"You're not the first to remind me of that, Madame. Please allow me, though, to explain my presence."

"And you couldn't have done that from the beginning? Instead of dirtying my floors, frightening my girls, and beating my musician?"

"Without the ruse, I thought I might be turned away at the door."

"You would have been." She stood up from her desk, and came around to meet him. She was an impressive-looking woman, he conceded. She had to be formidable, considering her difficult line of work. He'd met countless madams in his time as a police officer, but Nina Clifford was special. Many said she was as powerful as any man in Saint Paul, with the exception of James J. Hill, perhaps. He considered his theatrical entrance for a moment, and wondered whether it would further foul his standing in this city. On second thought, however, he was glad to have caused such a spectacle. He liked attention from those who pulled strings, and she certainly wouldn't forget him after this.

"There is a girl in your employ."

"You went to these extremes for a girl?" She gave a bitter laugh. "I'm sure she would be most impressed."

"You misunderstand, Madame. This is a girl that isn't supposed to be here."

"I look after every young woman under me, detective. I'd never let harm come to any of them."

"This is a special situation. She was forced into this profession, under the most revolting of circumstances. The man who kidnapped her, Emil Dander, was a vicious animal, whom I unfortunately knew all too well. I don't know how she found herself working for you, but I'm here to find that out."

Madame Clifford eyed him coolly, but he thought he caught a glint of concern.

Time to press.

"Do you know a Maisy Anderson? Is she here?"

"Detective, no one here works by that name."

"Yes, of course I understand that. She goes by something different, I'm sure. I believe she is connected to Jiggs Kilbane, if that stimulates your memory."

"And why would you be looking for her?"

"Her grandfather, a retired sheriff from Bemidji, came to claim her body from Dander's brothel. As it turns out, it wasn't her. The old man was hell-bent on finding her and taking her home. Jiggs Kilbane ended his search. He had the sheriff killed while he was sitting in his chair, cleaning his gun."

"I'm acquainted with Mr. Kilbane. He is a well-known businessman in Saint Paul. I am aware of his temper, but not of any capacity to commit murder."

"Listen, please, Miss Clifford." His knowledge of etiquette screamed at him not to do it, but he was determined to get through to her, and put a hand on each of her shoulders. She flinched, but stood her ground. He fixed his stare, and continued. "If she is here, and has anything to do with Jiggs Kilbane, you need to tell me. I am her champion, madam, of last resort."

"Because of this sheriff?" she asked.

He knew it. *She's here.*

"Yes, because of him. And because I've dealt with Kilbane before. I know what he's capable of."

She nodded, surrendering to the detective. "Follow me," she finally said.

Queen fastened his mitts on the lapels of Martin Baum's greasy suit, and hoisted him to his feet. He hadn't seen this bastard since the election, and wanted nothing to do with him now. How he was involved in this, Queen couldn't even begin to fathom.

"Does this chucklehead have any reason to be in your personal residence?" he asked Madame Clifford.

"No, no, of course, not. I'm never seen this man in my life."

"Then you have some spilling to do, Baum," he said, and gave the man a hard slap to his jowly cheek.

Baum tried to speak between halting sobs. "D-d-damn you, Queen. Damn your interference."

"And what am I interfering in?"

Madame Clifford spoke. "The door to the tunnel is open. I'm sure it has something to do with that."

Queen set Baum down, and examined the entrance. His lantern lit the first few feet of a corridor, braced by wooden beams.

"Where does it go?"

"To the Minnesota Club, Mr. Queen."

"From your *home?*"

"My house stands almost against the bluff. Follow this passage, and it will take you up through the rock and into the basement of Saint Paul's premiere gentleman's club."

The detective was impressed. The city's privileged patricians would be blackmailed if spotted coming through the front door of her establishment for a paid roll in the hay. It made perfect sense to have a discreet, back-door method of coming and going. Ingenious, is what it was. He turned back to Baum. They had a tainted history together, and Queen thought a change in tactics might improve his chance at information. So he lowered his voice, and did his best impression of someone who cared.

"I'm sorry for striking you, Baum. I'm looking for a young woman, and I think you know more than you're letting on. I want to help her, so tell me what happened."

"I'll never tell you anything," he snapped. "STAY AWAY FROM MAISY!"

That was too easy, Queen thought, with satisfaction and slight distaste. Baum knew who she was, which didn't necessarily surprise him. Martin Baum had always traveled in dark circles, hiding behind his jolly exterior to avoid suspicion. Getting him fired from the force had been one of his first goals when Doc had taken office.

He saw something clenched in Baum's fat hand, and yanked it away. Baum yowled, but Queen ignored him. It was a necklace, but not of a style he'd ever seen before. The chain was a leather strap, and the pendant that dangled from the end was a small silver turtle. It wasn't flashy enough for twinkle-footed Jiggs Kilbane, either.

"Whose is this?" he demanded.

Baum tightened his mouth and stared defiantly at Queen. He wasn't going to talk, the detective knew.

"I've seen it before," Madame Clifford said. "It's from the man who works for Jiggs Kilbane."

"Do you think she is in danger?" he asked her.

"I didn't before, but I do now," she said. "His guard, whom he called Henri. That necklace you hold belongs to him, I believe." She went to the entrance and reached for what looked to be a switch, punching the buttons three or four times. "The tunnel is wired with electric lights, but they're not working."

Queen wanted to ask her about her relationship with Kilbane, and how Maisy had come to work here, but time was too precious. They already had a head start, and he aimed to go after her. She seemed to anticipate his impulse, and took a kerosene lamp off the wall. She lit it with a match, and handed it to him. He quickly wrapped up the turtle necklace and shoved it into his pocket, pushing it into the middle of his bill roll.

"Go quickly," she said. "I should never have let them take her."

He nodded, took the lamp, and ran into the tunnel.

CHAPTER 12

Queen wasn't supremely tall, and at five-foot-nine above average in height, but he still had to bend his head slightly at points as he moved through the low-ceilinged passage. The dirt floor was uneven, and he could smell the stink of mold in the wooden beams. The lamp had plenty of fuel, which gave him a boost of confidence. But if someone was waiting for him ahead, they'd see him coming. He thought he could handle himself, though. As long as they weren't a good shot.

Suddenly he didn't feel so good after all, thinking about a bullet whizzing from the darkness and blasting into his chest. *Just put one foot firmly in front of the next,* he told himself. *Use the God-given brain that got you to the position of chief of detectives to finish your duty.*

His right knee started burning after only a few moments of sprinting, so he slowed to a walk. He knew he'd better take it gently, as a big climb, in some form, lay ahead. The only sounds were of the rocks that kicked up under his feet and his own breath as he sallied forth. He tried to imagine where he might be in relation with the city above. He knew the Minnesota Club bordered Rice Park on Washington Street. Streetcars were rumbling over his head, probably, at that very moment.

The tunnel started to steepen, and the pain in his knee continued. This has to be a tunnel for young men, he decided. Randy young men, who are willing to endure the brisk exercise and mildewy stink for a quick trip to heaven. Beer bottles and cigar stubs littered the floor as he toiled up the grade. He thought about Jiggs Kilbane to spur him forward, and the more he thought, the angrier he got. He wanted his hands on the neck of that rotten Mick, for Edna Pease, for Dix Anderson, and for Maisy.

He reached a series of short staircases, each followed by a slight slope, until he knew he had to be near the top. The tunnel finally leveled out, and there was the door.

He'd made it entirely through, and hadn't encountered Jiggs, his man, or Maisy. As no celebratory glass of champagne appeared from thin air, he took a moment to catch his breath and ponder the situation instead. They're hightailing it, he decided. He wondered if Maisy was fighting them, or going willingly. He thought about Madame Clifford again, and wished he'd learned more about the situation. She definitely knew much more than she'd revealed to him. Damn, he felt like a fool for passing that opportunity by. But every moment lost meant Kilbane was that much farther along.

The door was unlocked, and he slipped through after a pull on the handle. He noticed the furnace immediately, and realized his clothes might work to his advantage now. He was in the basement of one of Saint Paul's most elite club houses, a place where Kilbane would feel as snug as a bug in a rug.

"Where did you come from?" came a voice. He turned to meet the eye of a sleepy-looking janitor, washing a mop in a grimy sink.

"I saw three people come down," Queen lied. "Two men and one woman. I was curious so I followed them."

The man scratched his head thoughtfully. "Curious you say? I s'pose it was rather curious. I seen them, but it was one man, not two. He had the girl under his arm, I think. And they was going up, not down."

"Did the man have orange hair?"

"Not that I saw. It was short, I'd say, and white. And the girl was a real beauty. A delight on the eyes."

"How long ago did you see them?"

"Twenty minutes at least. The man was running."

So there were two, not three. Christ. And the man was carrying a full-grown woman at full throttle through an uphill tunnel that had winded Queen after five minutes. What was he dealing with?

"Queer query coming from you, chum. Were they your pals?" the janitor asked.

Queen ignored his question, took two dollars from his pocket and handed them to the man. "Can you get me out of here?"

"Hot-diggity and hells bells. Come this way," the janitor exclaimed with a surprised look. "You're mighty gen'rous for a coal-man."

They'd wound their way through the club house, past the bar, and through the dining hall before reaching the Washington Street entrance. Queen kept his eyes peeled, but every room was empty, and even the staff, it seemed, had disappeared. This was a segregated club, and a woman and a man together would have been considered the height of impropriety by the membership, so he expected that they'd probably scuttled through quickly, even while it was quiet. The janitor held the front door open for him, and Queen walked out into the fresh air.

"Where's your wagon?" the janitor asked him.

"Around the corner," said Queen. He looked down the sidewalk both ways, and then at the park in front of him. An elaborate fountain bubbled with water, and men wearing summery straw boaters sauntered by, but there was no sign of a man dragging a woman against her will.

He didn't know where to go, or what to do.

There were two options now, as far as he could make of it. Either find the man he'd been pursuing or go straight to the source, Kilbane himself. Could they be heading back to Kilbane's gambling house on University? If he committed to storming Kilbane's headquarters, he'd really be setting himself up for trouble. And he didn't want a repeat of the disaster that happened on his last trip to that unwelcoming joint.

Think, goddamn it, think. Where else could I be, if I were Jiggs Kilbane, on a Sunday morning?

And as if answered by God, he saw the twin spires of the Assumption Church rise over a line of trees.

He felt less guilty taking a bicycle from a jackass, so when the scorcher came flying down the sidewalk, scattering pedestrians, Queen simply reached out and grabbed him by his collar and shook him off his ride. After mumbling an insincere apology and throwing a handful of dollars onto the stunned dandy, he got on the bicycle and began to pedal. The spires looked like stacks of boxes crowned by pointed hats and were easy to follow, and the giant clocks on their sides displayed the time of eleven forty-five.

While he wasn't a Catholic, he was familiar with the second Sunday morning mass, and it would be ending soon. Even a killer like Kilbane wouldn't dare carry a weapon into a House of the Lord, and it was the perfect place to confront him. He still hadn't thought through what he would say, but his rage was about to explode at the thought of that grinning ape acting holier than thou, especially after what he'd done.

The bicycle was top-notch, and he pedaled to the church in a matter of minutes. The doors were still shut, and the street quiet, and he was glad that he'd made it in time to put on a show. When he reached the church's front lawn, he tossed the bicycle onto the grass and went to the side entrance. He opened it slightly, and the drone of organ music filled his ears. When was the last time he'd been to church he suddenly wondered? Years, probably.

And then he remembered. It had been just before his first major investigation on the police force. A fire had devastated a tenement building off Nicollet Avenue, and he'd walked through the burned interior of one of the apartments. He'd seen the charred bodies of an entire family, including six children, huddled in the corners, blackened like meat that had fallen into a campfire. After seeing that, he'd suddenly lost his taste for church. And once he began to gamble, drink, and stretch his own morals for admittedly personal gain, there was no turning back.

He had no problem with the upstanding, law-abiding folk who prayed in pews, but he hated the goddamn hypocrites. So when he easily spotted Kilbane, wearing a pink and orange striped suit, standing in line for communion, he didn't hesitate.

Queen prowled through the vaulted arch of the church's transept, past the front pew and to the aisle. His filthy clothing drew bewildered stares from the well-attired congregation, but he couldn't have cared less. He saw Kilbane snicker, but as Queen came closer his expression turned to recognition, and then fear.

Fear. The detective smiled and strode up to the gangster to stand eye-to-eye with him. Whispers washed through the onlookers like a wave, and even the priest put down his wafer in mid-delivery and watched, dumbfounded.

In a loud voice, Queen began.

"Ladies and gentlemen, I am a police detective in disguise." He pulled out his badge and waved it in the air. "This is Jiggs Kilbane, for those of you who don't know. He is a cold-blooded snake of the worst kind. He ran a low-grade joint in Minneapolis, where he enslaved young, vulnerable women and forced them to do unspeakable things to fill his accounts with ill-gotten chink. He's got sporting houses in Saint Paul where he does the same evil business now!"

Ladies' gasps punctuated the air.

This should do it, he thought. Kilbane's criminal empire was about to turn into rubble. He turned back to the gangster triumphantly.

"You murder at will, with no fear of consequence. You strut around town like you own it. You're nothing but a four-flushing butcher, and I was a witness to it. I saw you end a woman's life. Blast her down with a bullet, in my arms!"

A lady in the second pew stood, screamed, and then fainted. The congregation erupted in raised voices, some pointing at the gangster. Kilbane's body shook and his teeth rattled as he backed away from Queen, towards the opposite transept. *I've got this bastard*, Queen thought gleefully.

And then, a large, white-mustached man suddenly stood up, and hammered his hymnal on the pew in front of him. The crowd quieted as they identified him.

After a moment Queen recognized him too. Saint Paul Police Chief John O'Connor.

"What in holy hell is this about?" O'Connor's voice boomed through the nave, echoing against the stained glass windows. Queen stepped forward.

"I'm a police detective, sir . . . ."

"From Minneapolis. I know you. Harmon Queen, is it not?"

"Yes, sir, it is. This man, this farcical fakir is Jiggs . . ."

"I know who he goddamn is!"

Queen could feel the congregation cringe at the police chief's ill-use of the Lord's name. John O'Connor, however, was not a man to seem to care what others thought. He rumbled out of his pew and filled the aisle, directly between Queen and the gangster. He was a barrel-chested, intimidating bear of a man, if Queen had ever seen one. Fred Ames served as O'Connor's Minneapolis counterpart, but didn't have a tenth of the natural authority that this man possessed.

"Sir, I can explain everything to you personally. It's fortunate that you happened to be here as witness to this."

"Witness to your baseless accusations, you mean? This is not a court of law!"

"I realize that sir. It's just that . . ."

"This is God's house, you insolent son-of-a-bitch!"

Queen was stunned. What was the police chief doing? The detective was handing him Kilbane on a silver platter. He was a witness to the man committing murder.

O'Connor bulled his way up to Queen, and snarled.

"Give me your badge and gun, Queen. I'm placing your under arrest for instigating a public disturbance."

CHAPTER 13

When Maisy awoke, she almost gagged on the rag in her mouth. She recognized the pungent ether smell, and spit it out.

Her head swam with pain, and her clothing stank with sweat. She struggled to sit up, to focus on her surroundings.

The man who had taken her came into view. He sat in a chair near her feet, arms crossed. "I'm sorry for all of this," he said.

She realized she was on a table when it wobbled as she slipped herself off. The man reached out, in an attempt to help her keep her balance, but she pushed him away, and managed to stand up on her own.

"The chloroform was unfortunately necessary."

"To keep me from fighting you," she replied. Her bun had opened and fallen onto her shoulders and she pushed her hair out of her eyes.

He gave the barest of smiles. "Yes."

She nodded. "Where am I?"

"You're in a cave."

"A cave?"

"Yes, a cave. This was a saloon a few years back, but abandoned now."

I'll be darned, she thought, as she looked at the arched sandstone ceiling above her. It was cool and quiet here. A wooden bar lined the rock wall, with benches along the opposite side. Iron light fixtures hung from above, and the dim bulbs cast a burnt orange half-glow on the rough ceiling.

"Why are the lights on if this isn't an operating joint?"

"Mr. Kilbane keeps this place in working order for situations such as this."

Maisy was callused enough not to be too surprised by anything anymore. She'd seen what evil men were capable of. Finding herself here, in a damp cave, after an afternoon draped over a man's shoulder, hadn't fazed her as it might have another, more innocent, girl. The fact that Kilbane had a hideout made perfect sense, with his line of work.

"So," she said. "What now?"

"We wait for Mr. Kilbane," Henri replied, handing her a glass of water from a nearby table that was stacked with plates, folded napkins and utensils.

She took it and drank quickly, relishing the relief it gave to her parched throat. She handed it back, and he filled the glass again from a bottle on the bar. After another glass, appreciated more slowly this time, she sighed, and sat down.

Henri, seemingly satisfied at her compliance, took out a small book from his vest, and taking a seat, opened it to a bookmarked page. With nothing better to do, she tried to peer over and make out the words, but they were French.

"Is that an interesting subject?"

He looked up. "To me, yes."

"What is it about?"

"Nothing that a young lady should concern herself with."

"You've written notes in the margin, and they are English."

"I like to practice writing English when I can."

The man seems so calm, she thought. So unlike his boss. It didn't make sense, but little of the world did.

"May I ask you a question?"

"Yes," he said, closing his book.

"Why do you work for him?"

"He pays me well."

"Where is Trilly?"

"With him, perhaps?"

"So you don't know."

"No."

In her experience, men liked to talk. A few of them came only to silently rut, but others? They wanted to chit-chat on the dime. Tell her about their cold wives and their business troubles. When she did encounter a quiet type she had weapons of seduction to coax words out. But she decided her wiles wouldn't work on this one.

Henri, here, was different. Suddenly she was tired of pulling teeth.

"Is there a lady's washroom?"

He pointed to the end of the cavern, where the dim light scarcely reached. "It wasn't constructed for use by the female sex," he said. "But you're welcome to use it."

It was probably filthy, she thought, as she stood up. She sucked in her breath and tried to gather her skirt tight as she walked past Henri, but the gap between him and the table piled with eating ware was narrow. Despite her best intentions her dress brushed over the top, carrying glasses and utensils with it.

Glass smashed against the rough floor and forks and knives bounced and clattered alongside.

"I didn't mean for that to happen," she said as she bent down to pick up the mess.

"No, no," Henri protested. "Just go. I will clean it."

Maisy walked through the bar to the washroom, feeling a mixture of pluck and dread as she pushed her way through the saloon-style doors. This all was so exciting, she admitted to herself. Her early days as a captive in Dander's saloon had been spent cowering in corners, but she was different now. She'd been so afraid to disappoint her grandparents that she'd chosen instead, to slink into the shadows submissively. Her grandfather's death, she concluded, had freed her to care about others beside herself. Her actions were more selfless now. She felt a sense of purpose. For the first time in a long time.

She turned on the sink faucet and splashed cold water on her face. It smelled of sulfur, but felt good on her tired eyes.

And then she pulled out the knife from her sleeve and tested the point. *If I'm to die today,* she decided, *then I'll make sure I go down fighting.*

To my last breath of damp cave air.

Desperation makes a person resourceful. Baum had never been resourceful by nature, but getting clocked in the gut by that crack-faced man had awakened his brain, somehow. It had cleared the whiskey fog and sharpened his calibration. Maisy had asked for him. *Asked* for him! She wanted only one thing from him, and he was ready to give it to her, or give up his life in the process.

Despite his poor physical condition, Baum was still a police man. He had some experience in tracking suspects and had learned a lot about sleuthing matters from his friendship with Dix. It had seemed obvious to him that the tunnel would end somewhere up above, so after he'd shaken himself off in Clifford's basement, and brushed away her offer of help, he'd made a hasty exit. Up the outside staircase that connected Washington to West Third Street he'd wheezed and huffed, and then he'd waited.

Before long, the man had appeared on the street, setting Maisy into the back seat of a carriage, and driven off. He'd watched them as they crossed the Wabasha Bridge, and after wiping off his spectacles and putting them on, could just barely see them turn, towards the base of the bluff. The added bonus was that Queen hadn't been pursuing them. He was an idiot, Baum decided with smug satisfaction.

After making his way across the bridge, he'd walked along Wabasha Avenue, past angular industrial buildings lined up in little red-bricked rows, until he reached the steep limestone-faced walls that ridged the river.

His heart wasn't used to this much strain and stress, and it made its displeasure known by pounding like a pile driver in his chest. To ignore the sensation, he studied the bluff as he tramped down the road. A massive building suddenly appeared, built right into the rock. Bruggemann Brewery's malt warehouse and mill, according to the sign. This was a part of Saint Paul where the Germans brewed their beers, letting their kegs age and cool deep inside the hand-carved sandstone interiors. They drew their waters from the natural artesian wells deep below the earth. He hadn't tried this brand, but plenty of familiar breweries operated around here, he remembered thirstily.

Another five minutes of walking and he saw the man's carriage. It was parked outside a wide metal door that led into what he assumed was a cave. What he intended to do now, he wasn't sure. He was alone and weaponless, and for the most part, gutless.

He had pebbles in his boot, so he walked to the curb and sat down. His foot was in pain, and slightly swollen, making the boot, which was already tight around his fat calf, even more difficult to remove. After a hard tug, he manhandled it off, and let out a sigh as his foot hit the cool air.

"What the hell are you planning, anyway?" The voice came from behind. He tried to turn, but he felt a strong grip fasten onto his shoulder and the cold metal of a gun press into his neck. He dropped the boot and put his hands up.

The person came around and into his view. He wore a well-tailored suit and had broad shoulders, and his hair was slick with oil. He was young, too, but held the gun like he knew how to use it.

"Answer my question, old man."

"I'm just taking a walk. It's a nice day and . . ."

"Can the nonsense," the boy said. "You followed a man and a woman here."

"H-how do you know that?"

He gave a dimpled smile that ate up half his face. "Simple. I saw what you saw, and followed your hobbling carcass across the bridge."

"Wha-what do you want from me?"

The boy got on one knee, and looked him in the eye. "I want you to screw, Grandpa. Blaze a trail somewhere else."

"But I c-can't. The girl inside. I know her. She's in danger . . ."

"And you're a goddamn dirty old client who rolled with her once and can't get her out of your head. I know. You think she'll give you a free poke for your attempt at chivalry?"

He leaned in, and Baum could smell citrus. "There are men with guns in there, Grandpa, and they'll kill you as soon as look at you. Now get lost."

Baum winced as the boy grabbed him by the fabric of his coat and hoisted him up. He felt a kick in his buttocks that made him stumble forward.

"You old men always think you can take whatever the hell you want, don't you? You see a lady you fancy, and you can do what you please with her, is that it? To hell with you and all your patrician pals. If I find you lurking about again, I'll have to get violent with you. Go home to your wife."

Baum looked back and saw the determination in the kid's eyes. The boy was far stronger than he was, he knew, and without a gun of his own it was pointless for him to argue. Slowly, he began walking, back the way he came. He strained his ears for the slam of a door or a conversation.

Nothing. When he got to the brewery, he scuttled behind a beer wagon and waited for a shout, but none came. He dared himself to turn around, set back his fat shoulders, and pivoted, just in time to see the boy pull open the door to the cavern and then drop down to all fours and crawl inside. Part of him wanted to see what would happen, but the rational voice in his head spoke more forcefully this time, and told him to stay where he was and see how things played out first.

So he intently watched.

CHAPTER 14

She was sitting again, by Henri, as he read his book under the amber electric light, when the front door's handle clicked, and it slowly swung out. She could make out the sunshine as it streaked through the room, lighting a haze of floating dust. But no one entered.

Henri shut his book and got up.

"Stay here," he said.

She watched him as he strode to the door, unconcerned. His wool sash, tied tightly around his waist, was knit in an intricate design of red, yellow and green. She'd never seen anything like it before. At the brothel she had seen lumberjacks who sometimes would come to Saint Paul to spend their money, dressed in colorful garb, and they always made a spectacle as they trudged up the road from the riverboat landing. But Henri wore his sash over his suit like a military accoutrement. He was all business, and very serious. She had to admit that despite being her captor, his stern, fatherly bearing was growing on her. *I actually feel safe with him,* she realized with slight astonishment.

It was with more astonishment that she watched his body suddenly drop out of her sight.

She jumped out of her chair and ran to the door. Without even thinking, she pulled the knife from her sleeve and held it out.

Behind a table, she saw him, suddenly and ferociously locked in a grip with Dick. They both commanded great strength, and they had each other by the throat, rolling and grunting on the concrete floor. Dick was an athlete in his prime, however, and took the advantage, finally flipping Henri on his back, and pinning him with a straddle.

"Dick!" she screamed, and he looked at her, his wild eyes melting at her sight.

"Nellie! Are you all right?"

Then she saw Henri reach for a chair leg, and before she could cry out a warning he smashed it onto Dick's back with a horrible crack, showering their bodies with ragged wooden splinters. Dick had taken worse hits during his football games, he knew, but this one had stunned him for just long enough that Henri took his fist and knocked him hard in the jaw, sending him falling onto the floor.

She screamed again and rushed over to him, almost tripping over Henri and the rest of the broken chair. Dick held his hand on his bruising face and tried to shake his head.

"I thought I had the upper hand," he moaned.

Henri stood, brushing bits of wood off his jacket. He bent over the boy and drew the gun out of his pocket. Then he looked at Maisy, and the knife she held in her hand. He walked behind the bar, and pulled out two pairs of handcuffs.

"I love you, Nellie," Moonlight said, as Henri snapped the cuffs to his wrists, behind his back.

"I so wish you hadn't come, Dick," she replied. She looked at him, so miserable lying on the floor. He felt humiliated, she imagined; used to excelling at everything he did. What had he been thinking? This was a world he didn't belong in. Was he really so innocent about the nature of evil men that he thought he could traipse in with nothing but an athlete's constitution and somehow save the day?

And what would Jiggs Kilbane do when he learned of Dick's attempts to free her? That was the question that most distressed her. Her plan to stick the knife into Jigg's Kilbane's heart was finished, and now she had to worry over Dick's safety as well as her own.

Moonlight blinked fiercely, resolve smoldering in his eyes. "I'm going to be a policeman one day soon, Nellie. I've just talked to a detective in Minneapolis. He told me I'm guaranteed a spot on the force as soon as I graduate! Don't worry, sweetheart. They can't hurt me."

He can't be serious, she thought. Overconfident, yes. But not a fool.

"Henri. Don't listen to him. He's a thick-skulled idiot and in love with me." She paused, and looked at Dick with apology. She felt a tug of heartbreak at hurting him again, but evidently he needed more pain to get the message. In a few minutes Kilbane would walk in, and she didn't want the gangster to do to Dick what he did to Trilly Flick. Or easily worse, and her imagination ran wild with the potential tortures inflicted on her old flame.

"Please, just hide him," she pleaded to Henri.

The man with the cracked face took her by her arms and pulled her away from Moonlight. He bent down, made the sign of the cross, and then slugged the boy with a single, devastating blow. Moonlight's cheek slapped the cement and he closed his eyes.

Another scream from Maisy reverberated through the cavern. Henri ignored her, slipped his arms underneath Moonlight's, and dragged him behind the bar and through what appeared to be a kitchen door.

"What are you doing?" she cried after him, pulling back tears.

"Hiding him, like you asked."

"Is he dead?"

"He is not."

"But why did you do that? He never hurt you!"

"The boy hates his father," Henri replied, staring at her grimly. "An uncontrollable, venomous hate. The less he speaks to him, the better for everyone."

Maisy was confused. What did Dick's father have to do with any of this? He sat in some large office somewhere, commanding his workers to make rafts of money. What exposure did he have to bordellos and gangsters and guns?

Henri saw her expression, and shook his head.

"My dear," he said, his voice dropping low. "This boy's father is Jiggs Kilbane."

CHAPTER 15

The cell was cold, but the plate of potatoes and gravy next to him were colder. Queen was hungry, though. He picked up the spoon and heaped in a mouthful.

He was exhausted, and slumped against the stone wall. They'd put him in a cell by himself. He figured it was for his protection. If word got around that Detective Harm Queen was lounging about in Saint Paul's Central Station, he was bound to get attention. While it wasn't his home city, there were probably a few scoundrels locked up here that he'd laid a hand on in Minneapolis.

His mind was a jumble of emotion. He'd been close to reaching Maisy, so close that it had clouded his judgment and landed him square in the heart of the enemy. Who the enemy was, he wasn't sure, and that made things even more dangerous for him. Jiggs Kilbane, it seemed, had a genuine relationship with Police Chief O'Connor, which Queen hadn't believed until now. Jack Peach, Kilbane's former henchman, had alluded to it, but Queen had taken his words as lies. Who did he need to watch out for now? Kilbane, certainly, but John O'Connor had inserted himself into Queen's sphere, and that made him terrifically uneasy.

And then there was Karoline. As far as he could tell no one knew he was in jail, and that included her. She'd be gone first thing tomorrow morning, heartbroken, thinking that he'd broken things off, if he wasn't able to make it to her in time. She'd think the worst of him, he feared.

His immediate problem, though, was protecting himself. Without a gun for defense, a badge for intimidation, or a stack of green for bribes, he didn't know how he'd stop a guard from entering his cell and pummeling him into a mash of meat. He was vulnerable here, and that was a feeling he didn't like. The whole situation was far worse than he could ever have anticipated. He'd expected to deliver the goods today, and instead had been delivered himself.

"Detective Queen. You look lost in your thoughts."

He raised his head, and saw a young man at the bars with a thick black mustache, a gray suit, and a sharp-looking Homburg on his head.

"I'm Frank Frasier." He held out his hand through the bars. Queen walked over and shook it.

"I've heard of you," Queen said. "You're new to the detective game, aren't you?"

"I am," the man replied with a confident smile. "But I'm old to police work."

"You've tracked down and captured a fair share of criminals, from what I've heard."

"Just earning my salary, like any good officer of the law does." He gave Queen a friendly wink. "You've found yourself in a pickle, I see."

Queen was more than aware of Frasier. His name had been inked in golden phrases by newspapers on both sides of the river.

Frasier was a sleuthing prodigy, who'd risen through the ranks faster than Jesus on Easter morning. It was said that Frasier, without even a weapon, could disarm the most hardened criminal with nothing more than a steady gaze and a few select words. It was hard to believe, but now in person, Queen understood. Frasier was one of those men blessed with charisma. And he disliked the man for it immediately.

"Glad to finally meet you, Frasier. Now come straight with me. Why am I really here? Your police chief claimed that I was causing a disturbance, but I've been here all afternoon without a word from anyone. My suspicions are that something else is going on."

"I'll give you that courtesy of being straight with you, Queen. From one cop to another."

"That's appreciated."

Queen was slowly warming to the man.

"That was the original charge, but things have changed."

"What's changed?"

"Police Chief O'Connor had a talk with Mr. Kilbane about your accusations."

"And I'll bet Kilbane denied them."

"Yes. Not only that, but he claimed that you were the one that killed the prostitute. Not him."

Queen had had plenty of time in the cell today to think about what was really going on, and he'd figured a conclusion like this would materialize. When Kilbane had shot poor Edna Pease, he'd used Queen's gun to do it, just for insurance. Now Jiggs was calling to collect on the premium.

"So it's Kilbane's word against mine."

"That's about it."

"Do you really think a jury will choose the word of a gangster over a detective?"

Frasier shook his head sympathetically, with just enough condescension to make Queen bite his tongue.

"I don't know how to put things delicately, so I'll just say it. You're a well-known scoundrel, detective. You once jammed your pistol, while drunk, into someone's eye, at a saloon, did you not? You twisted and gouged at it until it came right out."

Queen had. He looked away from Frasier.

"That man, and a dozen others like him that you've beat down, will testify as witnesses against you. Rip your character to shreds on the stand."

"What about Kilbane? He's done far worse!"

"He has," Frasier admitted. "But do you think anyone in Ramsey County will have the courage to speak against him? You're playing against a stacked deck, detective."

"Well, what am I supposed to do, then? Just buck up and take it? Go willingly to jail for a crime I had no part in?"

Frasier tapped his fingers on a bar, hesitating. He stared Queen in the eyes, hard, as if to gauge his caliber. Finally, he spoke.

"Convince me you didn't."

"What?"

"You heard me. Convince me that it was Kilbane and not you. If you can do that, we can talk further."

"On my very life. On the life of my sister." He grabbed both hands on the bars and came as close as he could to Frasier. "On my word as a police officer."

Frasier grimaced. "Not good enough."

"And why the hell not? We've both taken the same oath," Queen growled.

"True, but I haven't broken mine. I know what goes on in Minneapolis. You break yours every day."

Queen thought for a second to ask him how he knew, but immediately thought better of it. He'd already revealed his knowledge of some of the low points of Queen's career, from ten years past. Why wouldn't he know what Queen and his cohorts were up to now? Frasier was whip-smart, and had ears. Plenty of stories were circulating, he figured, about the mitt games and other cons in Minneapolis.

"Well," Queen offered, "What if I found a witness?"

"A witness?" Frasier lifted his eyebrows. "The Pease girl is dead. Jack Peach is dead. You left his bodyguard in a mangled trolley on the courthouse lawn. Who else was there?"

There had been someone else there, in fact. He had no idea

where she was, but she'd seen everything.

"Her name is Trilly Flick. A girl that worked for Kilbane. She still does, as far as I know."

"And why would one of Mr. Kilbane's trusty whores testify on your behalf?"

"Because she owes me. She double-crossed me, and she owes me."

Of course Queen had no idea whether Trilly would even look at him, let alone come to his defense. She hadn't given him the time of day the last time he'd seen her. He couldn't think of any other way out of this, however.

He had to try.

"I'll have you know, Queen, that even if the clouds part from the sky and God himself floats down to find you innocent of this, it isn't necessarily over."

"Why is that?"

"Have you been following what's been going on in Saint Paul in the last year? Or have you been too busy laying track to the bank?"

Queen wasn't sure what he was talking about. He didn't want to answer the last part of Frasier's loaded question, though, so he just shrugged.

"John O' Connor trumps God in this town, detective. He's established something called the Layover System, as you apparently haven't heard."

"I've been busy, as you've apparently stated."

Frasier chuckled. "Well, let me entertain you with the tale."

"Do you have a cigarette?"

"Sure, why not?" Frasier took a smoke out of his case, handed it through the bars to Queen, and lit it for him with a match. He waited for Queen to enjoy his first few puffs before continuing.

"Police Chief O'Connor, frustrated with the excesses of city vice, decided last year to put an open invitation out to criminals in Saint Paul. In essence, he gave them permission to live within city limits, without fear of persecution or prosecution, in exchange for one thing. No crime in Saint Paul. No burglaries, no robberies, no shoplifting. No destruction of private property." He let those words sit for a moment, and Queen understood their weight. The streetcar fiasco in January had left a swath of destruction, a conductor in the hospital, and scores of frightened onlookers. The police chief knew Queen was behind it. The Saint Paul papers had blamed a lunatic for the crash. A lunatic who had never been caught, until now.

"So he plans to blame me for that, too?"

"It was you, wasn't it?"

Queen shook his head, partially out of shame, but also to deny full responsibility.

"Kilbane's man, Jack Peach, chased me with the intent to kill me, Frasier. I would be dead if I hadn't done what I did. Was it careless? Thoughtless? Yes. But no innocents died. And I got away just in time to save the life of a fellow police officer."

He meant Tom Cahill, of course, who'd been set to be burned alive by a hobo with a tile loose in an abandoned town just outside Hastings.

"That was never published in any newspaper."

"It wasn't, but I know where the officer lives, and I can confirm the story at your go ahead. A sheriff named Anderson too."

"I've read about him. The papers said he'd died by a hunter's bullet. He sounded like a good man."

"He was a brick, Frasier. One of a kind. But it was no goddamn hunter. Jack Peach shot him. Ordered by your boss's best pal."

It was quiet as Frasier digested Queen's words.

Frank Frasier was an honorable man, Queen knew. As straight

as a razor. The mention of Cahill and Anderson had affected him.

His colleague lit a cigarette for himself, and took a long draw.

"I can't let you out," he said. "But I'll make one call for you. Give me a name, and it's done."

Queen thought for a moment. Peder Ulland was the first person to come into his mind. Peder could get him an attorney, along with any other resource he required. The problem, though, was Karoline. If she knew he was locked in jail, she'd cancel her trip to Chicago out of worry. Admittedly, he liked the idea of Karoline staying in Minneapolis. Their relationship, however, was fragile at the moment. Once she found out his predicament, there would be no way, he feared, they would ever be together again, after she saw him through this ordeal. Would she even believe he wasn't guilty, with the full weight of the law and John O'Connor thrown at his face?

He was wracked with self-doubt, and he didn't want to take the chance. Better to choose the fastest way to find Trilly Flick and clear his name. It might even be done without Karoline ever knowing he'd sat in a damp jail cell. But he needed a person who would be willing to break the rules, like he was.

"Get me Chris Norbeck, at Minneapolis City Hall," he said.

"What's his rank?"

"Very rank," Queen replied.

"Sounds like a daisy," said Frasier. They shared a little laugh.

CHAPTER 16

"Is this where the goddamn party is?"

Jiggs Kilbane grinned as he staggered through the door, followed in by a line of men, some carrying sloshing bottles of booze. Maisy took in her breath at this unexpected group. She watched them enter rowdily, cursing and belching and laughing, and then felt herself shrink in her chair. With every hair on her head, she sensed potential violence. The fact that she was the only woman here had only heightened her fear.

"My faithful man," Kilbane proclaimed to the group, motioning to Henri. "Get behind that bar and pour us some drinks. I'm in the mood to celebrate!"

Henri gave a slight bow, and met eyes with Maisy for a second before pulling out glasses and setting them on the counter. Jiggs was drunk by the looks of it, and in a jolly mood. She had to remain tough, she decided, so she pulled her courage together and strode towards Jiggs. She felt lascivious stares from some of the men, but ignored them. Putting back her shoulders, she stuck her nose slightly in the air, and delicately held out her hand. She was determined to look every inch the professional lady.

"Mr. Kilbane, a pleasure to see you again."

His bloodshot eyes shrank into beads as he looked her up and down, until they settled on her outstretched hand. He snickered and turned to the man nearest him, a pale, porcine fellow who was coughing at his own cigar smoke.

"This is Miss Nellie Boyce, also known as Maisy Anderson, also known as the bane of my fucking existence!"

The man guffawed, and Maisy's head suddenly whirled with confusion. Did he say that because he was drunk? Or had their arrangement suddenly changed?

"I don't understand, Mr. Kilbane. When we last met . . ."

"Shut your gob, bitch," said Kilbane. "You turned Harm Queen onto me, and our relationship has gone the way of the fucking dodo-bird." He raised an eyebrow and let out a creaky burp. "Our business relationship, that is."

She took a step back, grasping the back of a chair for support. This was a bad box she was suddenly in, she realized with ice-cold clarity.

"The good news, is, dearie, that Harm Queen ain't ever gonna come bothering you again. He's in jail for fucking murder, and that is the true joy of the day. A reason to celebrate!" He raised his hands to his intoxicated chums. "Drink all you want, boys! This place has a goddamn bowling alley too! And if you're looking for female companionship, I've got that covered as well. It'll be expensive, I warn you, but well worth the green." The men around him gave an unruly cheer.

"Mr. Kilbane. I don't know who Harm Queen is. I've never met the man." She looked for a weapon of some kind through her peripheral vision while she forced a fixed gaze and a polite smile for the orange-haired killer in front of her. The knife she'd had tucked in her sleeve was gone, and she wasn't sure how she'd defend herself. Her grandfather's spirit coursed through her, though, forcing her to remain calm and level-headed. There had to be a way out. And if there wasn't, she would put up a fight before she let them take her.

Her days of letting men crawl over her at will were over.

Kilbane pounded his hand on the bar. He threw his head back and guffawed.

"Don't give me no sauce. You're a goddamn piece of meat, and nothin' more. You think you come from some noble fucking lineage? 'Cause your grand-dad was a *lawman?*"

He leered his hideous leer, and grabbed her face with his hand, squeezing it until the pain numbed her cheeks. "I had him killed. It was me. He was nothing but a troublesome snoop. Months from the grave, from what I'd heard. I just helped him with that last step in." He leaned forward and put his tongue in her mouth, and she gagged at the slippery ribbon in her throat. With all of her strength, she shoved him away. He tottered, balanced himself with a hand on a table, and giggled.

"Tie her up and take her to the washroom, and leave her on the floor. Whatever suits your fucking fancy."

"You got the first go?" the porcine man asked with a wheeze.

"Hell no," he snickered. "I just finished with her friend at my suite at the Ryan. Ain't no more wax on my candle, gents!"

She winced at the mention of Trilly, and then looked around, searching for a way out. There were men between her and the door and even though they were drunk, she didn't think she'd make it past them. Then she felt Henri behind her pull her hands behind her back.

"I am sorry for this," he whispered. "I'll try to make this bearable." He clasped a cuff to each of her wrists, but to her surprise, left them loose. And then she felt the prick of the knife as Henri slipped it back into her sleeve. Her heart burst in gratitude, and courage took hold.

She heard the lewd catcalls and whistles as Henri gently pushed her into the depths of the cave.

The first one to touch her, she told herself, was going to wish to God he never had. And then she would find Jiggs Kilbane, and finish him herself.

Baum's fear intensified as he watched the parade of carriages pull up to the cave's entrance. He'd hoped for a chance to kill Kilbane, but now his odds were lessening as each new rig appeared. He didn't care about his own safety anymore. He was a washed up, unloved, miserable drunk, and the world wouldn't miss him in the slightest once he left it. But he didn't want to try at this last one thing and fail. If his only choices were Kilbane's life or bust, then he was determined to go out with a try at redemption.

The brewery was quiet, and Baum didn't know whether it was because it was Sunday, or if the place was out of business. He didn't read the papers anymore, and his alcohol of choice was straight whiskey, but the windows looked dark when he peered in, and he thought it might be abandoned.

He rattled the door handle, and it was locked. Another carriage rolled past, but the occupants looked busy reveling inside. Nobody gave a damn about him, and while this normally left his soul in the depths of a bottle, he was relieved to be ignored now. He went over to the window, and closing his eyes, used his elbow to smash it in. Shards still clung to the frame, and he snapped them out until he'd made enough room to climb through. Some boxes sat in a semblance of a pile nearby, and he sweatily scooted them over until they formed a crude set of stairs. Once he managed to get his large body over the edge, and after he picked himself up from a fall that almost knocked the wind out of him, he gathered himself together to look around.

He was familiar enough with breweries to know that this was the malt warehouse. It was empty, except for a dozen fermenting tanks and the rich, lingering, biscuity smell of malt. Dust layered the floor. A staircase nearby led to what Baum assumed to be the cellar, where the barley went through its first process in its transformation to lager. To his right was a door, and he peered in. This was the malt kiln. A massive furnace centered on a tile floor would dry the sweet malt to make it ready for brewing. Farther back, he could see where the building's interior met the cave. Brick-lined archways curved over natural sandstone ramps, where he assumed barrels could be easily rolled out of the cave's cool storage and into racking rooms.

The afternoon sun still shone through the windows, giving Baum enough light to navigate. He licked his parched lips at the idea of a cold, frothy lager, and continued across the warehouse floor, past a door that led to what looked to be a cooling house. A gigantic ice machine, now quiet, was there to produce ice water to chill the refrigerator rooms. This had been quite an operation up until recently, he thought. There was a glut of breweries in the Twin Cities, though, all ready to fill any void left behind by this abandoned place.

Past that, he found a large office. This is what he had been looking for. Inside were four desks, strewn with loose sheets of paper. File cabinets with open drawers lined the walls. Baum searched through each, looking for a gun. When he had exhausted the file cabinets, he started through the desk drawers. Still nothing, except for a few pennies, which he pocketed, and some old candy, which he gobbled down.

He walked back out to the warehouse, and looked around. There was nothing here for him to use, he decided, with a despondent shake of his head. It was over. He could find a gun elsewhere, and come back later tonight, but the chance that Maisy still might be here, and unhurt, were remote. He walked back to the main door, and unlocked it.

As he was about to leave, he saw a large metal toolbox out of the corner of his eye, sitting against the wall, smothered with cobwebs.

Even a wrench or a hammer would be something, he thought. He went over and opened it up.

Blessed heaven above.

His heart leapt into his throat as he carefully took out six sticks of dynamite.

CHAPTER 17

Her hands were slick with sweat, and her chest was so tight she could barely draw air into her lungs. She jiggled the cuffs behind her back a little, finding comfort in the fact that they were still loose. But it didn't quell the sickening, horrible anticipation of the foul acts she knew would soon be expected from her. Fear, desperation and resolution collided inside her head, as she tried to calculate her odds of escaping without being raped.

Henri knocked open the saloon doors with his shoulder and led her inside the washroom. He turned to the line of men following them.

"Wait, please, while I prepare her."

"Prepare her? Ha! I can do that for myself!" cried the first man in line, drawing lecherous laughter from his cohorts behind him. "I'll rip off her clothes and knock her through like a game of nine pins!"

"Wait," Henri repeated. He looked at the man with a cold expression, the expression of someone not to be trifled with. The man's smile disappeared and he gave a reluctant nod.

Henri took her around the washroom corner, and they were momentarily alone.

"I can't fight them all off of me," she whispered. "If Jiggs was first, I could kill him and the rest might run. As long as he's here, though, I'm as good as dead if I go for his friends. He doesn't need me now, and he'll do me in without hesitation."

"I won't let that happen," Henri said.

"But you work for him. What will he do to you, if you betray him? He's a depraved lunatic. He'll likely bury you next to me if you turn."

"My dear." Henri's voice was calm. "Jiggs Kilbane means nothing to me. He is in my way."

In his way? Her mind couldn't register what he was talking about. Kilbane was the most powerful criminal in Saint Paul, and Henri's flippant words struck her with wonder. But she pushed that wonder aside. At this moment she didn't care, as long as he could get her out of this suffocating cave in one whole piece.

Martin Baum picked up a smoking cigar stub from the gravel in front of the cave door, and put it in his mouth. He had shoved a stick of dynamite between each button of his shirt, giving him the look, he imagined with relish, of a Mexican bandito's bandolier. They would be easy to hide, he thought, but also easy to access by reaching into his coat. His fat stomach actually allowed the dynamite to lie in place, and he silently congratulated himself on his creativity.

The door was unlocked, and when he opened it, the smell of must and tobacco smoke hit his nose, making him sneeze. No one paid him any mind, though, as he joggled his way in and scanned the interior. Ingenious, he thought. It was a saloon, built into the bluff. Revelers here could have the time of their lives, and the sandstone would absorb the hullaballoo. He looked towards the bar, and saw a man who held the attention of all the others. His carrot-colored hair stood straight up on his head, like the clowns he'd seen at the circus, and he wore a brassy suit checkered in blue and pink. He'd never seen Jiggs Kilbane before, but this had to be him.

He jumped at the sound of an echoing crack, and turned to see an arched entryway into a long bowling alley carved into the sandstone. Two lanes fit snugly inside, and he watched for a moment as a tipsy fellow tried in vain to send a ball down a straight line to meet his awaiting pins.

"I was goddamn robbed," the man managed to gurgle out between swigs from a glass of beer.

This was as good a place to start as any, Baum decided.

The cigar in his mouth was still burning, and he withdrew one of the dynamite sticks from his lapel. The tipsy man walked over at him and gave a silly, drunken smile.

"Is that real, friend?"

Baum touched his cigar to the dynamite's wick.

"Watch and see," Baum said, and pitched the stick as hard as he could. He watched it skitter down the lane to the end of the bowling alley. *I'll bet that's a strike,* he thought, just as the blast turned the alley into smithereens.

Once, Maisy, remembered, when she and her grandparents had lived in North Dakota, they'd been caught in the midst of a spectacular thunderstorm. The kind that electrified the sky like an H.G. Wells invention gone awry, and with matching thunder that boomed so deafeningly that your hearing went numb for minutes.

While the noise of this explosion didn't quite match that sound, it came close. She and Henri looked at each other, stunned for a second, and they ran out of the washroom.

Everyone's attention was turned to a cloud of dust near the saloon's entrance, and a figure, wobbling on a chair, waving something in the air.

"He's got an explosive," gasped the man who just moments ago had been bragging about how he was going to crack her open on the washroom floor.

She squinted her eyes to make sense of the outline. After a moment, a jolt of recognition put everything into place. It was Uncle Martin Baum. He had somehow followed her here, and was trying to make his amends. His fleshy body had undergone a transformation, she realized. He was stronger now, bolder, as he brandished what appeared to be a stick of dynamite in his hand. She saw fearlessness in his eyes. This would be the last time she would see him, she knew.

As she thought those thoughts, she saw his head turn in her direction, and the barest of smiles flashed on his face. *He sees me. He wants me to remember him, like this. Ready to die for her.*

A mixture of admiration and disgust shivered through her bones.

"We've got to get Dick," she suddenly said to Henri.

"There is a second way out," he said, under his breath. "There."

He guided her gaze with his cocked head to a jagged opening in the wall she hadn't seen before.

"That leads to a staircase, which will take you to the top of the bluff."

"And you'll bring Dick? And you'll kill Jiggs?" The words drifted from her mouth like music, she felt. That horrible man needed to die, and it didn't matter to her how.

"Not me," Henri said. Uncle Martin was shouting something now, and they looked at him. "Him. The one you had set to attack me in Clifford's basement."

"He was there because I'd summoned him to shoot Jiggs, not you."

"Well, he's here now."

Henri bulldozed his way through the crowd and up to Kilbane, who had moved himself behind the bar. The gangster looked shaken at Baum's spectacle, and a stab of satisfaction filled her heart. Henri whispered something into Kilbane's ear, and the gangster's face turned white.

Strip away the guns and the bodyguards and he's nothing but a gutless poltroon.

After a few seconds of struggling, she slipped out of the cuffs, and they dropped to the floor. The knife was out of her sleeve and in her hand in a second, and she dropped into the shadows of the unlit crevice Henri had pointed out. She could see that it opened into a large room, and saw the start of a crude stone staircase that wound up through the rock.

She knew, logically, that her best chance to escape was now, but she glanced again at Jiggs, and made up her mind in that instant.

God willing, if an explosion didn't kill them all first, she would end this day standing over the monster's corpse, and give her grandfather his proper revenge.

Baum had taken out an insurance policy against his life years ago, but had stopped paying the premium after his wife Joanne had made him leave. Even though she'd emptied their accounts and left him with nothing, he still loved her. He hoped she'd feel some remorse once he was gone. Or even pity. He wasn't choosy, as long as she felt enough to show up at his funeral with a kind word or two.

The real person to blame for all of his woes, he knew, was sitting in a comfortable chair in Minneapolis City Hall, counting his stacks of ill-gotten money. Detective Harm Queen was a fraud. He sat on his mighty throne, directing corruption like a conductor in an orchestra for the worthless mayor and his brother, but was jealous of anyone with any aspirations of their own.

Over the years, Queen had harangued and belittled him. He'd accused Baum of being a bad officer dozens of times in a dozen different ways. When Baum had tried to make a little money on the side, like every other cop on the force, Queen had quashed his business. He'd accused Baum of being a degenerate, just because he didn't approve of Baum's methods. And how did Queen have the right to decide what was moral and what wasn't?

Everything that strutting ass dipped his fingers in was corrupt. He fleeced men out of their hard-earned money and had them booted out of town. He shook down madams for green. So what if Baum had introduced a few young women who needed money to gentlemen of means? It wasn't any different than what the brothel madams did, except that the poor young girls *he'd* found kept far more of the money they earned.

Baum suspected sour grapes had led to his dismissal. Queen must have been insanely jealous of his ventures, and wanted Baum out of the picture so he could step in. Queen had told Baum that what he did was despicable, but how was that so? These young women were destitute, and fortunate that the men they met took such interest in their plights. Baum's work had bordered on charitable, but Queen had claimed he was taking advantage of them instead. What absolute poppycock and hypocrisy! Queen was a vainglorious tyrant who destroyed those who were smarter than him, and who figured out better angles. Baum had gotten too big for his britches, and so Queen made sure he was thrown out with the morning chamber pot piss.

Once he'd been booted from the police force, he'd quickly started circling the drain. His connections gone. His money gone. His wife gone. Oh, how he'd suffered!

But now, as he stood atop a chair, demanding obedience from the most powerful man in Saint Paul, his vigor had returned. And he'd caught the eye of Maisy, in the far back. She was safe, and that was all that mattered to him.

"Kilbane!" he shouted from above the din of the panicked cavern.

The gangster turned to a couple of men near him, goading them, he thought, to pull out their pistols and shoot him.

Baum would not let things go down that way. Placing the fuse of the dynamite to the end of the cigar, he lit it, and the room erupted in shouts. He tossed his second stick towards the bowling alley again, but this time it landed much closer to the heart of the festivities, and it was hell and Tommy. The blast ripped through the cavern with ferocious, brutal force.

The shock knocked some men down, while others grabbed their ears in agony, and rock rained down from the ceiling. The force of the explosion flung Baum from his chair and into the side of the bar. More dust rose, and he tried to shake the terrible ringing from his ears and the pain from his forehead where it had bounced against the foot rail. He crawled back up on the chair as fast as he could, fighting every urge to just lie on the floor and give up.

But he needed to keep the upper hand.

If these were to be his final moments on earth, then they would be on his terms.

As he fought for his balance he noticed that Kilbane too, along with his bodyguard, had fallen. Baum shakily pulled out another stick of dynamite and pointed it at his adversaries, who were getting back to their feet. Jiggs took in the chaos with goggle-eyed awe as he clawed himself up to the bar.

"All of you, leave!" Baum cried, as he circled the stick over his throbbing, buzzing head. "Except Kilbane. And you." He pointed the dynamite at Henri, who nodded back in understanding.

The cave emptied in haste, men just minutes before drunk out of their minds now sober and sure-footed, and they parted like a wave around him. Baum caught a whiff of fresh air and turned his head back for a split second, just long enough to see that the door had blown open. Bodies were crumpled on either side of the entrance, twisted and moaning, and he suddenly felt a wave of guilt ripple over him.

Remember why you're here, he told himself. *Your sole reason for this folly is to avenge Maisy*. And the police would arrive in minutes, police he knew were in cahoots with the bastard he was about to blow into pieces.

He scanned the back of the room. Maisy was no longer there, thank God. She'd found a safe place to hide, and it would allow him to end it all, here and now.

He lit the third stick, and hurled it at Jiggs Kilbane as hard as his out-of-shape arm could throw It landed at the gangster's feet.

Baum toppled off his chair and scrambled for cover.

After the second explosion, the saloon rocked with pandemonium, and the diversion allowed her to move closer without notice. She watched her old Uncle Martin, in command of the room, and despite her hatred toward him, she felt a twinge of respect. It was his moment, she understood. In his mind, he was her knight, and she was willing to let the game play out in that fashion.

As she got to the edge of the bar, she dodged into the kitchen door. Between the cook stove and the icebox lay Dick. The bruise on his face had swollen purple, but he was breathing normally, and she gave silent thanks.

"Dick." She patted his face, trying to revive him. He was out cold, still. Her worry increased. A well-aimed throw by Uncle Martin might land one of those dynamite sticks here, and she wouldn't ever forgive herself if that happened.

The fact that he was Jiggs Kilbane's son still hadn't fully delivered its impact to her brain. She didn't want to comprehend it now, either. She just wanted him out of here. But her strength wasn't enough to drag him away. His body was a mass of solid muscle, and he outweighed her almost two to one. She had to wake him up.

She hit him harder this time, but still couldn't rouse him.

Frustration mounting, she scoured her surroundings for something that might do the trick. The kitchen hadn't been used for a while, it seemed, judging from the dirt that layered the counters and stove top. She could see no water supply, either. Her eyes finally settled on a beer keg sitting on the floor, and she crawled over to it and screwed the spigot open.

Beer poured onto the floor, stale from the pungent smell of it. She cupped her hands until it overflowed through her fingers, and moved back to Dick on shuffled knees. His mouth was open slightly, and she let it trickle in. He sputtered and choked and then came to.

"My sweet," she cried. He grinned when he saw her, sudsy foam running down his chin.

"You look well," he replied.

She laughed and they embraced. Everything had changed, now, and she didn't want to be apart from him, she realized with every atom of her body. But they couldn't sit like this forever, as much as she'd like to, when something horrible was about to happen in the next room.

"We must get out," she said, her face turning somber. "Your *father*."

In his knocked-out sleep, she thought, he must have forgotten why he was here, because his expression instantly darkened.

"He took you, didn't he? He was the one that you were to become partners with."

"Dick, I had no idea you were related to him. I never . . ."

"I don't blame you," he interrupted, caressing her cheek. "He's a bad egg, Nellie. I've put up with his capers for long enough. But involving you in his deceits is where I end it. Where is he?"

Her eyes darted to the door, and she didn't have to say anything. Like an acrobat, Moonlight Darling jumped forward from his back to a full stand.

But the crack of a gunshot stopped him in his tracks.

CHAPTER 18

Baum waited for the dynamite blast, but it didn't come. When he uncovered his eyes a boot landed square in his nose, making bones split and crack. More terrible pain screamed through his head, and he put up his hands as a makeshift shield.

"My man was too fucking fast for you, codger," a voice sneered. "He stepped on the fuse." As the world slowly focused, Baum could see Jiggs Kilbane standing over him, hands on his hips. "You came to kill me, is that it?" Another kick slammed into his ear, turning the ringing into a full-blown church-bell clang. He rolled, feeling his body rise and fall over his stomach. Sand kicked up into his eyes and mouth from the cavern floor. Finally, he bumped into an upturned table, and he heard the gangster snicker.

"Who sent you?"

He tried to talk, but could only groan instead, as the pain stung in his ears and eyes and even throat.

"Get up." Baum felt Kilbane's hands on the back of his coat, tugging at him to stand. And he attempted to comply, finally staggering to his feet. Kilbane pulled the remaining sticks of dynamite out of his shirt and handed them back to Henri, who hovered silently behind.

"WHO SENT YOU?" he howled through rattling teeth. Kilbane looked like a teapot ready to burst. He bounced on his heels, and his hands jiggled along his sides like limp eels. Baum had lived a long life, but never in all of his experiences had he met a man who appeared to be as unhinged as this one.

Then the guard whispered something in Kilbane's ear. The gangster spread a greasy smile and let the man step forward.

"My name is Henri, *mon ami*. I've been hired by Mr. Kilbane to do his difficult work." He took out a handkerchief and handed it to Baum. "You poor shack of a fellow. Your nose is bleeding. Please use this."

Baum blinked his eyes. He could suddenly taste the blood as it dribbled into his mouth, and he wiped himself dry.

"Mr. Kilbane is not afraid of giving you pain. Not only does he not mind, but he enjoys watching it done by professionals. And I am experienced in the skills of giving it. You've had the sting of it just now, but believe me, *mon ami*, that is only the beginning of what you could suffer."

Baum heard Kilbane snicker again, and watched the gangster sit down in a chair, a bottle of whiskey in one hand and a glass in the other. This would be a show, Baum realized, and Kilbane was making himself comfortable in the front row.

"Now I have not always done this," the man continued. "My family was in the fur trade once. My father worked for the Columbia Fur Company, many years ago. While he did not procure the furs personally—there were Indians for that—he had developed the skills of the trade from a lifetime of work. He taught me, long after the muskrat was hunted out and the trade was in its decline, how to use the tools to catch food to provide for myself. For instance . . ." He took a small object from his pocket and held it into the light. "This is an awl. It was given to the Indians in exchange for furs. It can be used for stitching leather."

It had a wooden handle, Baum noticed, and a sharp metal point jutted out from its end.

"It can also be used for other things," the man said. "It can leave small stab wounds in a man. Hundreds, if done properly, while the man is still conscious. And they will hurt, *mon ami*. They will hurt more than a roll through a bed of nails, if executed with the proper skill."

Baum moved his lips, but nothing came out. He wanted to tell the man he understood, but couldn't make the words. The man looked back with sympathetic eyes, and stepped close to him.

"I understand your anguish, *mon ami*. I've seen the terrible things men do to each other. You've been stepped on, kicked and beaten by those above you. You've experienced immeasurable torment."

"Yes," croaked Baum.

"Here is a man who represents everything you despise about power," he whispered in Baum's ear. "He is the very effigy of authority run amok. Can you dispute this?"

He could do nothing but shake his head.

"Good," the man replied, and Baum felt him slip the cold handle of a gun into his hand. "Shoot him now," he breathed. "Do not hesitate." And he stepped to the side.

Moonlight Darling bounded over the bar with only his hand to support him. He landed next to Baum, who Maisy could see was trembling with fright. The smoke from the gun circled his head. She rushed around the bar, past Henri, and slipped under Dick's arm.

Together, they stared at Jiggs, who had fallen to the floor and lay on his back, holding his hands to his gut. It was a nasty, nasty wound. She looked at him, writhing in agony, his eyes bulging in surprise at how he'd been done in. She'd wanted him dead since she'd seen him bash Trilly's head, and had expected satisfaction at its conclusion, but was surprised instead that she felt only disgust and pity instead.

Henri motioned to Moonlight. "Your father is dying. Say what you have to say."

"But what about *him?*" Moonlight let go of Maisy and spun to meet Baum. "He shot my old man."

"Do you want revenge? Your father will be dead soon, and this man will hang for it. Make your peace, if you care to."

The boy turned back to Kilbane and got down on his knee, moving broken pieces of a whiskey bottle away. He picked up his father's hand.

"I despise you," he said, "for everything you do and you stand for. For the way you treated Mother. For your carousing and philandering and lack of nobility."

"Nobility?" Kilbane sputtered, blood dribbling down his cheek. "Do I look like a goddamn king to you?" He flung his son's hand to the side.

"You look like you're knocking at death's door, is how you look. Just go, Father. Close your eyes and pass on."

Kilbane struggled up into a sitting position. "Somebody get me a goddamn cigar," he suddenly shouted. "I don't want a penny stick either. Get me a ten cent Havana, for Christ's sake!"

Just die, Maisy thought. *Just die, you son-of-a-bitch.*

"You're a disgrace," Moonlight scoffed. "You make your green by cheating, stealing and murdering. You've lived your life selfishly. And now that your misbegotten ways have led you to this moment, you have a chance to atone. Apologize for how you've treated me. How you've treated Maisy."

"You ungrateful little shit," Kilbane spat. He snatched the back of Moonlight's neck and yanked it close to his crimson-stained shirt. The gangster's chest rose and fell with heavy wheezes, and Maisy couldn't help but glance at the ragged hole in his stomach, oozing with thick, dark blood.

"That fat fuck just gut-shot me. Why are you wasting your time on that fuckin' folderol when he's standing right there!"

"W-whatever he did to you, you deserved it, I'm sure."

"That doesn't matter. You've got to be strong, boy. Give out your licks like a man. Just because you've. . . you've. . . ," a wheezing fit overcame him, and he gasped for air. "J-j-just because you've got a college degree, and I ain't, don't void you of your goddamn duty. You ain't no Darling, no matter how much you hide under your mama's name. You're a Kilbane, for fuck's sake!"

Moonlight's eyes blazed, and he stumbled up, wrestling his neck from his father's grasp, suddenly unsure of what to do. Maisy put her hand on his shoulder, but he brushed it off. He turned again to Baum.

"I am under obligation," Moonlight said.

"Your life will be ruined," she cried. "Your father was going to have me raped, Dick."

"I just don't know," he muttered. "I don't know what to do."

She looked at Uncle Martin. Congealed blood clogged his nostrils, and his eyes were wet with tears. Trembling, she removed the gun from his hand.

I thought I could do this, she thought, fighting to control her panicked breath. *I thought that I could, but I'm not sure now.*

Her finger slipped onto the trigger, and she stretched her dainty thumb to the hammer, pulling it back. It was all she could do to hold it steady, but she gritted her teeth and aimed.

At her Uncle Martin.

"Atta girl!" cried Jiggs. "I knew you had pluck the moment I first laid eyes on you at Dander's brothel. How does it feel," he turned to Moonlight, "that this vicious little bitch has got more moxie than you ever had?" He threw his head back to laugh, but gagged instead on the blood that clogged his throat.

"What are you doing?" Moonlight gasped.

"You're a hero, Dick." Her senses were dulling, and she felt faint. "Children know your name. You've got a future, and I won't let you spend it in prison. If you feel so obligated to your father . . ."

"You're not a murderer. I won't let you do this."

The cave sat silent, as if waiting to see what she'd do next. Martin Baum had steadied himself, and wore a resigned expression. Henri stood by as serenely as a stone statue, and Moonlight looked overwhelmed with emotion. Then Jiggs broke the silence.

"What are you fucking waiting for? Do it. Shoot the pudgy shit, and get it over with." He gave a low, agonizing moan, and then it slowly crescendoed into a high-pitched giggle, finally climaxing in a hysterical fit of coughing.

She walked over to Kilbane and looked down without expression or remorse this time.

His eyes grew wide when she put the barrel against his forehead. Her aim was steady, and Jiggs fell back forever with her shot.

It was as if the steam had been let out from the entire room. Moonlight fell to his knees, sobbing into his hands. Baum looked exhausted, and sat down in a chair and stared into space. But Henri appeared to be nothing but business.

"My dear," he said. "You should have let him die on his own."

"I needed to do it."

"I know."

Henri took the gun from her, wiped the handle with his jacket, and placed it into Baum's sweaty hand.

"Do you understand what you have to do?" he asked. "Whether it is by the police, or by your own hand."

Baum nodded. Henri turned his attention back to Maisy.

"You are free to go."

"To where?"

"Do you have money?"

"Yes, some."

"Here is more." He counted out a dozen bills from a stack he pulled from his jacket pocket.

"This is too much. Why would you give me this?"

"Because I have a soft heart for the downtrodden. You've been through the mill, and need to start again. I have one more thing for you, by the way." He reached into the vest of his suit and took out the book she'd seen him reading earlier. "I know it is in French, but perhaps you can free some time to learn the language of love."

"And what will you do?"

Henri gave her a pat on the shoulder and smiled. "These are dangerous questions to ask, Miss Anderson, so let us part on these friendly terms, shall we?"

CHAPTER 19

He came far faster than Queen had anticipated, which reminded him he'd better thank Frasier for his promptness in making the call.

"How are things, Harm?" Norbeck asked with a chuckle.

"What do you think?"

"I don't get to this part of town as often as I'd like to. You know a good place 'round here for a plate of pickles and a strong drink?"

Queen turned away as Norbeck picked at one of his sores. It was all Queen could do to hold his miserable lunch in at the sight of the blistering scabs that crawled over his ex-partner's nose.

"Christ, Chris. Where is your ointment?"

"Oh, right," he said. He took out the container and dabbed it delicately on his face. "Feels better, Harm."

"I'm relieved to hear it. Listen." He leaned into the bars, trying to avoid Norbeck's breath, which smelled of rancid sardines. "I need you to do some things for me, Chris."

Queen had always had an odd relationship with Detective Chris Norbeck. They'd been partners in the past, and Queen had leaned on him many times before for personal help. While Norbeck could be readily counted on for follow-through, he made piss-poor decisions, too. As long as Norbeck was judge-sober, though, he was good in a pinch.

"I figured," Norbeck said. "I never expected to see you in air and exercise, Harm. Jail, tut-tut! I mean I know we're walking the line in Minneapolis, but Doc has our asses covered and . . ."

"Chris." Queen waited for Norbeck to realize he was talking too much. When Norbeck took a breath and gave a sheepish smile, Queen continued. "I need you sharp for me. Can you abstain for the next few hours?"

Evidently Norbeck saw the seriousness in Queen's expression, because he gave a firm nod and grabbed the bars with both hands for emphasis. "What do you need, Harm?"

"I need you to get me out of here."

Norbeck dropped his voice to a low, conspiratorial tone. "That's what I'm here to do, actually. I've got a message from Colonel Ames."

"What is it?"

He looked around to make sure that no one could hear. "Colonel Ames is worried about Doc, Harm. Really worried. The mayor found a note at his door this morning."

"What kind of note?"

"It had a threat written on it."

"A threat? What kind?"

"It said that he had to watch out."

Queen reined in his irritation. "Elaborate."

"It said that Doc was an enemy of the proletariat and a shill for the aristocracy and he should be punished for his crimes."

"What crimes?"

"For what he did to the Indians during the Sioux uprising. And for what he's doing in Minneapolis now."

"He was a goddamn doctor during the uprising. And it's the proletariat that got him elected mayor to begin with."

"Well, that's what the letter said." Norbeck gave a wide grin. "He's worried about being assassinated, Harm."

Queen ignored Norbeck's spectral smile. He was long used to the detective's inappropriate responses.

"Did the note mention that?"

"Nope. It just demanded that he confess his crimes, or else."

"Or else, huh?" Queen scratched his cheek. First, anarchist

scuttle, and now this. On the surface, it didn't seem particularly menacing. But knowing Doc, he was likely reinforcing his home with barbed wire and guard towers to counter the threat. This malcontent, whoever he was, really wanted to shake the Ames brothers up, and was certainly succeeding. And a threat was a threat, and it needed to be followed up. Unfortunately, he wasn't in a position to do anything about it.

"You really think there are anarchists in Minneapolis, Harm?"

"Well, there are definitely plenty of Socialists. It's one step away from that. And you were the one that questioned the boy at the university who said he was attacked by one, and never bothered to tell anyone."

Norbeck shuffled his feet. "It seemed kind of funny, at the time. I thought he was pullin' my donkey's tail."

"That a boy's finger was bitten off by a lunatic?"

"Well, yeah." Norbeck's face suddenly brightened. "But I got to meet Moonlight Darling! What a swell player he is!"

Queen hadn't been positive that word had gotten around yet about his discovery of Pock, but now he was sure it hadn't. Norbeck would have arrived with questions from Fred Ames about Pock's arrest, and why he hadn't been brought directly in front of the colonel for a personal grating. This was a lucky break, because he had no idea where Pock was since the trouble at Nina Clifford's place. He hoped that he'd stayed in the wagon as instructed and Big Snorre had taken him home.

"Chris, is word of my incarceration on the streets yet?"

"Don't know. News travels slow on Sundays."

Thinking about Peder had taken his mind to Karoline again. What were the chances she might have already heard about this fiasco?

"I need you to find Trilly Flick for me."

"That sweet little dish? Sneaking her in here just for a poke don't seem such a great idea."

"Do you know why I'm actually here, Norbeck? I'm being charged with murder," he hissed. "A roll with a prostitute is not exactly on my mind."

"Okay, okay. Got it." He gave Queen a sly wink. "Detective Frasier filled me in. Jiggs Kilbane sure don't like you, huh?"

"He shot Edna Pease . . ."

"The one who couldn't talk."

"Yes, her. Trilly was there, and saw everything. Get her here, and convince her to tell the truth, and I've got a chance to get out."

"We don't need to do that, Harm." His grin shone in triumph. "Doc is pulling strings."

"What does that mean?"

"He's already spoken to the mayor of Saint Paul. I don't know the business behind it, but you're going to go in front of a judge first thing tomorrow morning, and bail will be posted. You'll be out for a whiskey lunch! Ain't that just snappy?"

That was one hell of a helping of good news. Too late to see Karoline, but it would give him time to clear his name, which had to be his first priority. How Doc had managed to go above Police Chief O'Connor and make this happen, he couldn't even begin to fathom, but he wasn't about to argue. For this, Doc would get the finest box of cigars Queen could afford.

"Does Frasier know yet?" he asked Norbeck.

"Right after our conversation outside I saw John O'Connor approach him, looking perturbed as all hell. I'd imagine he knows now."

Queen rubbed his forehead, trying to erase a headache that had been building all afternoon. He had so much work to do. And Trilly was first on his list.

"I'm getting out, but only temporarily. Miss Flick still needs to be found."

"Colonel Ames wants you in front of him as soon as you're released. He said he's relying on you to figure out who's behind the note."

"Then you need to find her, Chris, because Jiggs Kilbane wants me dead. Can you do that for me?"

"Where do I look?"

"He's got a casino on University Avenue . . . ."

"I know it."

"And a suite at the Ryan Hotel."

"Which one?"

"Just pay the bellhop, for Christ's sake. You know how to turn over the trash bin and shake it out."

"What do I do when I find her?"

"Put her in a Minneapolis hotel, near City Hall. And put a guard on her. Do it personally if you have to. She's my only goddamn way out of this."

"I won't let you down, Chief of Detectives," he said with a salute.

"And don't drink until you find her. I don't want to find you all jaggy when I see you next."

Norbeck smiled wistfully and licked his lips. "I'll ignore every bottle of bug-juice that crosses my field o' vision, Harm."

CHAPTER 20

She'd taken him by the hand, and led him to the spiral staircase inside the cave, but Dick was lost in thought, it seemed, and missing a step. His face was dark and despondent, and while it troubled her, she was still far more concerned about getting out of the cave before the police arrived.

The staircase opened to a heavy metal door, hidden in a thick grove of trees at the top of the bluff. Henri must have assumed they were coming the same way, because he'd left it wide open. An early evening breeze cooled her face as she pulled herself out. Dick followed, and she stopped and confronted him when they were finally clear of the passageway.

"Snap to," she demanded.

"I'm trying." He rubbed his eyes and gave her his attention.

"There are a couple of things you need to know before I take another step with you. First," she said, brushing off her dirty dress, which smelled of cigarette smoke, "my name is not Nellie Boyce. It is Maisy Anderson. And before you question why, every sport in every house of ill-fame goes by a name other than her own."

He flinched, slightly, in understanding.

"Secondly, the man that shot your dad is an old family friend. The man I had always thought of as my dearest Uncle Martin met me on my first day in Minneapolis. He was supposed to take me to college, but instead left me with a gang of men who abducted me. That is part of the reason why I considered killing him. The other part, like I said before, is because I didn't want you to do it instead."

"So where does this leave us?" Moonlight asked, averting her gaze. She took his face and moved his chin up until he locked eyes with hers.

"You have to shake off your father's death," she said, hands placed firmly on her hips. "It's over, and, I'm sorry to say, was a long time coming. We're going to go, now, to where your father lived, collect whatever money we can, and then shut down whatever notorious business he had brewing. Then, I'm going to find my friend, Trilly Flick."

He nodded, slowly, in numb acceptance.

Finally, you're going to take me to this famous Detective Queen, who you and Uncle Martin and your father kept mentioning. He seems to have been with my grandfather during his last moments on earth, and I want to know what really happened." She was still out of breath from the walk up the stairs, and all of this talking made it worse. Once she regained her composure, she continued. "Do you have a problem with my plan, Dick?"

"Where does this leave you and me?" he asked.

"What do you mean?" she asked back, although she already knew the answer.

"The last time I left you said you wanted nothing to do with me. The situation has changed now. You don't have to fear my father anymore." His old charm suddenly reappeared, as he lit his lopsided grin and a loose lock of his oiled hair dropped into his eye.

She sighed, and tried to hold back her delight while keeping her shell of toughness intact. "Let's just make it through today," she said. "And I understand if you feel queer about what all's just happened between you and him. You don't have to put on a brave face for me."

Moonlight pulled a cigarette from his pocket case and put it in his mouth. She'd seen him only moments ago, debating with shaking hand over whether he could kill his own father, but now he was the very figure of coolness.

"For the record, my dear. I'm glad my dear old Dad got beefed. We can be together now. It's all worked out." He sucked the smoke down to ash, and flicked the butt into the grass.

It's going to take him some time for this to settle, she realized. But she would help him, for however long it took.

She had no one else.

It was all he could do not to bawl like a baby as he watched his darling Maisy disappear with Kilbane's demon-spawn son into the darkness of the cavern's rear crevices.

He looked at his pudgy, filthy fingers, wrapped tightly around the pistol's grip. He looked at Jiggs Kilbane's motionless body, doused in blood, a maniacal smile staring up at the ceiling through crimson-stained teeth.

Then he stared at Henri, the man who had placed the gun in his hand. Henri looked back with compassion in his eyes.

"Do you need some liquid courage, *mon ami?*" he asked.

What Baum really needed was his ears to quit ringing, and the dizziness and pain in his head to cease. And a drink could help considerably, he guessed.

He stumbled to the bar and watched as Henri poured a shot glass to the rim.

"Drink quickly, Mr. Baum."

Baum didn't have to be told that. His hand shook as he tippled the fire-water down his gullet and the warm burn brought incredible relief. He put the glass down and his shoulders dropped, as though a set of strings had been snipped.

"You must continue to protect Maisy," Henri said. "Confess to the police that you pulled the trigger."

"W-what will happen to me?"

Henri's expression turned grave. "You'll likely be tried and convicted of murder. And then, hanged by the neck."

"But only you, and them," Baum pointed to the back of the cave, "saw me shoot him! If everyone keeps quiet . . ."

"Look around you," Henri cut in. "These men died as a result of your rash decision to toss dynamite inside of a cave." He took a sip from his own glass, and wiped his lower lip delicately with his sleeve. "I will, however, hire a top-shelf attorney to defend you. Anonymously, of course. This, I can do, to give you a fighting chance."

Baum looked down at the floor, devoid of desire for this depressing conversation.

"I know you love her," Henri continued. "While it might seem disconcerting that she's with the son of her enemy, let me reassure you that he's a young man of sound mind. He will not follow his father's path."

"Does he love her?" Baum asked, dejectedly.

"I believe he does, yes." Henri gave him a heartening smile. "I know, underneath your suffering, that you are an honorable man. You've been dealt a raw deal by men in power. And I will make sure you're a martyr for our cause."

"What cause? What do you mean?"

"I mean that your name will be spoken far and wide with reverence, and you'll be elevated in our struggle, far beyond your death." Henri straightened his sash. "I must go now. A full force of uniformed ruffians will be here soon. Take care of yourself, Mr. Baum."

What kind of "cause" was he babbling about, Baum wondered? He watched Henri slip into the shadows, and then looked again at the gun in his hand.

There was only one man in power that Baum wanted dead, and

he was still out there, footloose and fancy-free, while Baum was about to go down for a mass of murders. Well to hell with that, he thought. To hell with that crafty holier-than-thou piece of shit.

And to hell with Harmon Queen.

He grabbed the whiskey bottle Henri had left on the bar, took a fat swig, and surveyed the room. Five bodies, he counted, not including Kilbane's, dead on the floor.

He spotted a large-waisted figure at the end of the bar, and recognized him as the one who'd been leering at Maisy before everything had gone to piss.

Baum pushed the body over, looking for the cause of the man's demise. Not a mark on him, he realized with satisfaction. His heart had probably exploded from fear. Baum slipped off his own shoes, took off his jacket and trousers, and proceeded to do the same for the man. They were close in size, he could see, and after a few moments of struggle they had switched clothes.

His new suit was flash. It was made of expensive linen, with a silk handkerchief and silver buttons polished to perfection. There was a bulge in the inside pocket, and he reached in to pull out a leather wallet, thick with twenty dollar bills.

His admiration of his new duds was suddenly interrupted when he heard voices outside the open door. Baum moved quickly. He grabbed the pistol that had shot Jiggs Kilbane and pushed it into the porcine man's palm.

I've got a temporary lease on life, he thought. It'll be hours, if not a day or two even, before the police realize that this man was not really Martin Baum. The instigator of this disaster, this multiple murderer, would still be on the loose. It would throw the city into panic, and make headlines across every newspaper in the state.

But he had some time before that happened. Time to exact his revenge on that son-of-a-bitch Queen.

He darted to the back of the cave, just as he heard the policemen cry out their discovery.

When Maisy and Moonlight reached the University Avenue building Kilbane used as his headquarters, the lights in the downstairs storefront were already on, in anticipation of evening activity. A slot machine sat like a squat, shining iron god in the front window, under a sign proclaiming the store the exclusive local distributor for the Mills Novelty Company. Moonlight led the way to the man behind the counter, past more slot machines, arcade games and vending contraptions. Evidently they were familiar with each other, as the man took off his hat and put it over his heart. He was tall, pale, and endowed with some of the largest ears Maisy had ever seen. She tried not to stare, and decided that if she were ever to wear a man's hat, a pair of ears like those would prevent it nicely from falling over her eyes.

"Sorry to hear 'bout your pops, kid. I got the call ten minutes ago."

Maisy was flabbergasted at how quickly the news had traveled during their thirty-minute cab ride. Why had the police found it necessary to call the manager of Kilbane's casino so soon with the news? How was that possible? Moonlight, however, either didn't think it strange, or didn't think about it at all. He seemed to be all business, and she'd never seen him like this before.

"Where's the money from this weekend's take, Diddles?" he asked.

"It was collected by your pops this morning."

"Why? Where did he bring it?"

"He doesn't like the weekend take sittin' around on Sunday," Diddles replied. "Mr. Kilbane's done it this way for years. Where he takes it, I never asked. Probably because I like bein' alive." He laughed a little at this.

"I've never paid attention before," Moonlight muttered.

"No offense, Moonlight, but I ain't never seen you here in any business capacity. I know you've been busy with your football and your girls, but you've been here maybe once or twice in the last four years? And only to play roulette. Never to see your pops."

"Are you blind, Diddles? Don't you realize your boss was completely bughouse?"

"Sure, his trolley was off a little, but him bein' unpredictable made him interesting. And he wasn't never bad to me."

"I can be unpredictable too," Moonlight said, and suddenly leapt over the counter. He slammed the cash register open with his fist and pocketed the cash.

"We need that to make change, Moonlight! What if someone wants to come in and buy a Little Wonder gum ball machine?"

"Don't tell me you don't have plenty of money upstairs, where the real action is," Moonlight snarled. "And until I get my affairs straightened out, don't question me, Diddles."

Maisy tried to set the comment about Moonlight's "girls" to the back of her mind. While they were both adulterous, she'd had no choice in the matter. She had been forced by circumstance to bed men for money. And honestly she didn't believe in her heart, because of her difficult place, that she was disloyal to Dick. She allowed herself no emotional connection to the queue of flesh-hungry men lined outside her door.

Dick, however, always had the freedom to choose. The freedom to be steadfast and true, and yet he still wasn't. Yes, he was a college boy, and full of vigor, and that vigor led to impulsiveness with other women, she knew. But why couldn't he stay faithful? She had freely given him what he wanted. Why couldn't that be enough?

And that led to an even more perplexing question. Why did she still love him so maddeningly, even with his infidelities?

But she stashed those thoughts into the attic of her mind. Dick was acting differently, rashly, and this was her current concern and priority. He was confused, she understood, and obviously affected by his father's death. He'd also never bothered or obsessed over money like this before. While she'd given him the idea to clean out Kilbane's cash, she still hadn't expected that he'd embrace it with such ferocity. His good-natured, easy-going charm had captured her heart once, probably because she'd had so much darkness in her life to deal with. But he was different now, and she hoped he hadn't changed for good.

"Come on," he said, taking her by her sleeve and pulling her to the exit. "My father's suite is in the Ryan Hotel. We can get baths and fresh sets of clothes there."

"Dick," she said, when they reached the sidewalk. He continued to drag her, but she planted her feet firmly. "Dick, stop."

"Nellie—I mean Maisy." He was flustered, and rubbed his brow in frustration. "We've got to get that money before someone else does. My father had enemies, and the word is already out on the street that he's gone. If we don't act fast . . ."

"We'll get there when we get there. Calm down. You need to collect yourself."

He turned to her, and kissed her. It was a forceful kiss, and felt both intimate and sad. They held each other, a long, slow embrace, and his body relaxed in her arms. Finally, he looked up, imploring.

"Let's leave town once we get the cush. Go west, to San Francisco. I want nothing to do with any of this."

"But there are things I must do first," she replied. "I need to settle my family affairs, and get my own questions answered. And find my friend Trilly. And you graduate this week."

"We'll take her with us," Moonlight said, his face cheering. "We can't stay, Maisy."

She thought for a moment, about her grandparents, and her overwhelming love for them. They would have sacrificed every possession they had in the world to find her and make her safe and happy. Her happiness and safety depended, now, on Moonlight Dick Darling. He needed her, and she him. She'd be able to start a business, with him by her side, in some far-off city, away from the horrible memories here.

And most important, she believed, her grandfather would approve of this decision. He'd have wanted her to be happy.

Her heart suddenly ached at the memory of his tall, bent figure, and she could still feel his calloused hand enveloping hers. Her grandfather had never been uneven in thought. He'd always known what to do. It was a slow revelation, now, that she'd be the one making the rational decisions in her relationship with Dick. It didn't change her love for the kid, but her expectations were taming at every turn.

"We'll go, right after your graduation ceremony," she told Dick. He nodded, looking grateful, and they kissed once more.

Maisy had heard stories of the Ryan Hotel, but seeing it up close, in all of its Victorian Gothic magnificence, filled her with mouth-dropping awe. It was a seven-story behemoth of arched windows, granite columns and balconies; built in red brick and banded by white sandstone. The tops of the pointed spires built above three elegant, European-looking towers seemed to pierce the blue afternoon sky.

They walked into the lobby and she immediately felt a pang of envy. Dick had lived here through his teen-aged years, with unfettered access to these opulent surroundings. Marble columns held up a spectacular vaulted ceiling, bordered by a dark-oak balcony and softly lit by stained glass windows. To hell with propriety, she thought, and slipped off her battered shoes, delighting in the cool, clean tile on the bottom of her sore, dirt-encrusted feet.

Men milled about the sitting areas, smoking cigars and sipping coffee. She felt their stares as they walked by, and suddenly was self-conscious over her filthy appearance. She made up her mind to give a defiant stare right back, but then realized, to her complete surprise, that the object of their interest wasn't her.

It was Dick. He was a celebrity, she then remembered, with a flutter of sudden shyness. They'd never been in public together before, but now that they were, a wave of girlish excitement washed over her like she'd never experienced.

Maisy tightened her hand on Dick's fingers, and they walked to the concierge's desk. He rang the bell, which summoned a young man with a gray suit and brown sideburns from behind a door.

"Mister Darling. Very happy to see you again, sir. Your father isn't here at the moment . . ."

"I know. He asked me to meet him in his suite."

The concierge bowed slightly and produced a key from inside a drawer. "For you, sir," he said, giving it to him. "Shall I send anything up to your room? A bottle from the bar, perhaps?"

Dick shook his head and handed him a bill, and Maisy was struck by how casually he tipped. This was so different than the devil-may-care fellow who had crawled up to her window in the dark of night.

"Come on," Moonlight said to her, his voice lowering into a whisper. "Let's get my money and go." And he took her arm.

Maisy had never been in an elevator car before, and her stomach knotted as it lurched and groaned its way upward. The elevator operator, a smartly uniformed man with a greasy smirk, shouted out the number of each floor with gusto. She held tightly to the iron railing, trying to steady herself.

When the car finally ground to a stop on the sixth, the operator pulled open the door and offered a cheerfully hollow "good day" to the couple. But Maisy noticed him give a knowing wink to Dick.

She suddenly realized the meaning of the gesture, with equal parts revulsion and confusion at its implication. Did she so look the part of a prostitute? Or was the sight of Jiggs Kilbane's son in the company of a young woman a familiar one to the elevator man?

"Dick," she said, as they walked down the plush, carpeted corridor. "He thinks that we are about to do something uncouth."

"Well, we could." He broke into his irresistible grin, instantly putting her mind at rest.

"We could," she agreed and gave a smile of her own. But her mind moved to her friend Trilly Flick, as Moonlight turned the key into the door's lock, and the idea lost its glow. She reminded herself that she had to settle her friend's position before she could turn to her own happiness.

The door to the suite opened and they entered. The place was extravagant, certainly. Expensive-looking art hung from the walls, and rich curtains draped the windows. But she found herself a little let down in the ordinariness of its luxury. What exactly she'd expected from Jiggs Kilbane's home didn't know, but assumed there would be signs of his sadistic side. Perhaps a medieval stretching rack, or an electrocution chair shoved between the settee and the fireplace.

"Trilly? Trilly?" She moved through the richly furnished parlor, poking her head into the first bedroom, and then the second. "She was here," she finally said, when she pulled open the heavy mahogany wardrobe. There were three dresses, one of which she recognized from Trilly's visit to Madame Clifford's house.

Her chest collapsed in gloom. Perhaps Trilly had heard the news herself and left? Had she taken her captor's demise as her opportunity to escape? Trilly had always had an independent streak, buried deep beneath her sultry appearance.

While disappointed her reunion with Trilly wasn't to be, Maisy felt a sense of excitement for her friend, too. They were both free of the gangster's talons, and the freedom was exhilarating. She hoped Trilly was taking advantage of that freedom now.

"Come here, quick," Moonlight called from the parlor. She arrived in time to see him removing a gold-framed painting of a sailboat from the wall, and could plainly see a large cut-out hole, where a massive safe sat on a sturdy shelf.

"Do you know the combination?" she asked as she moved up to Moonlight's side.

"It's already open," he replied, and swung the door so they could see its empty interior. "That double-crossing bastard."

"Who?"

"Henri," he mumbled. "Who else would have the combination?"

"I don't think so. He's a gentleman, I believe. And how would he have access to your father's personal safe?"

"Well who do you think it was, then? The ghost of Jessie James?"

"How much was in there, Dick? Do you have any idea?"

"Tens of thousands, probably. Besides his casinos and bordellos, he was involved in saloons, horses, opium dens, protection. You name the crime, and he was making money from it. Nuts," he said, stomping his foot dejectedly. "We should have come here right away."

Maisy suddenly put her hands to her face in shock and realization. Moonlight looked at her, surprised, and then figured it out, too.

"Your friend."

Could Trilly really have done this? Of course she could have. Why wouldn't she? She was smart, and could easily have learned the combination, a shadow behind Kilbane in her lithe, quiet step. While she selfishly wanted the money for her new life with Dick, the idea of Trilly making off with it admittedly gave her a liberating feeling as well. She would never hold a grudge against the girl for taking advantage of her situation.

"Wait," Moonlight said. "Look at this."

She bent closer to the object of Dick's attention, the safe's thick circular dial.

"Here." He pointed to a thumb print on the dial's edge, smeared in a white cream.

"It has a horrific odor," she said, wrinkling her nose. "I can't imagine Trilly slathering something like that on her body."

"I don't think so either, Maisy." He put his hand next to the dial. "Whoever left this print has a thumb as big as mine. And I'm guessing that he not only cut dirt with my father's money, but with your dear Trilly as well."

CHAPTER 21

Queen's eyes were closed, but he still heard the key turn the heavy lock.

He sat up, rubbing away the effects of his shallow nap. It was Frank Frasier, and the bars were wide open.

"I thought you said I wouldn't see a judge until tomorrow morning."

"Jiggs Kilbane is dead."

What the deuce. Queen didn't know whether to laugh or slam his fist into the wall. He'd still had some words for Jiggs, memorized and rehearsed for the past four months, but now it looked like he'd never get his chance to say them. However, the good news was that he was free to go, it appeared. If he ever fell off the wagon and took another drink, he'd make sure it was a double, in celebration of the bastard's death.

"Who killed the son-of-a-bitch?" he asked with a smirk.

"I don't know the details, yet. But it happened somewhere in the caves along the river."

"I guess O'Connor changed his mind on me, huh?"

"We've got nothing to hold you with, Queen. Unless this witness of yours ever materializes, no one except for you saw what really happened. The County Attorney doesn't think there is a case without her testimony."

"I thought you had my gun."

"We do, but no bullet or body to connect it to. Kilbane said he'd had her buried secretly. He was going to reveal her location once he was confident you were behind bars and he was safe."

Christ, this was a lucky break. A lucky, lucky break. Jiggs had been genuinely scared of him, by the sound of it, and he took great satisfaction from that.

It broke his heart that Edna Pease's body was hidden away in some unmarked place, but he was still selfishly grateful that he was free, and most important, that Karoline hadn't left yet. He could still, possibly, rectify their relationship.

"So I'm free to go."

"You are." Frasier handed Queen his badge, money and weapon.

"Any chance I can get my old Smith and Wesson back?"

"None," Frasier said. He stuck out his hand, and Queen took it. "For what it's worth, I don't believe you murdered anyone."

"Thanks," Queen returned. "And if you ever get tired of your overbearing boss, visit me across the river and I'll set you up nice."

Frasier cracked a smile under his well-oiled mustache. "I don't think you'd appreciate my presence in Minneapolis, Detective Queen. I'd outstay my welcome fast."

His clothes were filthy, so he was grateful when he exited the police station to find Doc's bodyguard, Fred Connor, manning Doc's personal carriage, and holding out a fresh suit and shirt.

"You must have had a chat with my sister," Queen said, while trying to contain a grin.

"She wanted to know where you were, Harm."

"And of course, you didn't say," he said as he climbed up next to Fred. Although the soft cushioned seats in back sounded nice after an afternoon on a cold, hard bench, he could never pass up a chance to talk with his good friend.

"Is there any chance I can convince you to detour to south Minneapolis before we visit the big man?" he asked, as the carriage bumped forward.

"You know we can't do that. I'm under orders from Colonel Ames to bring you directly to Doc's office."

"His medical office?" Doc was still an actual doctor, and although he was more than busy as mayor, he still used his spare time to visit his partner at their office on Nicollet Avenue and dole out advice.

"Criminy, no, Harm. He's petrified of being out in public with this threat hanging over his head. He's holed up in his City Hall office, with a platoon of armed officers sitting in front."

"What about appearances? Events? Is he planning on making his rounds? He can't keep himself insulated like this when he has a city to run."

"He won't come out until you find out who's behind that note."

Queen gritted his teeth, and the urge to have a drink washed over him like a Lake Superior wave. *Maybe if I got some decent food in my stomach at least,* he thought, *I could function better.* As if in answer, his stomach gave a nasty growl, which made Fred raise his brow.

"I've got an extra chicken sandwich my wife made me," he said, rustling through a paper bag next to him. He took it out and handed it to Queen.

"I'll give you my first-born son for this," the detective replied while unwrapping it, and blissfully took a bite.

"Hell, Harm, I wouldn't know what to do with a miniature version of you."

"I wouldn't either," Queen said with a chuckle. "But if you give him a glass of pop-skull, some poker chips, and a wastrel to throw in the pokey, at least he wouldn't wake you up crying in the middle of the night."

CHAPTER 22

Minneapolis City Hall was a wedged-shape four-story limestone building that sat where Hennepin and Nicollet Avenues collided. It was a place in its final years of life, overcrowded and under-maintained, as the city preferred spending its money on a newer version going up a few blocks away.

Fred Connor eased the rig to the curb, and Queen slipped behind the privacy of the carriage's curtained windows and changed into his fresh set of clothes. He found a can of pomade in the bundle, so he oiled his hair back and put some on his mustache to shape up the ends.

"Thanks for the ride, Fred," he said, as he put on his derby.

"Thanks for not trying too hard to redirect our route."

"I'll see you later," Queen said, with a tip of his hat.

A streetcar clanged by filled with smiling passengers, probably out enjoying the last of the weekend. He wished, for a moment, that he had a lazy evening ahead of him, as well. A leisurely Sunday dinner, with pot roast and potatoes, a cigar and a good book to follow.

Life was careening along a different course, however, and he had to tackle it head on. When he went through the door, his countenance changed. He was chief of detectives, a hardened officer, and it was his time to take the bit in his teeth. He scowled at the patrolmen and detectives crowded in the mayoral waiting room, and they, in turn, snapped to attention.

"Why are you all lounging around in here? This is no goddamn way to guard the mayor. I want two officers stationed at every door in this building. Check everyone wanting inside for names and weapons. If they don't need to be here, then send them home."

A chorus of "Yes sirs" and feet shuffling brought the room to life. The mayor's secretary, Thomas Brown, normally a meticulously organized and no-nonsense manager, seemed at the end of his rope. He looked gratefully at Queen as he stood from his chair.

"Please, detective, please go in."

Queen strode by, shutting the door behind him. The mayor's office wasn't spacious, but it was comfortable, accented in dark woods and rich fabric coverings. A picture of Ames as a younger man, probably from his first term as mayor twenty-five years prior, hung in a fancy gilded frame.

Doc sat behind his mahogany desk, looking anxious as hell. His gray mustache bristled, and heavy black rings circled his eyes. His brother, Colonel Ames, sat across from him with a grim expression. Two bottles sat on the desk, one empty and the other on its way.

They both stood for Queen, something he was used to from the usually jovial Doc, but never from the colonel.

"Harm!" Doc cried. He walked around his desk and embraced the detective. The Colonel shook his hand.

"I'll have to admit, I never expected a reception like this," Queen said.

"I'm glad your business with that filthy Irish gangster is over," said the mayor, who broke into a beaming, relieved grin.

"We had to move mountains," Colonel Ames added, "to get you that hearing."

"But it was all for naught, because Kilbane is dead," Doc finished. "Would you like a swig, Harm?"

He did, of course, but wasn't about to break his promise to his beloved. "Black coffee."

"Sensible, Harm. Sensible," Doc said. "We should be alert. Tom!"

His secretary hurried in.

"Bring in a pot of coffee and three mugs."

"Very good, sir."

The mayor gave Queen a long look before sitting on the edge of his desk. "Now that you're here, we can get this bastard behind bars. Did Detective Norbeck fill you in?"

"A little. He said that you received a note at your house."

"My house, goddamn it, Queen. My house! If you can't find sanctuary at your own precious hearth, then where on earth will you find it, let me ask you that?"

"Where is this note, Mayor Ames?"

"Here," said the Colonel, extending his thin arm. Queen took the envelope from his hand, and turned it over. It was plain, without writing, and manufactured of a heavy stock. Expensive, Queen thought. Not something a filthy gutter-traveling radical would be wasting his money on. Unless it was stolen, which was always a possibility when dealing with criminals of the low-down variety.

"So you think this was sent by anarchists?

"Read it, Harm. Read it and judge for yourself!"

Queen pulled the paper out and smelled it. He caught the faintest hint of a men's cologne.

"Do you recognize this smell?" he asked, holding it out to Doc. Doc took it and sniffed it.

"By God, Fred. It smells of musk!"

"Perhaps a well-groomed revolutionary," the Colonel muttered.

Queen took back the paper and unfolded it. The handwriting was neat and precise.

Mayor Ames

Curse you and your villainous ways. The very pillars of the earth wail beneath your heavy, heartless steps. May the devil himself consort you to the most fiery, terrible pit of hell and leave you there to burn and suffer for a hundred eternities.

Your years on this earth have been marked by atrocities and tragedies that you have been accomplice to. Nay, you have been more the instigator than naught!

Even as a young man, your march with Sibley against the native Sioux was marked with blood and misery.

Once grown into a "man," your deceptions and calculations proved to the world how like a wild, savage wolf you are. How noble you are, Ames, ripping apart the oppressed with the blood of innocents dripping from your sharp, patrician fangs!

Understand this. You have been illegally elected to office for your final time. Enjoy your last days on earth with fine Cuban smoke-sticks and a bottle of "bubbles" while you can. On behalf of laborers around the world, I will avenge their despair by taking your final breath!

Signed,
A concerned citizen

"Interesting," said Queen, folding the paper up and inserting it back into the envelope. "May I keep it?"

"Get it out of my sight!" Doc shouted. "Find this man, Harm, and put him in jail! Damn these dirty anarchists and everything they represent!"

The old man was working himself up into a lather, petrified of mysterious assailants hidden deep in the dark night. Fortunately, men like this did not frighten Queen. He felt at home amongst the low and desperate, although from this note, he wasn't so sure that was where he should start looking. The grammar and spelling were precise and proper. Whoever wrote this wasn't trying to play games, either, by attempting to mislead the police by misspelling words. He was who he was, and ready to cry it to the heavens.

"Do you have any enemies who might use a tactic like this to scare you?" Queen asked plainly, trying not to react to Doc's agitation.

"Do I have enemies? Without question, I do."

"Could this simply be one of them, trying to get a rise from you? Could it be, Mayor, that this wasn't written by an anarchist, but instead by someone with a personal grudge?"

Colonel Ames stepped forward, clenching his teeth. "We've considered that, Detective Queen. But that is why you're here, to determine the identity of the author. The note does cast a revolutionary tone, does it not?"

It did. What really struck him, though, was the specific mention of Doc's early life. Why would the writer hone in on what happened forty years earlier, but speak only in vague terms about the decades of actual corruption as the city's on-and-off mayor?

"Do you remember anyone back from your days with the Ninth Minnesota," Queen asked, "that you might not have gotten along with?"

"No, no. We were like brothers," the mayor said. "And need I remind you, I was a surgeon! I never fired a weapon at an Indian, nor any other enemy. I was too busy learning my trade with a saw."

That made sense to Queen, but he wasn't ready to let the letter's reference to the Sioux go just yet.

"Remind me, Mayor Ames, of what exactly you fought for."

Doc went back to his chair as Brown entered with the coffee. Brown started to pour, but Doc waved him away, and began the process himself.

"You said black, Harm?"

"Yes, sir."

"Here," he said, handing him the mug. He sat back down in his chair, and leaned back. The lines of worry disappeared from his face, and were replaced by a look of nostalgia. "Those days were glorious, Harm, simply glorious. Carefree and without a problem in the world!"

"Except for the Indians."

"Yes, yes. I was just a boy, really. Fresh-faced out of medical school. It was 1862. I'd just started my medical practice in Minneapolis when Indian troubles started brewing in the south and the west. I helped raise a company of volunteers for the Ninth and we rushed to the front to fight. I rose, Harm, rose, through hard work and pails of blood, to the rank of Surgeon Major."

"I know how proud you are of your service, sir. But can you think of anyone that you might have made angry during those years?"

"Angry? The war was popular!"

"It was popular with the side that won, but there were losers as well."

"The Sioux lost, as we all know. I'm sure they were more than a little sore. But what political power do they wield? They've all been rounded up and placed on their reservations, to live their lives, properly apart from the white man. What more do you want?"

"Were there sympathizers with the Sioux cause?" Queen persisted. "Some say they were hungry, and attacked out of desperation. The goods they had been promised in exchange for their lands had been withheld. Surely at least a few white men might have sympathized with them."

"I don't know, Harm," Doc said, in frustration. "Hell, there were some whites who lived with the Indians. Men in the fur trade, tied to the tribes by blood mixing."

The fur trade. Why did that sound familiar? The entire day had been a blur of motion, but somewhere, today, he had thought about it.

Of course. His hand dived into his pocket, and he wrenched his roll of money apart with his fingers. He felt the leather strap, and the outline of the silver turtle. The man he had chased: he'd worn this, along with a wool sash strapped to his waist. Didn't long-ago trappers and traders wear those same marks of identification?

"Detective Queen," the Colonel said, interrupting his thoughts. "This can't wait."

"I know, sir, and it won't. I've got some ideas on where to start."

"Where?"

"I think it is best if I don't bother the mayor with the details. Leave that to me and my detectives."

"As the police superintendent, I need to be privy to . . ."

"Christ, Fred. Leave him to his work. He has experience in these things."

"Thank you, sir. What does your schedule look like in the next few days, may I ask? I'll assign our plain-clothed detectives to stay with you at all times. I know Fred Connor is a crack bodyguard, but you'll need more help than him if something should happen."

"We're canceling the mayor's appearances, Queen, until you find the man who wrote that message."

"Aren't there important events . . ."

"Yes, and that is why you need to start working on this right away. I will escort you out."

Queen nodded, and turned to go, but Doc caught him with a firm arm around his shoulder. "You've always been my man, Harm, and you've never let me down."

"I won't this time, either, mayor."

Doc gave him a weary, reassuring smile. "I have every confidence you won't."

CHAPTER 23

The waiting room was quieter now, but a few policemen still milled about, with nothing to do. A door joined the waiting room to the police offices, and as Queen put his hand on the knob, he heard the colonel behind him.

"A word, Detective, if I might."

Queen wasn't surprised, as this was a common tactic for Colonel Ames. He'd be agreeable in his brother's presence, but then directly and often viciously speak his mind in private.

"Sir?"

"I want details of your plans, Queen."

"Today has been exhausting. I've hardly had a chance to catch my breath, let alone devise a plan. I need a night of sleep, Colonel, before I'm ready to tackle this."

"Don't be ridiculous, Queen. I saw your expression after my brother answered your questions about the Indian wars. You reached for something in your pocket . . . ."

"I've got nothing in them except money and a badge. Do you need to inspect those?"

"Listen," the colonel commanded. "I know about your friend Peder Ulland. He has ties to the Socialist Party. And where Socialists tread, anarchists are quick to follow. He is your path to the assassin. You've got to interrogate him, Queen. Force him to reveal his contacts. Make him give up the underground revolutionaries that are plotting against Minneapolis. Plotting against you, and me, and the very foundations of civilized government!"

Colonel Ames was his boss, but it didn't mean that Queen felt any personal allegiance to the man, nor any duty to surrender his best friend. Although Peder walked in the world of the destitute, uneducated and voiceless, it didn't mean that he was an active member of the Socialist Party. He also knew it wouldn't do a damn bit of good to try to convince the colonel otherwise.

"As we both know, Colonel, Mayor Ames in power is like money falling from the sky for you, for me, and for many others. I won't jeopardize this administration by allowing anyone with a grudge against the mayor to threaten his life. Let me do things the way I see fit. If I fall short, than you can punish me as you see fit."

"If you fall short," the Colonel snapped, "then our entire world will collapse, and punishing you will be the least of my worries."

Once he was away from Colonel Ames, Queen rushed to the detectives' room, which opened from the larger police assembly room. He booted three bulls out, shut the door, and picked up the telephone receiver.

"Operator, connect me to 2785 L-3."

Peder answered the phone with food in his mouth. "Hello?" he managed after a swallow.

"It's me, Peder. It's Harm."

"Harm," he said, "Vere are you?"

"I'm in Minneapolis."

"Ven Karoline came back vitout you today, ve tot da vorst."

"I know, and I apologize for worrying you. Things blew up."

"Vat do you need from me, Harm? Do you need any of my men for . . ."

"No, no. I've already involved you too much. I just need to see Karoline. I want to make sure that she's at your house."

"She's gone, Harm."

Queen couldn't speak. Gone? She wasn't supposed to leave until tomorrow morning.

"Ve heard dat you vere in jail. It vas too much for her to bear.

She couldn't stand the tot of you dere, so she bought a ticket for tonight."

"What? When?"

This couldn't be. He needed to speak to her, and smooth things over. He wanted her to understand why he did what he did. She had said she'd wait for him.

"So she's on the train now?"

"She left in a hurry. I yust dropped her off at de Milvaukee Depot an hour ago. She vanted to get dere early. She didn't vant to take any chances to miss her departure."

He put his hand to his vest pocket, but his watch wasn't there.

"What time does her train leave?"

"Half past six."

"And what time is it now?"

Queen waited for the pause.

"A quarter past six. Harm, I yust don't tink it's a good idea . . . "

He dropped the receiver and ran.

Milwaukee Depot was only blocks away, but it seemed an eternity to his tired knees. He kept running, though, running to keep his fiancée. Running to keep his friend. Running to keep his anchor. More than once he stumbled on the sidewalk, and cursed his forty-year-old body for not moving as fast as it used to.

The pain soon began ripping through his legs, as he hotfooted past fruit markets, saloons, hotels and finally the tangle of railroad tracks that marked his approach to the passenger depot. He could see the waiting, rumbling trains and hear conductors from behind the fence as he ran for the nearest door.

"What train is leaving for Chicago?" he yelled, as he pushed by a line of people to a ticket window.

"The first track," said the attendant, "but you need a ticket!"

He barely heard him as he willed himself to ignore the pain, and made a final burst for the departure gate.

CHAPTER 24

She'd insisted on finding Trilly when they left the suite, but Dick shook sense into her immediately.

"We need to eat first," he said. "Then we'll go back upstairs, and you can bathe and change into one of your friend's dresses. And I'll try to find a suit of my father's that doesn't look like a drunken hobo's upchuck. Then, we'll think about our next step."

She agreed, and decided she would enjoy her time with Dick. Her fear for her friend was tempered, she realized with some guilt, by the excitement of freedom and time alone with her beau. It was wonderful to have a dinner with him in a real restaurant, with real waiters, and from a menu with a dozen spectacular choices. There was wine as well, and a lit candle, and she soon melted under the spell of the restaurant's soft atmosphere.

Madame Clifford had taught her how to conduct herself like a lady at the dinner table, and she was now delighted to have the opportunity to put those skills to full effect. She knew the right fork for the salad, and the right spoon for soup, and was thrilled to use them, for once, without the heavy veil of expectations hanging over the meal.

Moonlight still had his college manners, and she'd had to stifle a laugh as he tackled his chicken with greasy hands. He ate like he hadn't eaten in days, and even ordered a second meal, which made her throw her hand over her mouth in mock shock. He was surprisingly cheery, considering a thief had made off with a fortune that belonged to him. She knew the reason why, though. She could see his eyes glazed with love for her, and she felt giddily happy in return.

Then, her thoughts turned to Trilly again, and her mood darkened.

"Where do you think she could be, Dick?" she asked, as a cheese and fruit plate arrived, along with fat slices of chocolate cake.

"Whoever took the money has her," he replied.

"Yes, yes, that has already been established," she said impatiently.

"My darling," he replied, putting his hand on hers.

"It's just so frustrating. They could be anywhere."

"But we will find her. We have each other, and can do it together."

She smiled at his sweet words, and grasped his fingers in hers. He pulled them out with a little grin.

"I've got to go to the boy's room," he said sheepishly.

"Yes, go."

He walked away, and her attention turned to the candle on the table. It flickered seductively, and she took a sip of red wine while she watched its glow. This was her first real night out with a man, she thought, simply for the pleasure of his company. While it was scarred slightly by the nature of the day's events, she decided, again, that she wasn't going to ruin the moment.

A man dressed in a tuxedo strolled through the dining room singing an Italian aria with a lilting tenor voice. She vaguely recognized the tune, but couldn't place it. It didn't matter, however, because the words, even in a language she didn't understand, set a romantic mood. She watched him walk from guest to guest, smiling and bowing when someone handed him a coin. The singer walked past tables, making patrons turn and listen. She felt as though she was being lifted to heaven, enraptured by the melody and the scene.

Then a man walked in. He was on a big drunk, she could tell, by the way he swayed. And there was something queerly disquieting about his face, but hard to make out from across the room. She watched him walk up to the singer and clap in his face, but he couldn't quite get his hands to work together. The singer gave an uncomfortable nod, and took a step back, but the man tilted forward, grabbing onto his coat.

"What the hell are you doing, chum?" Moonlight asked, emerging from the corridor. He took the man and pushed him backwards, into a table. The man and the table collapsed together on the floor.

"Stay down."

The man lifted his head, leered at the room, and gave a repulsive wink before finally lying still.

She watched Moonlight kneel next to him, and wipe his finger on the man's nose. He held it up for her, and she gasped.

It was covered in a slimy white cream.

"Get up, you son-of-a-bitch," Moonlight shouted.

"Who turned the lights on? Why's the room spinning?"

"I need to speak to you," Moonlight said, and he pulled the man up.

"Get in line," the man slurred. "I'm a pop'lar fella."

Moonlight put the man's arm over his shoulder and dragged him out, apologizing to the maître d' and handing him money.

Maisy gave a rueful smile to her waiter, and took out her own purse to lay some coins on the table. She followed them out into the lobby, where Moonlight had laid the man on a sofa.

"Who are you?" he demanded.

"Detective Chris Norbeck, at your beck and claw." As she got closer, she could make out better the man's bulbous nose and red-stained face. She looked at Dick, and he returned the look with a shake of his head.

"He's incoherent," Dick said. "He knows his own name."

Dick patted the man's jacket and trousers, finally pulling out a badge.

"He's a cop, all right. From Minneapolis."

"Say, ain't you Moonlight Dick Darling?" Norbeck rubbed his eyes and licked his lips. "I seen you and your fingerless friend a few days ago. You remember? My compliments, once more on a elegant ol' season. You got quite a set o' haunches on you."

"Enough about me," Moonlight said. "We know you were in Kilbane's room, and you had your sticky hands all over the safe. Where's the cush?"

"Looks like you've got a corker there, young buck. I'd expect no less, of course."

"What were you doing in my father's room?"

Norbeck's eye's lit at this question. "Your father? You don't say, huh? A Gopher football star whose pops is the notorious Jiggs Kilbane! What family dinner freakery that must have been!"

"I asked you where the money is."

"Don't have it," Norbeck replied, weakly lifting his arms and holding out empty hands. "It was already gone."

"What were you doing there?"

"I was looking for a bird named Trilly Flick. You know where she's shakin' that dairy air?"

Maisy covered her hand with her mouth, and fought back a choke.

"I need a glass of water," Norbeck choked in turn.

"Maisy," Moonlight said. "Can you get him some?"

"Maisy, you say? Maisy *Anderson?*" He leered again.

She felt her face blush at the sound of her last name. *How does this disgusting man know Trilly, and how does he know me?*

Norbeck seemed to notice her reaction. He licked his finger and smoothed down an eyebrow, in a bootless, last-gasp effort to look presentable.

"You got to come with me, Miss Anderson."

Dick grimaced. "And why the hell would I let her do that?"

"I've got someone who has been looking for you for a long time, and he's going to do a goddamn back flip when he lays eyes on you."

"Who?"

"Detective Harm Queen, sweetheart. We have to get a cab. Now."

CHAPTER 25

Queen sat on a bench, his head in his hands. The pit of his stomach had sunk to the soles of his shoes.

The train was closing its doors when he'd skidded onto the platform. He'd been so out of breath, so desperate, that he hadn't been thinking straight, and he kicked himself now for not brandishing his badge to keep the train from leaving.

But all he could think of to do was to run up and down the length of the train, peering through windows to catch a view of Karoline. He tried to call out, but the shrill hum of the waiting engine made it difficult to be heard. Then the bells began their rhythmic clang and the crankpins turned as the train began its slow departure, and he scanned the windows for any sign of his beloved. There was none. She hadn't seen him, or if she had, his presence wasn't important enough for her to leap out and into his arms.

He wasn't used to crying, and fought like hell to keep the tears from coming out as he tried to decide what to do. While he knew, deep down, he couldn't leave, a part of him was tempted to buy a ticket and follow her. The hell with all of this, he thought. He was tired of the manipulating colonel, he was still shaken by his arrest in Saint Paul, and from the deepest reaches of his aching bones, he was plumb exhausted. He could leave everything behind with a wave, and find his place in Chicago, by Karoline's side.

It was a pipe-dream, though, and nothing more. He had to protect the old man, who was like a father to him. And not only protect him from an assassin's bullet, but also from himself. The Ames brothers' cloak of corruption was thin, at best. While it still covered the city, there was no one except for Queen to keep it from being stripped away. He was the glue that held the entire racket together. And he was the only one who could prevent the foxes in the henhouse from tearing each other apart.

He lit a cigarette and smoked it, watching the stars twinkle through the gaps in the truss-roofed shed that sheltered the platform. He thought about going home for a good night's sleep, but only momentarily. It was still early, and there was still work to be done.

So he put on his derby and limped back to City Hall.

He was at his desk in the detective's room, when Norbeck stuck his head through the crack of the door.

"Hey, boss. How goes the battle?"

Queen stood. "In, Norbeck. Now."

The detective slunk forward, and Queen could smell the reek of alcohol and cigarette smoke on his clothes.

"Goddamn it, Chris. I told you not to drink tonight."

"You told me not to tipple 'til I found her."

"So you did?"

"Nope," Norbeck chuckled. "She was gone when I got to Kilbane's place."

"So why are you here, and in this state? There are other places to look, for Christ's sake!"

"I found someone else I knew'd you'd want to meet."

"And who in God's name is that?"

Norbeck pushed the door wide open, and a young lady walked in, wearing a billowy, forest-green dress. She was lovely, with round cheeks, deep blue eyes and blonde hair pulled back under a peacock-feathered hat. There was something about her air, her poise, that immediately reminded him of someone. It was an expression of defiance, although on her it was a beautiful defiance. Her eyes burned with independence and self-determination.

"Er . . . good evening Miss . . . ?" He glared at Norbeck for an introduction.

She held out her gloved hand. "A pleasure to meet you, finally, Detective Queen. My name is Maisy Anderson."

Queen closed his eyes, and then opened them. If Karoline could be here to see this, she would understand, finally.

He leaped out of his seat and took her hand, fighting to contain a smile.

"Miss Anderson. I've been searching for you."

She smiled back, and it was all he could do not to fall over at her beauty.

"I'm so sorry to have wasted your time, sir. Detective Norbeck, on the way over, explained the troubles you've put yourself through to find me."

"I am thrilled, Miss Anderson, that you are alive and well. I was close this morning to locating you . . . ."

"I know, now. Thank you for trying to find me."

"My pleasure." He didn't know how to continue, what to say. Miss Anderson, however, seemed to sense his hesitation, and began telling him everything that had happened to her from the very beginning. Norbeck, usually not known for his sensitivity, even shut the door and left to give them some privacy. And Queen sat, transfixed, as she explained what had happened to her for the last two years, from her betrayal at the station by Martin Baum all the way up to Dick's altercation with Norbeck at the hotel.

Many things struck Queen during their conversation. As soon as Maisy had mentioned Trilly Flick's name, his mind raced back to the last time he'd seen the other girl, and how she'd treated him with flippant disregard. He'd made love to her just hours before, but realized too late that she had used him for information, with every intent to cast him aside.

He could still see Trilly's pouty lips in his head, and the stunning eyes whose lashes could bat for the Millers baseball team. Then he felt that momentary lust that had gotten him in trouble to begin with. When he finally found Trilly, he'd do his best to convince her to tell the truth about Edna Pease's murder to Police Chief O'Connor. If she refused, then he'd put her on a fast train to the farthest corner of the country. He wanted no more of that trouble. Now that Kilbane was dead, he decided, she'd probably high-tailed it out of town already.

Baum's involvement with the Anderson family certainly both surprised and dismayed him. He'd always hated Baum, and seen him for the despicable bloodsucker he was. Baum's insistence on side business, business that did not fit into the natural flow of city graft, had been the reason for his dismissal. It had angered Queen that Baum had been running his own rackets, rackets that took advantage of the innocence of girls, and the idea that he'd snatched Maisy under the nose of his best friend made his blood boil in fury. Maisy said Baum had insisted that he hadn't been able to protect her from the men that took her, but Queen's intuition told him something completely different. He knew, he just knew, that Baum had arranged for them to enslave her, and he'd been paid a pretty penny for the service. If Baum wasn't tucked away in jail right now, Queen would find him and kill him.

He'd also learned about how contemptible a slug Jiggs Kilbane was. If anyone deserved a gut-shot it was him. But as much as he hated Baum, Queen realized that his actions might well have saved Maisy's life on a washroom floor.

The other two men Maisy mentioned piqued his interest the most. He'd just met Moonlight Darling earlier in the week, and had been impressed with his quick thinking and ready smile, but it was hard to believe that he was Kilbane's son. How on God's green earth did a kid with a head on his shoulders like Moonlight ever spring from the seed of that ridiculous gangster? She mentioned that the young athlete was sitting outside, questioning the cops in the assembly room about the life of a policeman. He was eager to shake the young man's hand and introduce him to Doc, who would be tickled to have the sports star in the rank and file. It would be a publicity coup to end all publicity coups to have Moonlight Dick Darling battling bad men on the streets of Minneapolis.

His questions to Maisy, however, focused on the man she called Henri. The only thing he knew about the man was that he had worn a turtle necklace, and that he'd worked for Jiggs. When she'd told Queen that this Henri had given Baum the gun to kill Kilbane, his brain was racing with possible reasons why.

"Tell me what the man is capable of, Miss Anderson, if you please."

"He's not as bad as he seems, despite his carrying me away on his shoulder," she replied, with an embarrassing little smile that revealed how silly her words sounded. "He tried to protect me. He was a gentleman."

A gentleman? Out of respect for Maisy, he bit his tongue. This man was no more a gentleman than the janitor who scrubbed out the latrines at City Hall. And at least the janitor put in an honest day's work.

"Tell me what you learned about him, during your short time together. Did he have any quirks? Any distinguishing features?"

"He speaks French, I assume because he is. He insisted on giving me money."

"Anything that would tell you about his past?"

Queen saw the reaction to his question on her face. She remembered something.

"Please, Miss Anderson, if you can."

"Just before he gave Martin Baum the gun," she started slowly, pursing her lips as if to recollect better, "he mentioned something about growing up in a family of fur traders. My heart was beating too loudly to hear every word, but I remember him pulling out a tool, and showing it. He said it was for stitching leather, but suggested it could be used on the human body. An awl, I think."

A gentleman with a sadistic side? Queen wondered what kind of stitching he did in his spare time. For a man to replace Jack Peach, he had to have some measure of cold-bloodedness inside him.

"Is there any other reason he gave you, besides the mention of his skill with an awl, that would lead you to believe this Henri is something more than he seems? Perhaps someone with a radical bent?"

She thought again for a moment, and again, her face flashed with realization.

"Yes, there was something else he said."

"What?"

"I don't remember the exact words, but he'd suggested that he had far bigger plans in his future than as a henchman. I'm not sure how radical that is, but it struck me as queer."

"And from what you know of him, do you believe that's true?"

"He is very smart, Detective Queen. And he seemed sincere in his claim."

With every bit of information gleaned about this man, Queen decided, he was more and more worried.

CHAPTER 26

Maisy didn't know what to make of Harm Queen. He was vaguely handsome. Not youthfully, charmingly handsome like Dick Darling, or handsome in a crippling, disturbing way like Emil Dander, but he had his own formidable presence. It wasn't height, or girth, or muscle that made him good-looking. He was attractive instead, she thought, because he was comfortable being who he was. His dark, fierce eyes and graying hair were born of experience. Cold, hard experience, dealing with society's worst elements. She felt nothing wrong with him. In fact, the very opposite. He was a defender. Someone who watched over the weak, and it drew her to him. But something else drew her, too. He was troubled and dark, in some way, and that intrigued her.

His questions finally seemed to be finished, as he leaned back in his chair, and gave a small, unexpected sigh. He had something else on his mind, she thought, besides all that went on today. There was something personal, a look in his eyes that bordered on sadness. It wasn't her place to ask, but it made her curious.

"You've been most helpful, Miss Anderson. Do you have a place to stay the night?" he asked.

"Dick is arranging our rooms, at the Pioneer Hotel, across the street."

"Those are comfortable lodgings. Doesn't he have a place of his own near the University?"

"He does, but women are not allowed there."

"Is there anything I can do for you?"

"What do you mean?"

"Anything you need? Notions, clothes?"

"I'm fine, Detective Queen."

"Good."

"I will be looking for this Henri, as you might imagine, vigorously. I hope you'll be staying in town for a while?"

"Dick and I haven't discussed our plans, but he has his examinations this week, so I'll be left to my own devices. He's asked that I not leave the hotel."

"I can't imagine, now that you have your freedom, that you'd be so willing to promise that."

"It's only until he graduates. Then we'll see what happens."

"And if he were to be offered a position on the force? What then?"

Detective Queen was a barrage of questions, and she now understood why he had risen to Chief of Detectives. She had nothing to hold back from him, but didn't have answers either. She didn't want to stay in Minneapolis if she could help it, but she and Dick were still in the infancy of their relationship, and had had no opportunity to seriously discuss their future. He'd make a good policeman, she thought firmly. And while a life of anxiety over his safety was not ideal, at least he'd take the opposite side of the law from his father.

"We'll see, I suppose. I will telegraph my grandmother as soon as I can, to see her."

Queen's face immediately betrayed him, and her heart smashed into pieces.

"I'm so sorry for more bad news, but I'm afraid that she's passed on as well. According to Sheriff Anderson, it was her heart."

It was all too much to bear, and she closed her eyes for a moment, to collect herself. Her sweet grandmother, who had raised her, was also gone.

"I can see that you're tired, Miss Anderson, and I regret that I had to deliver that news to you. Perhaps you should rest, now, and we can talk again soon. Let me escort you out to your beau. And here is my business card," he said, taking one from his desk drawer. "Please call on me if you ever need me. Ever."

"I do need to think, Detective Queen, on all of this. But may I ask you a question, before we part?"

"Certainly."

She took a deep breath. "Can you tell me how my grandfather died? Do you know what happened?"

"I was there. Outside the door, anyway. He'd been sitting on a porch, cleaning his gun, when a man named Jack Peach gunned him down. Peach was Kilbane's right-hand man."

"That is not how I would have imagined my grandfather's demise, being taken like that."

"He was at an extreme disadvantage, and couldn't get a draw. But you should have seen him minutes before." Detective Queen's eyes suddenly gleamed. "He took down a twisted, disgusting man, who had kidnapped a small boy that he'd befriended. It was, my dear— and I never give unwarranted compliments—it was spectacular."

Maisy nodded. That was the grandfather she knew and loved.

Her head filled, suddenly, with a thousand more questions. She wanted to know the details of her Grandpa Dix's last days on earth. Where was he buried? What had happened to the farm in Bemidji? So many things needed to be sorted. And she knew she would have to call on Mr. Queen again soon.

"Very well," she said. "Thank you for your time, sir."

She held her hand out, and he kissed it this time.

"I have a lifelong commitment to your welfare, Miss Anderson. So believe me when I say, any time. And I have something else for you."

He reached, once more, into his desk, and withdrew something heavy, wrapped in cloth. It clunked when he put it on the desk, and he gave her a nod to remove the fabric.

My God, she thought, as she slipped it off, and looked at the glistening barrels of her grandfather's pistols. He placed the retired star she knew so well next to them.

"They're yours," he said. "Out of my safe-keeping and back to the family they belong to."

Maisy stared at them, imagining them in her grandfather's holsters, strapped around his lean waist, and couldn't keep back her tears.

"Wrap them up," he said gently, "and keep them safe."

When they walked into the assembly room, Queen was amused to see Mayor Ames at a table, sitting across from Moonlight, with a look of joy on his face. A score of policemen had also gathered around, enthralled by the presence not only of Moonlight, but of their own mayor, who rarely visited the assembly room.

"Damn it, Queen!" he roared. "Why didn't you tell me that Moonlight Dick Darling would grace us with his presence tonight!"

"Well, here he is," Queen said, "and this, sir, is Maisy Anderson. Do you remember back in January . . ."

"Of course I do!" He jumped up and took her hand. "I hadn't had a chance to meet your grandfather on the last visit, but I'd read about his accomplishments in his obituary. What a hero he was! A bona fide hero! His service during the war was exemplary, along with his time in the Dakotas."

"Thank you, Mr. Mayor, for your nice words."

"Think nothing of it. And now, I hear, you've met a football hero, and stolen his heart," he said with a knowing wink.

"She has, sir," Moonlight said, giving his half-curled grin. "And so nice to see you again, Detective Queen!"

"This boy wants to be a policeman, Harm," Doc blurted. "Have you heard?"

"In passing, sir."

"When can I swear you in?" Doc's face was earnest and serious. "You have a job, my boy, whenever you want it."

"After the graduation ceremony," said Moonlight, unable to contain the excitement on his face. "I want to discuss it with Miss Anderson, first, of course." He looked at her imploringly, and she gave back a slightly forced smile.

"The commencement! The day after next! You will be there! I'm giving the address!" Doc's expression turned from anticipation, suddenly, to disappointment.

Queen knew what was going on in his head. Colonel Ames had forbidden any appearances, and Doc was now realizing that this probably included a speaking engagement at Minnesota's most prestigious university. Doc turned to Queen, and Queen could read his mind. *Find the man who threatened me as soon as you can.* Queen raised his brow to Doc, to affirm that he had received the message clearly.

Queen saw them out, and onto Hennepin Avenue. Their hotel was only a block away, but he still sent one of the two patrolmen guarding the door to escort them to their rooms.

Day had given way to night, and the electric lamps that lined the streets were glowing under the cool night air. As he walked to the streetcar stop he saw the White Elephant Saloon across the avenue, and recognized a couple of acquaintances smoking cigars in front.

What did Karoline's departure mean, he suddenly wondered, about his promise not to imbibe in a touch of the bottled courage? If there was a single moment in his life where a double whiskey would right a mass of ills, it was now. Even a single, just to ease his knee joints, he thought, would service.

"Thinking of going in there?" came a voice from behind him. He turned back and looked down to a slight fellow, holding a pencil and notepad in his soft-looking hands. "If you go, I'll be happy to accompany you," the man said with a toothy grin. "The notorious Harmon Queen, out for a night on the town, gets pitched out of a window for insulting some poor joe while in a jingled stupor. Read all about it in the morning edition!"

"Who the hell are you, again?" Queen asked. His hand instinctively curled into a fist.

"Freddy Bonge. Crack rag reporter for the *Tribune*. I follow you in the papers, detective. You make good copy."

"Well, there's no story here. Go bother someone else."

"Well, there could be a story," Bonge said, with cheer in his timbre. "There are two guards posted to each door of City Hall, out of the blue sky. What would ever lead to a decision like that?"

"Why do you care?"

"Because the *Tribune* has an office here! And if something sinister is going on, those of us who work here, along with our readers, of course, have a right to know."

This was the last thing in the world Queen needed to deal with.

"It's nothing. Go away. Make tracks."

"But it is something, and I will not." He licked the tip of his pencil, and posed himself to write. "From what I can see, Detective, you have two choices. Either you tell me what is going on, or I focus my attention on your little escapade in Saint Paul today."

"How do you know about that?" Queen snapped.

"You confronted the Chief of Police in the middle of a church! Did you think that it would stay a secret?"

Threats like this were not something that Queen ever put up with. He had his own ways of dealing with snooping reporters, but those ways required time, and time was the one thing he didn't have in this investigation. He thought for a moment, and then he came up with an idea. It was a sour one, but it would buy him a little more freedom.

"All right, Bonge. I see your point. Let me show you something, may I?"

He took the turtle pendent out of his pocket and placed it over Bonge's notepad. Bonge slid his pencil behind his ear, and examined the piece.

"Does it have something to do with the guards?"

"Yes, but what I'm not sure of yet." Queen bent down slightly to meet Bonge's eyes. "Let me make you an offer."

"What kind?"

"A simple one. You tell me who made this necklace, and I'll give you the exclusive on the story."

"And how would I know who made this?"

"I've read your 'Out and About' section, and I know you have your finger on the city's pulse. You wrote a story a few weeks ago called 'Our Native Soil,' where you interviewed pioneers from Minneapolis's bygone days."

"What does that have to do with *this*? And I thought you didn't know who I was!"

"Go find some goddamn pioneers who know who made this. And I lied. I know you, because of the piece of trash you wrote about Sheriff Anderson."

"That was a story of human interest . . . ."

"A story that ridiculed the man to the point where he found no support in the city."

Bonge raised an eyebrow. "Does this necklace have something to do with Anderson's death?"

"Not directly. In a roundabout way, perhaps."

"I felt bad hearing about the codger's demise."

"Well, then, do me a favor and find out where this necklace came from. If you help me, once this case is put to rest I'll sit down with you and tell you everything."

The reporter threw the pendant up in the air, and caught it. A grin plastered over his face, and Queen wondered for a second how a human could have teeth that big.

"Exclusive," Bonge said. "You'll hear from me first thing tomorrow."

CHAPTER 27

The envelope was delivered to Queen's front doorstep the next morning. The boy, a sweet faced little lad with an oversized cap, reminded him of another boy he knew named Petey. He hadn't seen or heard from him or his brother Ollie for weeks, and he hoped that the lack of news meant they were fine. He gave the kid a nickel, and as he scampered off Queen opened the envelope. The necklace was inside, and he slipped it out and read the paper.

James McGirk
604 E 22nd St
With Great Regards,
F. Bonge

Queen's livery was just around the block from his home, and in only a few minutes he was spurring his horse Arthur forward. The address wasn't far from where he lived, and before he knew it, he was at his destination. It was a two-story brick building on the corner of Twenty-second Street and Portland Avenue.

He walked under the sign "Olson Butchers" and through the storefront's entrance, and was greeted by a young man behind a counter, wearing suspenders and a work shirt, rolled up at the sleeves. Slabs of bacon sat in front of him, alongside a meat cleaver slimed with blood.

"Can you tell me if a man named James McGirk lives here?" Queen asked, with an easy smile.

"Jeg snakker ikke Engelsk," the man said, shaking his head.

"McGirk," he repeated. He pointed up.

"Oh! Yah, yah. Mika Girk. Mika Girk."

He left the counter and took himself back outside, to an adjacent door.

"Mika Girk," he said once more, and pointed up again.

Queen had learned a few words of Norwegian from his days with the Ullands.

"*Tusen takk*," he managed, and went up the stairs.

There were two doors at the top, and he knocked at the one on the right. After a moment, he heard shuffling feet, and then the sound of lock unlatching, and it opened. An ancient-looking man answered, bald in the middle and a mane of white hair in the back. Bits of dried white skin dotted the shoulders of his wool jacket.

"Are you James McGirk?"

"Who's asking?"

"Detective Harmon Queen of the Minneapolis Police Department. May I come in?"

"I suppose so."

Queen noticed the slight lilt of a Scottish accent. The man shuffled back to his parlor, and found a seat in a ratty-looking chair. Queen followed, and was jolted by the appearance of the room. Shelves hung from every wall, stacked high with books and bric-a-brac. A roll top desk sat in the corner, heaped with paper. Cobwebs stretched across corners and dust balls skittered across the worn floor. From his chair, the old man watched the detective taking in the disarray.

"You ever seen this much shit in yer life, lad?"

Queen laughed. "Someone told me you could help me with something," he said.

"I can barely walk to the toilet. What could you want from me?"

"This," Queen said, and took out the turtle pendant. He rubbed his fingers on it to clean off the lint, and handed it to the man.

"My work," said McGirk.

"There's no mark of identification."

"I know me own goddamn work." The man motioned to a wooden chest on the floor. "Can ye open that for me, lad?"

"Of course."

Queen brushed his hand over the surface. It was intricately etched in an old Celtic design. He lifted up the top.

"Pull out the innards."

A metal box was inside, and he handed it to McGirk. The man set it in his lap and opened the lid, his eyes sparkling at its contents.

"This is my life, lad."

Queen leaned over his shoulder, and looked at the pieces. There were sets of cone-shaped silver ear bobs, crucifix pendants, and brooches with beautiful patterns of triangles and half-moons circling their edges. The craftsmanship was extraordinary, Queen thought.

"I learned how to shape silver many, many years ago, back when Indians and traders used them for decoration."

"It is handsomely done, Mr. McGirk." He pointed to his turtle pendant. "Do you happen to remember who you sold that one to?"

"This one is very simple," he said. "I made many variations, hundreds and hundreds probably, over the years."

The detective felt the bitter sting of disappointment. He was hoping it might be a little more special than it looked.

"Thank you for your time, sir."

He turned to go, but felt McGirk put his hand on his waist.

"Wait a moment, lad. It's garbage."

"Garbage?"

It's nothing more than a cheap piece of costume jewelry."

"Are you certain?" Queen asked, taking the turtle and looking at it again.

"I made a dozen of them about fifteen years ago for a local play.

I don't normally work in common metal, but I needed money."

"Where, Mr. McGirk? Where did you sell them?"

"To a Captain W.W. Hill," he replied. "At the Theater Comique."

Queen knew the Theater Comique intimately. While it had been closed for four or five years now, it had also easily been the most notorious theater in Minneapolis history. Since the early '80s Captain Hill had run the place with an eye for profit, and he'd pursued that profit by creating the most jaw-dropping, titillating and scandalous reviews in the city.

For a number of years in his wistful youth, Queen had frequented the place regularly, and had on more than one occasion woken up in the arms of a young starlet of the stage. He remembered those years with the utmost fondness, and almost regretted seeing the inside of the old place now that it had changed.

Captain Hill led him in. He was a gruff but amiable man, who walked with a cane now, but had been one of the great promoters of his time.

"I'm renting the building to the Salvation Army, Queen," he said, as they walked through the lobby. "They've converted the saloon into barracks, and the bar into a goddamn church! They use the theater auditorium for their 'Come to Temperance' talks. Not my cup of tea, but they pay their rent promptly."

Gone were the colorful posters of can-can shows and vaudevilles, replaced instead with bleak, sober warnings of a life without repentance. The gaiety had been drained, Queen thought, with regret. They stopped in front of the old ticket window.

"I remember standing right here," Queen said. "When I met the Black Diamond."

"He was a bruiser," Captain Hill said proudly. "I sold out that boxing match in a single hour."

They walked into the theater itself, down the aisle, up the steps and across the footlights onto the stage. The heavy maroon curtains still hung, faintly smelling of smoke. He remembered with exquisite fondness the stunning young ladies who flitted their brief skirts, and warbled their "au revoir" songs here. Queen was trying to focus on the task at hand, but he was so struck by memories that he found himself lingering near each nook and cranny.

"What we're looking for is packed away downstairs," Hill said.

Queen remembered where the staircase was that led to the space below the stage. He'd kissed more than a few girls under the creaks and stomps of performers oblivious to the romance brewing below.

"Snap out of it, man," the captain said with a scowl. "Stop being so damn sentimental."

Queen followed Captain Hill to the basement, and they walked past the rows of dusty costumes and props to a wall of boxes.

"You said I bought these little trinkets fifteen years ago? That would make it 1886. I was selling out every night by then."

"Do you remember any show with a frontier theme? A show that might have included fur trappers or Indians?"

"Here is the box with the old programs," Hill replied, and handed it to Queen. "Have at it, son."

Queen skimmed through them with his fingers. They weren't in any order, so he had to look at each title and date.

Captain Hill, evidently not interested in the lull of silence, filled the air with his blustery lungs.

"These shoes," he said, kicking a box, "were specially made for the silver-clog dancers. And this hat," he said, as he rummaged through another, "was for one of our seltzer bottle comedians. He was a genuine fellow named Jack Tempest if I recollect correctly, and he always followed a wonderful quartet called 'Taylor's Sunburnt Aristocrats' . . ."

"I think I found it," Queen interrupted, holding up a program.

Captain Hill put on his spectacles, snatched it from Queen and held it close to his face. "Ah, yes. This was a long time ago. It was a serious play, which didn't do well, but the actors were earnest. It was about a group of French voyageurs who were captured by a vicious tribe of Injuns. The chief forces the leader of the group to marry his daughter, and then a brutal battle . . ."

"Who were the actors, Captain Hill? The actors that wore the pendants? Were any of them named Henri?"

The captain scanned the program with his finger. "No, no. No actors named Henri. But here," he pointed to a name. "According to this, one of the characters was named Henri. The main voyageur, in fact."

"Who was the actor that portrayed him?" Queen asked, his excitement rising.

"Seaver Loftus," Hill said. He stopped for a moment, silently mouthing the name. "I haven't seen Seaver Loftus in years. I'd forgotten his name, even."

"Was he that unobtrusive?"

"As an actor, yes. Very forgettable, but I still gave him a chance. He not only starred in this debacle, but he wrote and directed it, too. He studied history for a good year in preparation."

"Why did you let him do it, if he wasn't any good?"

"He was a hard worker, and I respect hard work. I don't remember what he did before he came here, but he had been in his forties, already, when he'd come under my employ. That is a late start for an actor, but he certainly gave it his best college try. He started by selling whiskey and beer, peddling it about for the audience. Then he worked his way up to stage manager, somehow, and then became a utility actor. He'd black up and go on at the end of the minstrels, and then take a role in the farce in the finale. He'd wanted to be a variety star, but didn't have the talent for it."

"So he left?"

"Yes. One day, probably not long after this Injun show. The reviews had been scathing enough that I ended it after just a week. He collected his pay the day it closed, and never came back."

"Do you recall any animosity he had towards anyone here?"

"He'd broiled in his own fat over the reviews, and was furious at me for stopping the show. And I'd heard that after he left, he tried to convince some of the other actors to leave, as well."

"Why?"

"He wanted to make some kind of statement. He'd been treated unjustly by the powers that be, I guess. And then I heard later that he'd found work in another theater in Saint Paul."

Seaver Loftus, Queen repeated to himself. *You aren't quite the experienced bad man I figured you to be. In fact, you're nothing but a failed ham actor who had landed the role of his life as Kilbane's muscle.*

Doc's got nothing to worry about, he decided, with fresh assurance. And now that he knew who he was dealing with, he only needed to find him, pinch him, throw him in the pokey and finish this up.

CHAPTER 28

Queen had barely had a chance to sit down at his desk when his telephone rang.

"Harm," came the voice from the receiver. "Is that you?"

"Peder, I don't think we should be talking on the phone right now."

"Ya, ya, I know vat you are saying, but dere is someone at my house, vaiting for you. She vants to talk to you yust as soon as she can."

She came back.

Karoline came back.

His heart started slamming against his ribs, and he felt his skin go warm. She'd changed her mind and had returned to mend their divide.

"I'll be right over, Peder. Did Karoline sound merry-hearted? Excited to see me?"

The phone went quiet. Then Peder spoke in a dry whisper.

"It's not Karoline."

"Who could it be, then?" And then, he slap-bang realized who it was.

She'd had the nerve to show up to the very same place where they'd last exchanged words: the Ulland house. He'd felt guilty enough already, when they'd tumbled together in Peder and Karoline's parlor, and he didn't want to be reminded of his mistake again.

"Did she say anything?"

"She said she missed our hospitality, and hoped ve didn't hold vot happened against her. Harm, she sounded sincere."

Of course she did. She was a deceptive, conniving bitch who

could switch on her feminine wiles with a one-two shake of her waist. He'd hear what she had to say, he decided. Try to convince her to redeem herself by acting as his witness in the Edna Pease matter, and then he wanted her out of that house immediately.

"I'll be there when I can," he said, and hung up.

As he rushed through the assembly room a patrolman approached him, looking tentative.

"Sir, there is a lady here to see you."

"Her name?"

"Miss Anderson."

"Show me where she's waiting."

The officer led him outside, where she stood on the sidewalk. She wore a white dress and a white hat with a single plume, and carried a purple parasol in her hand, her S-shaped silhouette ravishing in contrast to the dirty, bustling street. Absolutely ravishing, he noted, with some guilt at the observation.

"Why is she standing out here?" Queen asked angrily. The officer, taken aback, paused to formulate a thought, but Maisy spoke first.

"I insisted," she replied. "It isn't his fault. Last night we made such a scene."

"I know I invited you to call on me whenever you felt the need. Unfortunately, this is a particularly inopportune time." He looked at his watch, as if to emphasize his point. "Duty calls."

"Does it relate to Henri?" she asked.

He debated whether to tell her who it related to. He knew that she was eager to see her friend, but he also wanted to keep Maisy far from harm's way.

There was always the possibility of a trap when it came to Trilly, but he was armed, and wise to her duplicitous ways. Peder, too, would have his own men there. There was no reason not to invite

Maisy along, Queen decided. Her presence might actually ease the tension of the meeting. And if the tart little treasonist attempted to seduce him again—well, he didn't want any excuse to succumb.

"I'm on my way to see Miss Flick."

Her lip twitched, and Queen could see she was surprised, but also trying to hide it. "I'll go with you, Mr. Queen, and I won't take no for an answer," she said.

More mettle today than yesterday, he decided. She's a chip off the old block, he thought with admiration.

"My gig is in the livery across the street," he said. "Come with me, if you'd like."

They'd talked about her grandfather the entire way to the Ulland house. He'd been patient with her questions, and explained the entire story from the beginning, starting with his discovery of poor Ellie Van Allen's body outside Emil Dander's brothel in Hell's Half Acre, and up to Anderson's funeral. Maisy seemed relieved, he thought, to hear a truthful account. She admitted that what bits and pieces she knew had come only from the serpentine tongue of Jiggs Kilbane, and looked as though she'd been refreshed by a Lake Calhoun summer breeze as they pulled up to the house. Her cheeks glowed pink with cheer, and he was selfishly glad that he was able to gaze upon something so damn rum.

"Thank you for taking the time with me, Detective."

"You are most welcome," he said, giving her a smile, but feeling tremendous dread inside at the thought of seeing Trilly again.

Queen helped Maisy out of the gig, and they went up the path to the front door. Chickens were pecking in the bits of green grass that had managed its way up through the dirt yard. He waved to Big Snorre, who sat on an empty apple crate, working on devouring the box's former contents piled high on his lap.

"Hullo Q-veen!" he boomed, waving back with a dripping core in his massive hand. He tossed the remnant to the chickens, who squawked and flapped around the treat.

When they reached the door, Queen apologized under his breath.

"Please don't take offense that I don't hold it for you, Miss Anderson, but I'd like to make sure things are clear. Do you mind waiting here for a few moments?"

She nodded and opened her parasol, and he went in. The parlor smelled like lavender as he looked around.

He half-expected to see Trilly undressed and lying on the sofa, ready to bombard him with her curves, but that wasn't the case. She sat, upright and proper on the edge of an armchair as he strode in. She looked up, with those intoxicating eyes, and her pouty lips parted in a devastating smile.

"Harm Queen, as I live and breathe."

"You look well, Miss Flick."

"Miss Flick?" she laughed. "Have we grown so far apart?"

"I'm engaged to Karoline Ulland."

"Well, that's just the thing," she said with a touch of sarcasm. "Although she seems far too pure for your roving ways."

"Miss Flick," he said, sitting in the rocker, and masking his nerves. "Let me be blunt. When I last saw you, you had just sold me down river to Jiggs Kilbane. When I was locked in his office, with Miss Pease dead in my arms, you made no effort to show your concern then. How you're able to imply, with a straight face, that somehow I'm in the wrong for not showing some intimacy, is complete lunacy."

"Your skyrockety language don't fool me, Harm. But go on, if you need to."

"What I need, Miss Flick, is for you to tell the truth. I need you to walk into Police Chief John O'Connor's office and explain to him that it was Kilbane who killed Edna, and not me."

"And why the hell would I do that? I ain't gotten nothin' from you yet," she purred.

He'd expected that she would want something, and here it was about to come, he thought with animosity.

"You'd do it out of decency, and for the memory of Miss Pease. And because you betrayed me, and owe me the truth."

She gave another laugh, but it was bitter this time. "Don't you know that I blow with the wind? It was nothing against you, sweets. I got no loyalty to anybody. What do you expect from me, with the life I've led?"

"Just tell me what you want in return."

"Now you're speakin' my language." She took off one of her gloves, and idly examined a fingernail. "I want Kilbane's green," she said, without looking up.

"It's not yours. It's his son's money."

"That don't matter to me. That's what I want from you. If you give me your word on this, I'll tell the police the truth."

"So tell me where the money is, and I'll think about it."

"The man called Henri. That ain't really his name, ya know."

"I do know."

"Ha!" She gave an approving nod. "You are good at what you do, ain't ya?"

"So what happened at the hotel? Why didn't you get the chink first?"

"I didn't know Jiggs was dead," she said. "I didn't know until Henri came back, by himself. He cleaned out the safe and left me."

"He didn't want anything from you?"

"No!" she scoffed. "And what the hell kind of a man is that?"

"Tell me where he is, and I'll consider your request." He paused, and gave her a wry smile. "That is, if you really do know. After you parted ways, I'd imagine you were officially out of his circle."

"He told me, 'fore he left." She put her nail in her mouth, and nibbled on its end. "I don't know no better way to clean 'em," she giggled.

"Why would he tell you where he'd gone?"

Trilly shrugged her shoulders. "Because he don't care? Or because he couldn't help himself?"

This was a set-up if he'd ever seen one. While the man might be only an actor, he was a cunning bastard. Perhaps he really considered himself a bona fide revolutionary, and thought he had the brains to lure Queen into a trap. He knew from their earlier chase that Queen was impulsive, and ready to go dashing into the middle of a thunderstorm just to see the goddamn lightning up close.

And then there was this trickster in front of him. He trusted her about as far as he could throw her. But he truly believed that she'd sell out her former accomplice for a fortune in cush if she thought she could get away with it, and there was an element of truth behind her greedy motives.

He chose to ignore, for the time being, the obvious fact that the money rightfully belonged to Moonlight, and by a probable wedding, Maisy Anderson. Whatever promises he had to make to Trilly he would, because he didn't give a rat's ass about breaking them to the conniving jezebel.

"All right, Miss Flick," he finally said. "Tell me where he is, and you have a deal."

He waited on the walk, a cigarette in hand, while Maisy had her reunion with Trilly. Out of respect for Maisy, he gave them their privacy, but selfishly wanted to be as far away from Trilly as he could get. He felt that if he'd been in there another twenty minutes, she'd have had him in her carnal clutches.

And it would have been his own fault, he shuddered in guilt.

Maisy emerged, smiling, and he was happy she'd had her moment. Whatever his own feelings were, these two women had a shared experience together. As frightful as it must have been, it drew them together, and he understood.

Her eyes twinkled as he took her hand and assisted her back into the seat next to his. The gig had been for him and Karoline, and while he hoped that would still be true, and soon, he took the opportunity to enjoy being next to Maisy, and to share a ride on a beautiful day.

CHAPTER 29

"Good work, Detective," the colonel said from behind his desk. "We should have this finished by the end of the afternoon."

"It won't be that fast," Queen replied. "I did as you told me, and called Frasier. He has to work on a case for O'Connor, and insisted we wait."

"Damn it. I want this rascal behind bars, as quickly as possible."

"And I do as well. But it was your plan to work with the Saint Paul police."

"That's because I don't want you to repeat what happened back in January when you were let loose alone in that infernal city."

"I was forced off a train at gunpoint."

"Yes, yes," Colonel Ames said, motioning his hand in a vague dismissal. "The point is, I want no more embarrassments. When do you anticipate moving on this?"

"Detective Frasier insists on this evening, under the cover of darkness."

"Make damn sure it's tonight, then. I want no nail-biting tomorrow morning at graduation. And how sure are you that this won't get muddled up? Do we have our man for certain, Queen?"

"I believe so, sir."

"This is what I don't understand. If this fool really has that much money, why would he risk his own life over nothing more than political diatribe?"

Queen had wondered this himself. But another actor, John Wilkes Booth, had once bet his future to make a statement. Seaver Loftus's words in that letter dripped with animosity towards Doc. And even during his time at the Theater Comique, Loftus had tried to rally his fellow actors against Captain Hill. Perhaps he felt more confident now, having secured a vast amount of money, that he could fund whatever deviant ideas trickled out of his head.

"He is behind this, I'd bet my brass on it."

Colonel Ames slammed his hand on the desk. "Then take care of things," he growled.

The end of the business day came quickly.

Queen confirmed a meeting time and place with Frank Frasier. He'd considered asking the detective if he'd received his own blessing from Police Chief O'Connor, but then thought the better of it. Frank Frasier was a "by the books" officer, and had done what he needed to do on his end to ensure cooperation. O'Connor had to know that Queen would come with or without his approval. He was sure the Irishman had concluded that Frasier's involvement was far better than to have Queen running roughshod through the city on his own.

There was no need to go in a disguise, this time, Queen thought, thankfully. Arthur was fast and reliable, and his gig was light. It was a perfect vehicle to get in and out of Saint Paul fast. He snapped his horse forward out of the livery, and entered the chaos of Bridge Square, the heart of commercial Minneapolis. A streetcar whizzed past, its gong sounding through the crisp air. People were on their way home, and he jockeyed for position with the other wagons, carriages and occasional sputtering automobile as he maneuvered towards the center of the avenue.

"Mr. Queen, Mr. Queen!"

There were so many sounds that he couldn't tell at first where the voice was coming from, but he yanked the reins to a halt when he saw Maisy come running up.

"Miss Anderson," he shouted, looking behind to make sure a wagon wasn't about to come barreling down on her. "Get out of the street!"

"Please let me aboard, Detective!"

Before he could say another word, she had run in front of Arthur and around to the passenger's side. They were right at the edge of a track, and he could see, from a distance, a streetcar moving towards them at a fair pace. She'd be clipped if she didn't get out of the way.

"Yes, yes, get on," he yelled.

He reached over to take her hand and she climbed up.

"That wasn't a very smart thing to do."

"I'm accustomed to peril." She turned to him and gave him a grateful smile.

"Your hotel is just over there. I'll turn around and . . ."

"No," she said, with a determined expression. "No."

"Miss Anderson, you can't accompany me. I have important business, and you have to get ready for your beau's important day."

"Trilly Flick told me where you were going. I want to come."

He looked at her clothes, and accepted that she was dressed for action. She wore a checked canvas wheeler skirt, with a divide that allowed her to move her legs more freely. It was meant to comfortably sit on a bicycle seat, but it would be good for movement all around. Her outfit was completed with a cloth shirtwaist, gloves, a hat, a tie and a bag, all in somber shades of gray. The bag he looked at again from the corner of his eye, as they bumped their way up the avenue. It was stuffed with what he suspected was one of her grandfather's pistols.

He said nothing, and they continued on.

An hour or so later, and she'd found herself back along the bluffs of Saint Paul. She'd never expected to come here again, and drew a breath as she caught glimpses of Little Italy on the levee, its dead-looking little shacks spread out amongst the mud and the weeds.

She was determined to gather her pluck, and see this adventure through to the end. It was both exciting and frightening, searching for the man who had tried to save her from Kilbane. She hoped that her presence might keep Henri alive, if things got too sticky. She would never endanger Detective Queen, but she still felt some loyalty to the man they hunted.

Unlike her, Queen was looking unconcerned about the night ahead. He rode with his face forward, lost deep in thought, and wearing the forlorn expression of someone who missed a girl. Maisy was also sure he was peeved at her for forcing herself into his buggy. Her expectation was that he'd attempt to drop her off somewhere before they reached Henri's hideout, and she planned to fight him tooth and nail on that decision.

When he suddenly turned the gig, it startled her for a second. She could feel the wheel on her side dip as it went slightly off the road, and then they began driving up-hill. The brothels lined along the road were all familiar to her, especially the one at the very end, and she suddenly understood his plan.

"You'll be safe here," he said, putting the reins on his lap. "Madame Clifford will be happy, I expect, to see you, and perhaps apologize for her part in your misfortunes. When I'm finished with my business, I'll be back."

She looked at the house. The lights were blazing, and she could hear the tink of piano music from inside. There were men inside, men whom she'd known in carnal ways, who would assume when she walked in that she was still an inmate for sale. She suddenly felt sick to her stomach at the thought of it.

"Detective Queen. I will not. This is nothing I want any part of."

"No one is expecting you to go to work, Miss Anderson. Just to sit in the parlor, with a glass of wine maybe, and catch up with your friends."

"No," she said, gripping the seat with her hands. "I will not. And if you force me from your buggy and into the door, I'll find a way to leave, and make my way on my own to find you. Trilly told me where you're going, so it's no secret."

"You can't let that happen, Queen," someone said from the dark. She followed the voice to a man who approached them. He was slender, mustached and stood straight as an arrow in his black suit and Homburg hat. "It's dangerous down on the landing at night. Far worse might happen to her if she wanders about alone."

Queen gave a grimacing nod. "Frasier, I'd like to introduce you to Miss Maisy Anderson. The granddaughter of Sheriff Dix Anderson."

He gave a quick bow and a smile, and held up a gas lantern. "Detective Frank Frasier, Miss Anderson. A pleasure to meet you."

"Likewise," she said. "Are you coming with us?"

"If there is room on the seat," he replied.

"If Miss Anderson doesn't mind the close quarters," Queen said, trying not to glower, "we'll have to make do."

This was not part of the plan, Queen thought, as he maneuvered the gig back down the hill towards the river. It wasn't a place for a woman, especially the granddaughter of a man he'd made a pledge to. When they reached the bottom, Queen strained his eyes to survey the landing, quickly darkening from the setting sun. He knew that gangs of toughs, hobos and drunken lumbermen all milled about on the river's edge at night, looking for trouble.

There was no real road, just a mess of railroad tracks with dirt trails alongside, but his gig was light and small, and a reliable vehicle for these conditions. Arthur wasn't easily spooked, either, at the hoots and laughter emitting from the shadows as they moved towards the steamboat landing.

"Tell me again what you know," Frasier said, his words rattling as they hit a deep bump.

"This man, Henri, managed his way into Kilbane's inner circle after Peach died," Queen said. "His real name is Seaver Loftus, and his real occupation is actor. He's got a houseboat moored somewhere along the landing, but it's old and unseaworthy, and he's making arrangements to buy a new one. In the meantime, we think he's planning, as part of his final bon voyage celebration, to harm Mayor Ames. He's got a grudge against men in power, and he's connected the mayor, in his ill mind, to some of the atrocities committed against the Sioux during the uprising forty years ago."

"Good Lord," Frasier replied. "That sounds convoluted. But he doesn't sound particularly dangerous."

"I know, from personal experience, how clever he is," Maisy piped in. "I saw him talk my Uncle Martin Baum into shooting Kilbane, but he let me go. I don't fear for my own safety when I'm around him, I can assure you."

Queen could hear the squeak of the seat as Frasier crossed his leg over the other knee. Almost imperceptibly, he heard the detective take in his breath.

"Do you have something you'd like to share with us, Frasier?" he asked.

"I have sad news, for the lady." The light of the lantern rose as the detective held it near Maisy's face. "I'm afraid your uncle is dead."

Upon hearing it, Maisy gasped, and held her hand over her mouth. "Are you certain?"

"We've no one to identify the body yet. His wife doesn't have a telephone, although we've sent her a telegram, requesting her at Central."

"What does he look like?"

"An older man. Balding. Spectacled. Fat."

"And what was he wearing?"

"A moth-infested brown suit, as dirty as the bottom of the Mississippi."

Queen tried to remember Baum's outfit when he'd encountered him in Madame Clifford's home, but the light had been bad and he'd been too preoccupied to pay proper attention.

"Those are his clothes," Maisy said. "Good riddance."

They crossed, silently, under both the Wabasha and the Robert bridges. A number of times Queen had to go over one of the criss-crossing railroad tracks, and it made the gig bend and lurch. On one particularly frightening tilt, he felt Miss Anderson tightly clutch his arm. He felt a flutter of excitement at her touch.

"Up ahead," Frasier said, pointing through the darkness. "Lambert's Landing."

Saint Paul's Union Station suddenly appeared on their left, lights twinkling inside. A series of railroad yard buildings lined the bank, and next to them, on the river, five steamboats sat, diagonally docked.

"Are you sure it's here?" Frasier asked. "This is not a landing for houseboats."

"This is the information I have," Queen replied, as he stopped the gig along a stone embankment. They all got down, and Queen patted Arthur on the head. "I'll be back soon," he said.

Frasier led the way with his lantern, and they crossed the tracks to the river. The river looked still, although he knew it was deceptively so. The Mississippi had an undercurrent beneath its calm surface that had drowned many poor souls. As an engine whistle wailed in the distance, they walked along the river's edge, peering down at the steamboats from between the yard shacks.

A man appeared, sitting on the upstairs deck of a particularly plush-looking steamer. Dim lantern lights lined the rails and the man waved at them through the darkness.

"Ahoy!" Frasier shouted in return. "Have you seen a houseboat, perchance, in these waters?"

Queen winced at Frasier's piercing tone. He had heard that the detective was forward, but giving away the element of surprise was stupid and careless. Nonetheless, Frasier got his answer. The man on the deck nodded enthusiastically, and pointed to the next boat over. "There's a shabby old dinghy anchored on the other side," he called, "manned by a crew of mangy-lookin' mongrels!"

Christ, Queen thought. He sounds like a pirate in a Robert Louis Stevenson novel.

Frasier was already on the move, down a set of stairs toward the water, and they followed, Queen making sure that Maisy was safely between them. A narrow wooden wharf hugged the bank, and they crept along, past the second steamboat.

"Stop here," he whispered. Frasier turned, looking amusedly at Queen.

"Getting cold feet?"

"I don't want Miss Anderson to take a step further. We don't know what is waiting for us."

"Yes, we do," Frasier replied. "A failed actor, to use your words. This will be over in ten minutes. Let her watch things unfold if she cares to."

"I won't," Queen declared. Her safety was a heavy responsibility, and he'd already taken this too far. "Please, Miss Anderson, stay here."

She wanted to continue, he could sense. However, she nodded her consent.

"Take out your pistol," he said. She nodded again, and unbuttoned her bag. It looked like a cannon in her dainty hand, but she pulled back the hammer like a professional, and he heard Frasier chuckle.

"I think Miss Anderson knows how to use that six-shooter."

"My grandfather took me target shooting when I was little. He made sure that I knew my way around a gun."

"And is she spoken for, Queen?" Frasier asked, with an admiring stare.

Queen ignored his question, and turned to her. "Keep an alert eye."

"I will. Please be careful as well."

"Not to worry. I play a caged game, miss." He turned to Frasier. "Let's go."

CHAPTER 30

The boat was where the river pirate had said it would be. It was an ugly looking heap, a crude cabin built atop what looked to be the hull of an old scow. The letters were hard to read, but he could make out the words 'LES MAGNIFICANTS' painted along the side. If an acting troupe owned a boat, in his mind's eye it would look exactly like this.

"Let's figure out a way to board," Queen whispered.

"Nonsense," Frasier returned, and picked up a tin can, hurling it at one of the cabin windows. "Time to give it up, Mr. Loftus!" he shouted. "Come out with your hands high!"

Silence, for seconds, and then a light turned up inside.

"See," Frasier said, with a nudge at Queen's shoulder. "If you show them you mean business, then even the lowest life forms will give you respect."

Queen felt his anger rise at Frasier's patronizing tone, and fumbled in his brain for a quick and appropriate retort, when he saw two figures on the dock running towards them, with what appeared to be guns in hand.

"Watch it!" Queen yelled as he pulled his revolver out of its holster and pushed his way against the shelter of the bank. His foot slipped off the planks, and he suddenly went into the water, but it was only knee deep. He regained his balance, crouching low. "Get down," he hissed. Frasier paid him no mind.

The darkened outlines came into view. They were both gaunt-looking men, dressed in gaudy vaudeville costumes. What in tarnation were these two all about, Queen wondered? Were these motley fellows really associates of Loftus? And why did Frasier look so goddamn unconcerned? Queen drew a bead with his revolver at the bedraggled actors, but Frasier was already striding towards them, blocking his shot.

Christ, he's going to get himself cut down.

And then Queen remembered the stories of Frasier's coolness, and realized he was watching the man in his element.

"Put your guns down," Frasier said with a resolute voice.

"Hell no," cried one of the men. Queen could see their expressions now, and they were even more surprised than he was over Frasier's brash behavior.

"I don't want to repeat myself," the detective said. His pace didn't slow, either, and the men in front of him panicked at his approach. The taller of the two shoved his gun in his pocket, and threw up his hands. Queen couldn't believe what he was seeing. The other, who was more skittish and, Queen suspected, tight in the throes of booze, backed up, but still held out his gun, pointing it shakily at Frasier.

"Don't come near me, bull," he shouted. "You're nothing but mindless muscle for industrialists!"

"You're a smart young fellow," said Frasier. "You recognize that I'm a Saint Paul detective. There's no point in continuing like this, son. Put it down and chuck up your hands like your *comrade.*"

Queen was transfixed at his absolute boldness, and felt a twinge of jealousy that he would never be so brave. But a sound from the houseboat drew his attention, and he turned to see the man he had chased, with his wool sash swaying from its knot at his side, untying the boat at its bow. Then the man moved to the side, and pulled a long wooden pole off the deck. He shoved the end into the water and walked it along the starboard side, inching the boat from its mooring.

Frasier glanced back too. "Make sure he doesn't leave, Queen," he shouted.

"Hell," Queen muttered, thinking about his bad knees. He pulled himself from the muck and crawled onto the wooden-planked wharf. The houseboat was drifting into the river, but blindly leaping across the dark watery chasm was out of the realm of possibility. Instead, in desperation, he scoured the pier, finally settling his eyes on the steamboat docked next to the houseboat's slip.

Its gangway was extended, and Queen clambered aboard. He ran along the side of the deck as he holstered his pistol, matching pace with the houseboat. The man who pushed the pole was on the other side and out of view, but he was obviously a muscular brute, because it was easing out much more quickly than it would have under a normal man's power.

Queen knew his opportunity wouldn't last, and with great regret he hoisted himself onto the wrought-iron rail. With steeled attention, he watched the houseboat's movement, and realized it would soon be too far away for him to jump.

He gritted his teeth, bent his knees and leaped to the houseboat's deck. He landed, rolled, and grabbed his knee as it screamed in pain. Willing himself to ignore the searing burn, he grabbed his pistol from its holster and pulled himself onto his feet. He felt the cool river breeze on his neck, and turned around to see that he'd landed in the boat's aft. If the houseboat had been a few feet farther away he was certain he'd have dropped into the dark, choppy current.

A noise, like a heavy footstep, suddenly came from the top of the cabin. He took a step back and craned his neck up to see, and then felt the weight of a body come down hard on top of him, knocking him down. The gun flew from Queen's hand, and he heard it skitter across the deck. The man who pinned him stared directly into his face. He had a cropped head of white hair, and a face lined like a deep maze.

"*Mon ami*," he said. "I have nothing against you personally."

"How about the fact that I take orders from Mayor Ames?" he huffed, trying to catch his breath. "Does that change your opinion of me?"

"I do not know Mayor Ames," the man said with a little frown. "But he is from Minneapolis, no? Why would you come here, just for me?"

"Why would you send the mayor a letter threatening to kill him?"

"I don't believe," the man said with a gentle smile, "that I'm under any obligation to answer you. I have the upper hand."

"You're wax, Loftus. The jig is up. I know your real name, I know your history at the Theater Comique and I know you're suddenly tin-rich."

"Ha!" The man shifted his weight onto Queen's chest, crushing it with his own. "You know the truth, eh? Or is it simply the truth as you perceive it?"

"I know you're not French. I know you had Martin Baum rub out Kilbane, and I know you took a raft of green that was never yours."

"From what I've heard," Loftus replied, "you wanted Kilbane, how do you Americans say it? In a domino box? I did us both a good turn."

"Quit with the one-minute act, Loftus. You're as American as John Philip Sousa conducting 'Stars and Stripes Forever' on a Fourth of July picnic in Washington D.C."

And this mercurial grifter also knew who Queen was. It wasn't actually such a surprise, he thought. If Loftus had the brains and moxie to toady his way to Jiggs Kilbane's right side, he'd most likely done some thorough research on potential adversaries. And Loftus had performed plenty of research as a failed playwright, had he not? It would have been easy for him to gather his information and bide his time, while using his evident stage combat skills and acting ability to infiltrate the gangster's inner circle.

One thing was obvious: the man was tough as nails. He had the detective on the ropes, after all. Queen barely had room to wriggle under Loftus's weight.

"I understand that your brief foray into the world of play writing fifteen years ago poisoned your views towards Captain Hill and your critics, but how does that lead to anarchy?"

"I owe you no explanations, detective." He put his hand around Queen's throat and began to slowly squeeze. "I'm giving you the courtesy of actually speaking to you now, because I pity you and your false beliefs. Even under more casual circumstances, I'd refuse to acknowledge your phony authority. But none of that matters now. Your doctor will be dead at tomorrow morning's graduation ceremony, and there will be nothing you can do."

Queen could do nothing more than give a short gasp as his windpipe closed. Then pure panic followed as his head went light and he watched the skyline of Saint Paul begin to spin in a million flashes of electric light. He grabbed at Loftus's forearms, but they were made of solid muscle and didn't budge. This is not how he wanted things to end, he told himself, tears welling involuntarily in his eyes. In desperation he pounded on the man's back, and then jabbed at his face, but his aim was wobbly and his strength was weak, and Loftus remained calm. Not even a flinch.

Queen's chest heaved as he fought for a precious breath of air. His eyes closed, and he fought back the darkness that was trying to take grip. Loftus bent over him, tightening his death-choke even more, and Queen felt his hands tearing at the wool sash around the man's waist, trying to rip it off. He thought for a split second about forming a garrote with the fabric to strangle his attacker.

But then the man's coat fell open and Queen heard a clink against the wooden deck. His fingers probed and he snatched the object up, feeling its shape to confirm its identity.

It was an awl, it was sharp, and it was his goddamn lucky day.

Queen swung it into Loftus's shoulder, and felt the man's fingers release his throat. He heaved the awl forward again, this time into Loftus's chest. His foe grunted and fell back with a grimace, holding the wound with the palm of his hand. Queen lunged for his gun as he sucked in the wondrous night air, grateful to be breathing again. Revolver in hand, he whipped around, but Loftus was gone.

Then a sound of a splash, and Queen dragged himself to the side and looked over. Loftus was swimming now, swimming upstream at a breakneck pace. That takes one hell of a load of stamina, he thought, to brave the icy spring water. He watched in awe and disbelief as Loftus moved past the Robert Street Bridge, his arms arcing through the water in strong, swift motions.

CHAPTER 31

The desire to be part of the action was too strong for her to stay back. She'd hiked up her skirt like a sailor, sneaked forward to the sounds of the detectives' voices, and had watched, enraptured, as Frasier had strolled up to the men without even drawing his weapon. She then saw Queen board the steamboat, jump to the houseboat, and scuffle with Henri on the deck. She'd also heard the splash and was worried that Detective Queen might have fallen overboard. She'd run back to where she'd seen a rowboat bobbing in the murky water close to the dock, and had clambered in and started rowing.

There was nothing a man could do that she couldn't, she knew, thanks to her grandfather's careful tutelage, and she'd rowed boats many times in the lakes of northern Minnesota. It was easy for her to get her rhythm, and soon had reached the edge of the houseboat's rusty hull. She looked up, and Queen looked down.

"You were supposed to wait."

"I apologize for not minding your request, detective, but time is of the essence. He's almost to the island."

She held her hand to the scow to stabilize the rowboat, and watched Queen lift himself over the side and drop into the boat with a grunt. They looked at each other for a moment in the bobbing boat.

"Thank you," he said. "I'll take those oars, Miss Anderson, if you'd be so kind."

While she knew she could row the boat across the river herself, she didn't want to get in the way of chivalry either, so she acquiesced and passed the handles to him. He began his clumsy strokes, and coughed a little to get his breath.

"Perhaps it is better that you watch for where he goes ashore. My eyesight isn't as good as yours, I fear," she lied.

"Very well, Miss Anderson." He twisted his torso to see over the dark waters, and she took back the oars. They glided forward through the night, under the sweeping city bridges. It was twenty minutes of firm rowing before she caught a glimpse of Henri, swimming under a patch of moonlight. He was headed towards Harriet Island. Above the black water stood a long pavilion with a series of doors. A peaked gable in the very center appeared to mark the main entrance from the beach side.

"Those are the Saint Paul Free Public Baths," she said, to break the silence, and because her nerves were tense. "Have you heard of those, Detective Queen?"

"Only second hand, in conversation. How do people get to the island from the opposite side?"

"There is a long footbridge which connects the two. It opened last year for the first time and the new season starts in July. Many people in Saint Paul have no water to bathe in, and it's healthy in the summer months. Only two pennies, for a suit, towel and a cake of soap. Madame Clifford escorted us twice, last year. She warned us not to burn our backs while sunning," she said with a grim chuckle.

Queen looked back at her, but wasn't willing to share her joke. She got the sense from him that young women in brothels did not amuse him in any way.

"Let me at those oars, Miss Anderson. You've had enough," he said, and before she could answer, he had taken them from her, and was pulling with all his might on a slow but firm course towards the brink.

The shore of Harriet Island had no easy place to land, at least not with the river this high. Two feet of water covered the white-sand beach, and it lapped up against a cement embankment. Maisy sunk the oar into sand and tried to keep the rocking boat steady, as Queen stretched his foot to dry land. His knees creaked and cracked but he managed to pull himself to a full stand.

"Hand me the rope," he said. She complied, tossing the end into his hands. He tied it to an iron mooring sunk into the concrete.

"Shout if you need me," he whispered, and turned to survey the grounds.

The moon's light spilled across the set of stairs nearest him, revealing wet footprints. They led to the pavilion, and he followed, watching the windows and doors for any sign of movement.

Queen considered what he'd actually do if he caught this rogue actor. Seaver Loftus was twenty years older than him at least, but in far better physical condition. Queen had his pistol, which was his only chance, but it was a good one. There had been no sign that Loftus had a gun of his own, so he hoped that would be his advantage.

The watery prints led up to one of the pavilion's doors, but then continued on. Queen tried the door. It was locked. He continued along the building's side, watching the prints get fainter and fainter, until the water had disappeared and he no longer had a trail. His finger touched his revolver's trigger, and he listened for any noise. The scuff of a shoe on a cement pathway, perhaps, or the heavy breaths of a man who had just swam across an ice-cold river. Seaver Loftus, however, if near by, was skilled at keeping silent.

Once he reached the end of the pavilion, he eased his way around the corner, and continued forward. Even in the dark, he could tell that it was a beautifully groomed space, with trimmed grass and large shade trees to help keep people cool as they ate their lunches in the heat of summer. What a wonderful place to visit with Karoline, he thought, then immediately kicked himself for thinking it. He was chasing a possible assassin, and could ill afford idle thoughts of love.

"Detective Queen."

He heard the voice from above, and slammed his body against the wall. There was no way this bastard was going to jump from a roof onto him again.

"Detective Queen. I don't have a gun."

"I figured so."

"I'd like to make a deal with you."

"Why would you do that? I thought you don't speak to people in positions of authority. And I, as sure as hell, am that." Queen was ready to collapse, and this man had climbed up onto a building after swimming up river. How did he do it, and what was his game?

"I have a good vantage point here," the actor called down, "and your friend, the Saint Paul detective, is approaching the foot bridge. It's the only way out, except for your boat."

"Why don't you make a deal with him, then?"

He heard Loftus give a weary laugh. "We both know he doesn't make deals."

"But I do?"

Another laugh. "Yes. You work for Mayor Ames."

"Who you want to kill."

"The thought had crossed my mind, I will admit."

"But now you don't?"

"I will leave Minnesota tonight, I swear, and never, ever come back."

A trickle of dirt fell over the side, and the man's feet suddenly swung over.

"I have to sit down, Detective. That swim made me tired. Please, let me tell you my terms."

Queen said nothing, and rubbed his sore shoulder.

"I have over ten thousand dollars in a satchel next to me, and I'd like to give you half of it. How much do you make in one month?"

"Seventy dollars."

"I know you have other sources of income, detective, far greater than your petty salary. Those of us who pay attention to these things know that you're on the take in a thousand different ways. But five thousand can make you that much more comfortable."

"You're a hoo-doo, Loftus. A charlatan and a petty thief. You've been prancing about town faking a French accent and pretending to be a gangster. How do I know you're not working a sharp bargain on me right now?"

"I'm simply a humble actor, detective. I'm not a con artist. I only want a way out of my unfortunate situation."

"And If I'm so goddamn rich, why do I need your cush?"

Loftus slid off the roof, his satchel in hand, and landed like a cat in front of Queen.

"Once corrupt, always corrupt, *mon ami*." He handed the bag to Queen and smiled.

CHAPTER 32

A raindrop splattered on his forehead, and he opened his eyes. Next to him, her head on his shoulder, was Maisy.

The detective straightened carefully, so as not to disturb her. They had fallen asleep on the seat of his gig.

He looked up at the ominous sky, swirled in gray shades, and he pulled his derby down tight. How in the hell could they have fallen asleep in the worst part of Saint Paul? He patted his pockets, and his gun was still there. So was his watch, and his roll of bills. Had they really made it through the night without being robbed, beaten or worse? What a lucky turn that had been.

Then Arthur, who must have heard him wake, gave a whinny, and it brought Maisy's head up.

"Good morning," he said.

"We were only going to close our eyes for a few minutes," she said groggily. Her shoulder lingered on Queen's for a moment, and the detective felt a guilty stir of arousal.

"It was longer than that."

"What time is it?"

He looked at his watch. "Nine-thirty."

"But the graduation ceremony starts at ten. And I've been out all night! What will Dick think?" Alarm eclipsed her face, and she looked at Queen beseechingly. "We must go. I must change!"

They jerked forward, and headed back along the tracks the way they'd come. A morning mosquito buzzed in Queen's ear, and he slapped it dead on the side of his neck. He wiped the blood on his sleeve. The only blood shed last night, he thought gratefully, and mulled over the evening's events in his head. He'd remembered asking Frasier to both phone and telegraph City Hall to get a message to the Colonel that his anarchist had been captured. With any luck Doc is back in his old jovial spirits this morning, he thought, and eager to give his speech.

"I slept in the boat on the way back across, didn't I? I don't remember how things ended last night," Maisy admitted.

"Loftus was arrested, without being harmed."

"I'm glad for that," she replied. "Did he ask about me?"

He shook his head. "There was no time. Frasier marched up and snapped on the cuffs before we could make small talk."

"But did he know I was here?"

"He knew we had a boat. He must have seen you from his perch on the roof. You couldn't see him, I gather?"

"It was too dark."

"Well, it's all for the best." With a snap of his wrist, he encouraged Arthur to pick up his speed.

"Do you have a cigarette?" she suddenly asked. Queen lifted an eyebrow, surprised, and dived into his pocket for his case. "Help yourself," he said, clicking it open with one expert hand.

She put one in her mouth, and he reached for his matches, but something else from his pocket fell to the floor.

"Can you pick that up for me?"

"Certainly," she said. She bent down and snatched the letter that threatened Doc between her fingers. Before Queen could protest, she had the envelope open and was hurriedly reading the paper's contents.

"Miss Anderson," he said, "please, you cannot read that. It is evidence . . ."

"Who wrote it?" she asked, her voice tight.

"I cannot divulge . . ."

"Was it Henri?"

"That is a police affair and . . ."

She scrambled for her handbag, and ripped it open. First came the .45, and she tossed it on the seat. Then came a small book, and she opened it wide and began tearing through the pages, looking, it seemed, for something specific. She finally settled on a page, brought it up to her face, and let out a moan.

"What is it?"

"Pull over, now."

He saw the wild expression on her face and yanked Arthur to a stop.

"What did you find?"

"Look," she said, pointing to some scribble on one of the page's margins. "This is Henri's handwriting. There are lots of loops and flourishes, and it's messy." Then she shoved the letter at Queen. "This handwriting here is neat and legible. They look nothing alike!"

Son-of-a-bitch, Queen thought. Son-of-a-bitch.

This wasn't over yet, it seemed.

Queen considered finding a telephone to call City Hall and warn them, but he knew the Ames brothers wouldn't be there this early, and tracking them down would take too much time. It would be faster, he decided, to drive straight to the campus himself.

They blew past the State Capitol, and turned west on University Avenue, right past Jiggs Kilbane's gambling resort. He wanted a nice direct route to the University, and this was it. The avenue was a pleasant one, marked by stately homes and the occasional store or commercial building, and as they drew towards the half-way point to Minneapolis, the houses got more spread out, interrupted now by fields of wild grass and farmhouses.

"I'm sorry we don't have time for fresh sets of clothes," he said.

"What will we do when we get there?" she asked him. Her

fingers tapped on her bag.

"You won't do anything," he said. "And I must insist on that. There will be thousands of people attending, and if something terrible happens, things may erupt into a chaos that no police department could ever control."

"What will you do, then?"

"I'm not exactly sure, honestly," he replied, giving her a sideways glance. "I never quite know until I'm faced with the danger head on."

"Like Frank Frasier."

"Except I don't walk up to armed men with my hands in my pockets. I'm no fool." But after he said it, he realized the words rang hollow. Frasier had done just that, and made three arrests in his composed and uncompromising fashion.

Maisy stopped talking, and dropped into deep thought, it seemed, staring through the passing scenery. Her concern about Moonlight was obvious, and it touched him greatly. After all of the torment and grief she'd endured, she could still find a place in her heart to love.

There was something about this woman next to him, this woman who had fallen asleep on his shoulder so innocently, without fear of scandal or shame.

It was some intangible, wonderful quality that he couldn't quite articulate. She had both the grit and the goodness of Karoline, but just enough of Trilly's bewitchery to give him a fit of impure thoughts, if he allowed it. He thought during his search for her that he'd find satisfaction once he'd made her safe. But now, he realized, he wasn't satisfied simply to have completed his task. There was a genuine affection, far deeper than a mere acquaintanceship.

And he had no idea how to act on his thoughts. And he knew that for her sake and his, he never should or would.

They continued to ride silently along, thumping and shaking over a section of decaying cedar block road. Towering trees soon ushered them to the edge of the University of Minnesota campus. The streets were lined with carriages, and he could see a streetcar emptying out students and their families to partake in the ceremony. He pulled out his watch and looked at the time. It was ten o'clock. They'd made good time, but still were late. The commencement would begin shortly, and they needed to get there immediately.

To start with, he decided to assert his authority as Chief of Detectives and took the gig right up to the Armory. The Armory was an imposing structure with the shape and aura of a Norman castle. It was a three-story building constructed of white brick, and broken by a massive tower. Laid out in front was a huge drilling space for student officers-in-training. To its side was Northrup Field, where Moonlight had led his Gophers football team victorious over a host of visiting schools.

It was drizzling steadily now, and the sky was overcast. He could make out, at the head of a giant procession of people, the university president, Cyrus Northrup, dressed in a purple gown, a gold tassel swinging from his cap. Mayor Ames was next to him, looking regal in his own flowing robe, and clearly enjoying the pomp of the occasion. The rest of the regents and faculty followed behind them, leading a massive group of proud graduates and their families to the Armory's auditorium, where the speeches would commence. A gust of wind suddenly whipped across the group, destroying coiffures and absconding with hats, but the mood stayed bright. Even the University of Minnesota marching band's bass drum player managed to keep his drum steady through the unexpected breeze, as they played a rousing march alongside the joyous procession.

He took the gig as close to the Armory as he could without raising suspicion, and left it standing in the middle of the road leading to the building.

Queen turned to Maisy. "What are the chances of you waiting for me here?"

"They aren't good, detective. I desperately want to see Dick."

"I'll escort you to the building, but at least do me the favor of staying in back. Can you promise me that, at least?"

She nodded, and he knew it was the best he would get.

She took his arm, and they half-walked, half-ran to the building. Her breath, soft to his neck, was warm and sweet, and he savored their brief, intimate trip together, despite his apprehension over assassins and anarchists.

And in what seemed like only a few racing heartbeats later, they were at the front door. He'd made it in just the nick of time, but for what, he didn't know.

CHAPTER 33

The auditorium was packed, so much so that students in shirtsleeves were carrying in folding chairs to make seating in the aisles. Maroon and gold bunting hung from the ceiling, creating a festive atmosphere for the ceremony. Queen pushed his way through, searching for anyone he might be able to rally: patrolmen, detectives, or Colonel Ames himself, but crowds were thick and it was noisy.

Propriety had gotten the better of him once they'd passed through the entrance. He needed to look official, and not as though he were out on a romantic campus stroll, so he'd separated his arm from Maisy and moved ahead of her in his effort to make the most of his short time. But she was still running behind him, immediately breaking her promise to stay back. He almost had to laugh at that, that he'd had any expectation that Maisy Anderson would do anything other than what she wanted to.

And it endeared her to him even more.

He felt her tap on his shoulder and he turned. She pointed to a balcony above them, where Moonlight Darling was holding court. A mob of fans had gathered around him, waving their programs and clamoring for an autograph. The kid's grin stretched across his handsome face, joking and laughing with his admirers.

"Dick!" Maisy suddenly screamed through the hall, so loudly that it cleared the rest of the din. Moonlight looked back, saw her, and waved his hand until Queen was sure it would fall off.

"Hello! Hello Maisy! Where have you been?" he cried in return. A couple of his friends grabbed his arms and then, in a flash, they'd lowered him from the balcony, and men below clutched him and brought him down. The auditorium erupted in cheers, and Moonlight took off his hat and gave a silly bow. Then the mob in the aisle parted, and he galloped towards Queen and Maisy, amidst a flurry of ardent applause.

Queen looked at Maisy's enchanted expression, and was shocked that he suddenly felt a jolt of jealousy course through him like electricity.

How could he be envious of this young man and woman, who had found love through such fortuity? The kid was smart and good-natured and protective of Maisy. It was everything she needed and deserved. Nonetheless he knew he was failing miserably at masking the pain on his face. When he looked up at the approaching Moonlight Darling, the boy gave him a strange glance. He knows, thought Queen, a wave of unease enveloping him.

Christ, he realized. I've just bared my soul to the kid. And if Moonlight comes any closer, I'm going to baste his face with a right hook.

Without a word to Maisy, the detective disappeared into the crowd.

A man in a black coat and white clerical collar walked onto the stage. He opened a Bible, and everyone began to hush.

"Detective Queen is off in a hurry," Moonlight observed in a whisper to her, as they embraced.

"He's busy doing his police duties," she replied, not able to withhold a smile. She was sure he'd missed the real meaning of what had just happened, but she was too giddy to care. Moonlight Dick Darling, in the middle of a giant auditorium, had just publicly professed his love for her, and only her. He could have his pick of any young female here, but he chose her. Her!

Her fears were finally starting to melt away. This was no secret visit in the dead of night, with no one to see. He wasn't embarrassed or ashamed of her, and his shout to her in the balcony was all the proof she'd needed. There was no way she could ever express to him the overwhelming relief and delight at this moment. So she simply smiled again, and was surprised when he blushed.

"I've got no family here," he said. His slick black hair had flopped into his eyes again, and she gently pushed it back into place. "Would you mind sitting next to me?"

Of course she wanted to be beside him, but she also needed to help Detective Queen. She felt Dick take her hand in his, though, and it felt so good to be with him on this special day, and to share it with him. He led her to the front row, and they sat down.

"I want to marry you, Miss Anderson. I want to jump out of this town and marry you. We can go today, as soon I've got my sheepskin."

"But you've been offered a job . . ."

"Which was real swell, I suppose, but I don't want it. I've packed our bags," he said, a faint smile on his face. "President Northrup has asked me to say a few words to my classmates. Once I'm finished, will you meet me outside? My father's carriage is waiting, with a man to drive."

"Where will we go, Dick?"

"You'll see," he said. "You won't want for anything, sweetheart. I've got plans for us. How would you like to live out life with me in a little cottage by the Pacific Ocean? Right up on the bluffs amongst the seagulls?"

"It sounds wonderful," she said, and held his hand against her cheek. What joy, she thought dizzily. It was joy that she'd never imagined experiencing in her life. She decided, at this very moment, that their relationship would start afresh. If he could continue to feel this way about her, even with her prostituting past, then she could forgive him for his dalliances as well. And the fact that he'd made such plans! Perhaps she was too quick to judge him on his maturity. He was making decisions for them, decisions that she approved of with every ounce of her being.

This, she thought, was what happiness truly felt like. The anticipation of their new life together was almost too much bliss to bear.

The lights dimmed, and the crowd grew silent. And as the minister started his prayer, Maisy's head snapped out of her dream and back to reality.

There will be no special day if someone murders the mayor. Of course she and Detective Queen weren't sure it would happen for certain, but she couldn't live with herself if it did unfold, and she had sat idly by, watching the spectacle from the front row like a variety show.

I need to find a way to help. He's been so kind, and patient with me, and I want to prove my worth to him.

But the aisles were jammed with people, Dick hung tightly onto her hand, and the ceremony had begun.

"Come with me," Queen ordered, as soon as he spotted the duo of blue-coated officers standing near one of the exits. They stiffened, saluted, and followed him to the auditorium's foyer. It was close to empty now, as the last guests were trickling in.

"I'm not certain, but I think someone may be planning something devious today," he said. "You need to be alert, boys."

"But sir," one of the policemen replied, "we were told that the threat was over. Didn't you capture the anarchist behind the note?"

"No," he said, gritting his teeth. "I don't believe I did. How many of you have been stationed?"

"Only six of us. There were meant to be more, but the colonel canceled the extra details."

"Where is the colonel?"

"I don't know, sir."

Damn it, he thought. Any single one of the six thousand in attendance could be armed and ready to storm the stage, and there would be little he could do.

He walked back into the auditorium, and jostled himself through the aisles, under mutters from those he bumped and prodded. The prayer was over, and one of the regents approached the rostrum to make an introduction.

Queen scanned the balconies, looking for anything strange or out of place. Most of the faces were shadowed, however, and too many to sort. It seemed like such a monumental task, but he continued his search, feeling desperation in his throat, even as he heard Mayor Alonzo Ames' name, and a thunderous round of applause.

The mayor's familiar, booming voice belted out through the auditorium. "This splendid institution is the product of democracy; it is the implement of the purest democracy on earth for its security and its advance . . ."

Then suddenly he sensed a movement, just above him. He looked at the billowing bunting, tied to beams that crisscrossed the ceiling. And he saw the glint of metal. He watched it for a moment, and it disappeared. He rubbed his eyes and looked again, and then saw what he could have sworn was an eye blinking back at him. It was a man, suspended on the beam, and the man was holding a rifle. He was certain of it. And the man had seen him, in return.

Queen didn't know what to do. He couldn't shout out the danger. It would cause mass panic, and hundreds might be hurt or even killed in a mad dash for the doors. He knew he couldn't climb up there himself. The beam was narrower than his width, and even if he didn't lose his balance and plummet to the floor, crushing people below, what the hell would happen if he reached the man, who could simply twist back and shoot him dead? He looked again, but fortunately the decision was made for him. The man had seen him, and also seemed to have lost his nerve, as he scurried over the beam like a rat and back into the darkness.

A rat.

A *rat*.

He quickly racked his brain. Who in this world reminded him of a rat?

Holy hell, Queen thought. Could it be Pock?

He barged his way to the rear exit, stumbling over bodies and stepping on feet, and burst through into the foyer, just in time to see Pock bolt down a side stairway, rifle in hand, and straight to the front door.

"Pock!" he yelled at the top of his lungs. "Pock! You'll never get away!"

Pock was nothing but skin, bone and lean muscle. He flew down the steps and towards the drill ground, pumping his arms and legs through the rain like a well-oiled mechanical toy. Queen could barely catch his breath as he made it outside, and watched the man dash away, far faster than he could ever hope to.

And then he watched Pock fall.

It had been the rifle, and it had caught between his legs. The little man tumbled three or four times and then splattered on the soggy ground, arms and legs sprawled at his side.

Queen motioned to the two officers, and they sprinted out to collect him. They dragged Pock back, and he collapsed at Queen's feet.

"It's not what you think," he moaned. "It's not what you think."

Pock's eye patch was missing, probably from the fall, and his dead, milky eye stared to the right, as if guarding his flank from an enemy.

The detective kneeled down and grabbed him by his filthy collar.

"Did you really think you'd get away with this?"

He shook his head, and moaned again. "I ain't no anarchist, Queen. I ain't no anarchist."

"Could have fooled me. You and this goddamn rifle. First you shoot a girl off of a fence, and now you try for the mayor of the city."

Pock's head snapped up, and his good eye hammered into Queen's.

"You don't understand. I wasn't gonna shoot him. I was gonna protect him."

"Protect him from who? Who were you aiming at?" He snatched Pock's necktie and wrapped it around his hand. "Tell me, or I'm gonna cinch this so tight your peeper's gonna pop like a whip cracker."

Pock tried to shimmy away from Queen, but he took a handful of coat buttons and yanked him back.

"Spill, Pock. *Spill.*"

The man shrugged his bony little shoulders. "No one in particular, Queen. Ever vigilant, that's me. Like an eagle from the sky."

Queen stood up, and gave Pock a kick in his side. "Take the little shit to Central Station. Tell Colonel Ames we've got our man."

Moonlight rose when Doc's long-winded speech neared its end. Maisy knew it because she saw President Northrup in the wing, looking sternly at his watch.

"Go now," he whispered, and gave her an orange-scented kiss on the cheek. "I won't be long."

She watched him get up and move into the shadows of the stage's wing. Doc wiped a bit of spittle from his cheek, and finally stopped talking. The crowd applauded in rousing fashion. The mayor lit a grin under his bushy white mustache, and gave a brief bow. Maisy felt a great wave of relief envelop her. No one had made any attempt on his life. It had been a vile jest, and nothing more.

And then she felt a tap on her shoulder, and Chris Norbeck plopped into Moonlight's seat.

"Ain't this majestic?" he asked her with a wink. "All these chirpy bookworms wigglin' their tails in unison."

"Detective Norbeck . . ."

"Ah, call me Chris. All my sorry excuses for friends do. Care for a nip o' the necessary?" He pulled out a flask, and offered it to her.

"No, no thank you. I was just about to go . . ."

"But yer fella's about to talk!"

"Yes, but I need to visit the washroom."

"Hoots! Look at this," he said, ignoring her, and proudly held out a copy of the program. "I got yer beau's autograph. And he even wrote me a personal note. What a crack swell he is!"

She wanted to push it away, but he looked so genuinely earnest that she took it and read it out of pity.

Hello Chris

Glad to know you. Hope to meet you one day for a smoke-stick and a glass of bubbles.

Yours,
Moonlight

"I figure he means champagne by that," Norbeck said, looking thrilled at the prospect of an evening of drinking with a football star. "I prefer whiskey, but I'll fumble through the fizz for him."

Maisy's heart exploded in her chest. She opened her bag and tore out the envelope, ripping it open and yanking out the letter. Queen hadn't asked for it back, and she took advantage of his carelessness to hold the letter next to the program with shaking hands.

They were from the same writer, it was easy to see. She couldn't even begin to fathom it. She slid back into her chair, feeling utter repulsion in her realization of what had happened, or what was going to.

And then a huge cheer echoed through the auditorium as Moonlight Dick Darling strode to the lectern, a football under one arm and his diploma in the other. His lopsided grin took in the adulation, and then he looked at her and his smile grew bigger.

Did he see the shock in her face, she wondered? How could he not?

"Mayor Ames, would you mind stepping back out here for a moment?" Moonlight asked, and Doc strode out, beaming. They shook each other's hands and the football player spoke again.

"I know that this is highly irregular," Moonlight continued. "But I wanted to say how grateful I am to my professors for all of their encouragement. While I knew some thought me incorrigible . . ." The crowd bathed the room in laughter.

Maisy fumbled for the clasp on her handbag, trying to snap it open. Her hands were wet with sweat, and she wiped them on her dress.

". . . they had faith in me, and showed me how hard, dedicated work can bring success."

Is this why he wouldn't write to me, she wondered? Had he been covering his tracks, on some outside chance she'd discover his plan? She pulled out her grandfather's pistol, gripping it hard.

She lifted the weapon, and looked at Dick's stunned face, his jaw dropping as his eyes met hers. Her mind screamed with confusion, and her heart screamed with despair.

It couldn't be him.

Yet it had to be.

Her thumb pulled back the hammer in an instant, frozen in fear that she was wrong.

But she wasn't.

Dick reached into the seam of the football under his arm, and she caught the glimpse of an ivory handle. It was the matching pistol to the one she now held. She stared at the movement of his thumb, and how it moved towards a glimmer of metal buried in the football's stuffing.

And then she felt a stab of pain, as Chris Norbeck's hand came down on her arm, and the pistol clanked to the floor.

It was a blur to Queen as he watched it unfold. He was too far away to get to the stage, and he knew a clear shot was impossible.

And he'd forgotten, in his panic, about Doc's burly bodyguard, Fred Connor.

Connor leaped from the wings and before Moonlight could use his own weapon, he'd tackled him to the floor.

It was a sensational tackle, one that Moonlight, he was sure, hadn't seen in four years of dodging linemen and dashing for touchdowns. Connor pulled back his fist, the ruthless boxer inside him primed to throw the knockout punch, but the kid had already thrown up his hands. The gun in the football suddenly went off, sending bits of leather onto the stage. The crowd stood motionless, stunned.

Queen dropped his arm, gun in hand, to his side, watching the drama end as quickly as it began. No one had been hurt by the gunshot, thank the Lord above.

"What the deuce?" he muttered, and bent over to get his breath.

He looked up to see Doc's face, pallid with fear and befuddlement. Queen took advantage of the hush in the auditorium to make his presence known.

"Please, do not panic. I am Detective Harm Queen of the Minneapolis Police, and the danger is over," he shouted, raising up his badge and maneuvering his way to the stage. He shot up the stairs and strode to the lectern. I hope to Christ everyone keeps calm, he thought.

He watched Fred Connor yank Moonlight up onto his feet, and he saw him whisper something to the kid. Moonlight nodded weakly, and hung his head as Connor led him off stage. Queen looked at Doc to make sure he hadn't been harmed, but the old man was just shaking his head, still dazed.

Then he looked in the front row, and his eyes locked with Maisy's. Her lovely blue eyes were wet with tears, and he felt sickened at her anguish. Norbeck was still restraining her, but Queen shook his head at the detective, who released her arm.

Queen didn't know what to say. He looked to both sides of the stage, relieved to see President Northrup finally walk out to address the crowd. *I need to get Doc out of here,* he realized, and took the old man by the arm and led him out of view.

CHAPTER 34

Queen and Connor exchanged grim nods. Moonlight sat cuffed, on an upturned mop pail, his head between his legs.

"Is Doc all right?"

"He's lying down. There are two men with him, to make sure he isn't disturbed."

"Good," Queen replied. He thumped Connor between the shoulders. "Christ, he's lucky to have you, Fred."

"First bit of action I've had in a while." The bodyguard ran his hand over his hair, looking slightly amused. "What just happened?"

"I'll find out, soon enough." People were beginning to gather around. Curious, Queen knew, about their school's most famous student and his stage show. "Let's find a private place to question him," he said.

Queen lifted Moonlight by the arm and they led him from the darkened wing, past the onlookers, and into a room just off of a hallway. It appeared to be a makeshift greenroom, and Queen immediately shoved Moonlight down into one of the chairs as Connor closed the door.

"What were you thinking?" Queen growled, pushing Moonlight's head in frustration.

The kid looked up, a glint of anger hiding under glassed-over eyes.

"I-I-I'm not saying anything."

"You're not saying anything," Queen repeated, kicking the air in disgust. "That doesn't cut any ice with me. I know you were gunning for the mayor, you idiot."

Moonlight gave a low growl, pulled back his saliva, and spit a wad of cheesy mucus onto Queen's boot.

"You want to hear the truth? He's an oppressor. A despot. All of you are, who carry badges or wield authority like battering rams, running willy-nilly through the city without the fear of retribution. Imposing your will on the defenseless."

"Doc Ames, an oppressor?" Queen gave a bitter little laugh, shrugging off, momentarily, the shock of Moonlight's animosity towards him. "Of all the people with any modicum of power in this state, Doc is the least oppressive of any of them. Kid, he gives free medical care to anyone who asks. Can't turn a soul down, especially someone hard on their luck. He hands out hot meals and buys rounds after funerals!" The detective sat on the armrest of the chair next to Moonlight's. "This makes no goddamn sense. He offered you a job just yesterday, and you took it! What the hell gives?"

"He needed to be knocked off of his high and mighty horse. Brought down a few pegs, so he might realize what he's done."

"Listen, Moonlight. You're not in any way like your dad. You're not a murderer. I think you've been dunned."

The lad cringed, and Queen glanced at Connor, who winked back.

"Seaver Loftus put you up to this. Didn't he? Your father's thug?"

Moonlight closed his eyes and shook his head.

"This wasn't your idea, no matter how hard you might try to convince me." Queen took a cigarette out of his case. "Fred, do you want one?"

"I'm obliged, but no."

Queen lit his smoke and pulled a drag. The kid was a jumble of emotions, he knew, and didn't have the fortitude to assassinate the mayor in cold blood. Between the stress of a recently deceased father, final examinations and his romantic pursuits, the lad was ripe for being taken advantage of. All he needed to do was to calm

Moonlight down and explain the folly of using this ridiculous radical discourse anymore. Frasier had the real criminal, Seaver Loftus, already behind bars, and that is what mattered. If he could prove that Loftus influenced the kid somehow, a conspiracy charge could permanently seal the actor's fate.

Perhaps Queen could even twist things about a bit, and convince the mayor and the colonel that the threat had begun and ended with Seaver Loftus. Moonlight had a larger-than-life personality on campus, and who wouldn't believe that this was anything more than an ill-conceived prank? The star back of the Golden Gophers, firing a gun in the air through a football, in silly celebration of his graduation.

"Kid," he said. "Tell me the goddamn truth, and I think I can make it all go away."

And then his plan suddenly went to hell. Without warning the door flew open and Maisy rushed in, followed closely by a flustered-looking Norbeck.

"Oh Dick!" she cried when she saw him. "What have you done?"

Moonlight's eyes widened in surprise when he saw her, and then they narrowed in rage when he looked back to Queen.

Maisy gave a little gasp at his transformation, and Queen's heart wedged in his throat for the confrontation he knew was about to come.

"I'll tell you the truth, Mr. Queen," Moonlight snarled. "I was never going to kill anyone but you."

Maisy stopped dead in her tracks and absorbed Dick's words. Just minutes ago she'd wanted to rush into his arms, to apologize for raising a pistol at him, to plead for forgiveness for doubting his intent. In those moments after he'd been rushed off stage, she'd instantly regretted her decision to raise a weapon against the man who loved her more than life itself. There was more to the story, she told herself, as she'd battled the shaken crowd for the stage staircase, and then frantically tried each backstage door to find where Queen might had taken him. It'd been a mix-up, she was certain. There had to be an explanation for his brash and stupid action.

And now, she'd heard it.

She looked in horror at Detective Queen, who'd been so kind to her in the last day. Not only had he carefully and calmly answered all of her questions about her grandfather, but he'd also put up with her impetuous, headlong personality with the highest patience.

Queen looked back at her, and she was startled to see something more than mere compassion looking back, and it struck her harder than the back of Emil Dander's hand. Did Detective Queen have romantic feelings towards her? Had Dick found out? And if so, how could it have happened without her knowing any of it?

"Dick," she whispered, her face flushed and her eyes about to burst. "What do you mean?"

Her beau rattled the cuffs behind his back, and gave a groan. "Henri and I were friends, or so I'd thought. On the few occasions I'd visit for family dinner, my father would inevitably get sloshed and berate me in front of anyone within earshot. Henri must have sensed my frustration and anger. One day he pulled me aside, and said that he'd have him killed for me."

"That's a tall tale," Norbeck exclaimed, and gave a low whistle.

"I in turn," Moonlight continued with a sniffle, "only had to write a letter to Mayor Ames. Henri dictated, but it would be in my handwriting."

"Did the contents of that letter not arouse your suspicion?" Maisy asked, her nerves trembling at his revelation.

"Small price to pay, my dear, to have ol' Dad taken care of. You know how much I hated him. And so did you! It was for both of us in the end."

"But you knew that Henri planned to assassinate the mayor!"

"He said it was only a jest. Meant to put a bit of fear in the old man. Nothing more. But he was the one that took my dad's green, I'm sure of it, so I've got no reason to protect him."

She gave a glance to Queen, to see his reaction to all of this. The detective looked back, his face grave, and he shook his head.

"He meant for you to go down for this, or he wouldn't have asked you to do it. We can still get you out of this, Moonlight," he said. "Half of the people in the city have pointed a gun at me at one time or another, and I don't hold it against them. Why don't we let . . ."

"Screw!" Moonlight shouted with a feverish eye, quivering like a caged terrier ready to row before a dog fight. "You've handled me roughly, Queen. You'd like to make off with my woman? Is that it? I'd pound you into the floor if these cuffs weren't around my wrists. You're too damn fresh!"

More posturing over me, Maisy thought, and it made her sick to her stomach. This was a culmination of two years, she abruptly realized, as nothing more than an object of attention. She was a pretty little curio, high on a cabinet shelf, and these men all fancied her and then fought over her like a piece of steak in a poor house. Dander, Uncle Martin, Jiggs Kilbane. Even Detective Queen and Dick. They all desired her, and she wasn't sure she'd ever given them a real reason to. It was all so out of hand and insane. It was like she was a billiard ball on a pool hall table, getting knocked about without any say on her own fate.

"I don't know what I've done, kid, to make you think this," Queen said, his face slightly pale. "But a simple misunderstanding is an outrageous reason to kill someone."

"It was more than that," Moonlight croaked. "Maisy's uncle came and found me last night. He told me what you were really made of. He said you raped girls as a pastime, and that y-y-you'd do it to her. Like a mad, randy dog, he said!"

"He's alive? Is this a joke? Baum is a damn liar. I would never hurt the hair on a woman's head."

"It's no joke, Queen. He swore on his own daughter's grave that it was true."

"He doesn't have a daughter," spoke up Maisy. These were ludicrous accusations, and Dick was a fool to have ever believed a slippery sentence from Uncle Martin's mouth. She felt no emotion, either, at the thought of the fat old fraud still wandering the earth. She was exhausted, she suddenly realized, from all of this blind love, and wanted nothing more than to walk out of the room and not see any of them again. The loss of her grandfather, whom she hadn't even properly grieved yet, would be her priority now.

"Where is the bastard?" Queen snarled. "Where is he?"

"Long gone," said Moonlight. "On a train, far away from Minneapolis."

So it was at that moment that Maisy chose to exit. She turned to the door, not caring what happened in the room next. All she could think about was the feeling of absolute liberation in her decision.

"Maisy!" cried Moonlight, desperation in his voice.

"Miss Anderson," Queen said, taking a step towards her. She saw a hint of sadness in his eyes.

"Good bye," Maisy said, without turning around. And with a good, hard slam she shut the door.

A smile slipped across her lips, as she anticipated the possibilities.

EPILOGUE

Queen sat in a café, across a nicked-up table from Freddy Bonge, sipping cups of lukewarm, coffee-tainted water. It was a scorching hot day, and the fan whirled lazily above them. Bonge mopped his brow with a table napkin, taking in the story.

"So where is Baum?" he finally asked, picking up his pencil and touching it to a page in his notebook.

"As far as I know, he's on the other side of the country."

"How about Kilbane's money? The ten thousand big ones?"

"I don't know," Queen lied. The detective, in fact, did know. He had snatched the satchel of cush from Seaver Loftus just before the charlatan's arrest. Queen had meant it for Maisy, but after she'd stormed out of the Armory he'd let her be.

So, the fat stacks of tin were his for the moment. Stashed away in a safe little spot in the wall behind a radiator in the kitchen. Ready to use on a rainy day.

And he'd lied to Bonge about something else too. Well, not exactly *lied*. Instead he'd chosen to give the reporter only a bare skeleton of the real story, leaving out the drama of Moonlight, which he'd managed to officially wash away with the dishwater.

Both the colonel and the mayor agreed after hearing the yarn in its entirety that it would be better for everyone to keep the kid out of jail. They'd decided together that passing Moonlight's miscue off as a prank would avoid making the Minneapolis Police Department look incompetent, or God forbid, the administration look like an assembly of weak-kneed ninnies.

Of course there had been thousands of witnesses to Moonlight's misguided monkeyshines, but Doc Ames had tweaked the story of the gun in the football to make it appear that he'd been part of the jest all along; feigning fear when the pistol fired, but having a good ol' laugh over the "harmless" high jinks afterwards.

And there certainly would be no more invitation for Moonlight to join the ranks. Queen couldn't have that after their sour conversation backstage at the Armory. He didn't trust the kid as far as he could throw him, but, admittedly, he still liked him enough to want him to make a successful future. Hopefully that future would be in another state, far away from his father's tainted legacy, but he guessed that he'd see him again soon, in some way, shape or twisted form.

"So," Bonge said, leaning back in his chair. "You've painted a lovely picture. A rabid Irish thug in cahoots with a broken-down thespian. Add to that the malcontented drunkard Baum and you've got quite the hurly-burly on your hands. Anything else? Anything you're keeping close to your sleeve?"

"Like what?"

"A motive, Queen. What business would a drowned old pooch like Baum have cavorting with Saint Paul criminals? What dragged him off of his flea-infested mattress?"

The detective took a sip of his coffee. *I know what this damn snoop is up to,* he thought. *But I won't have Maisy squeezed through a wringer so the* Tribune *can peddle copies.*

"I haven't the slightest guess, Bonge. Why don't you find him and ask him yourself?"

The reporter grinned his toothy grin and pushed a newspaper across the table.

"Page twelve of the *The Bemidji Pioneer*. Not a rag you see in Minneapolis often, but I've managed to get my mitts on a copy. You'll find it interesting, I'm certain, and perhaps it'll jar loose your memory. Now if you'll excuse me, I have to make a call," Bonge stood and stretched his rubbery little arms high into the air, giving a lazy yawn. "Are you picking up the check, Detective? We word-slingers, whilst able to wax eloquent over innumerable subjects with wondrous ease, get paid in nothin' but bananas."

"I get it," Queen replied. "If Shakespeare had a trained monkey, it'd be you."

"Correct," Bonge chuckled. He scooped up his notebook and hat and scurried out of the café.

The reporter's prying questions left an acrid taste in Queen's mouth. But their deal was finished, now, and he could turn back to managing the Minneapolis rackets. He downed the last of his coffee, pulled out a coin, and laid it on the table. After a moment of hesitation, his curiosity aroused, he opened the paper to page twelve.

Immediately, his attention turned to a column under the headline "Town Notes". His eyes darted through the humdrum village news until they finally rested on a name he recognized.

Miss Maisy Anderson came up from Minneapolis Saturday. She is the granddaughter of former sheriff, D. Anderson, and here to settle his estate.

Queen felt a fleeting glimmer of regret at her mention. And all of the questions he'd been torturing himself with over the last few days rose back to the surface. What had he done to make her turn her back on him? How could she have ever deduced his true feelings, when he'd tried his damnedest to hide them from his own self? Christ, she is so lovely, he thought, as he closed the paper, folded it up, and stuffed it in his jacket pocket. Such a smart young woman, one who had pulled herself from the muck with immeasurable tenacity. He thought that he even might love her, but a growl from his throat tore that ill-conceived idea into bits.

He would be a father to her, not a lover. That was his role, and it was what she deserved. If she needed him, he would come.

Even if it meant killing Martin Baum. Or putting Moonlight Darling behind bars. Or suffering the company of Trilly Flick.

Whatever it took.

He wouldn't let her step off another train platform and into the arms of hell again.

But until the time when he was needed, he had his own work to do. And before he fell headfirst back into the city's machinations, he needed a proper christening. With a dry mouth and high expectations he took another coin from his pocket, and added it to the first.

"Waiter," he shouted, his fingers beckoning in impatient unison.

"What can I get, you sir?"

"Whiskey," he said, before the question even ended. "Double overalls from the top shelf and a Gluek to chase."

"Two shots and a beer," the waiter repeated.

His oath to Karoline was about to be smashed to pieces, but she was long gone and he was sure he didn't care. Back to making the goddamn green, he thought with a grimace. And a ready, open spigot of liquid fortitude would make it go down so much sweeter.

HISTORICAL NOTES

I was very excited, I must admit, to introduce Frank Frasier to *The Big Mitt* fold. Frasier was a real-life superhero, and the man police chief John O'Connor counted on to chase down high-profile criminals and keep his city safe. Frasier had the wonderful reputation of being able to make his arrests with nothing but his commanding presence. In June of 1901, he was still at the very beginning of his detective career, but later that summer, when Vice President Theodore Roosevelt visited the Minnesota State Fairgrounds to deliver his "speak softly and carry a big stick" speech, Frasier was hand-picked by Roosevelt as the Rough Rider's personal escort and bodyguard. I thought Frasier would be a great counterpart to Queen, as their investigatory styles and ethics are on opposite ends of the law-enforcement spectrum.

Nina Clifford is also an important part of this story's plot, and she was a very real woman who has taken on almost mythical status in Saint Paul history. In her time, she was as important a figure in Saint Paul politics as the police chief himself. Her bordello was considered the top of the line, and she entertained Saint Paul's elite for many, many years. One of Saint Paul's great unresolved bits of historical urban lore has been whether a tunnel existed between Nina Clifford's home and the Minnesota Club. Honestly, there is still no definitive answer. Back in 1997 a brief window of opportunity opened, courtesy of the Minnesota Science Museum, which was expanding its facilities. Unfortunately, archaeologists, while able to excavate the Bucket of Blood saloon and many of the brothels lining Washington, weren't able to fully explore the basement of Clifford's personal residence. Their concern was that it was too close to the actual bluff supports, and didn't want to interfere with that structural system. And while the Minnesota Club building has long been a cornerstone of Rice Park, it wasn't actually built until 1915. But because the Minnesota Club building and Clifford's brothel (which operated from 1889 to 1929) are entwined so tightly together in Saint Paul lore, I chose to move that history forward fifteen years for the benefit of the plot. Interestingly, the Metropolitan Hotel, which preceded the Minnesota Club building, was the headquarters of another gentleman's group, called the "Twilight Club". So, it isn't a stretch to assume that the relationship between Nina Clifford and the randy men who frequented her establishment, (just a drunken hike away) had a business relationship that went far, far back. And the Minnesota Club building today still has a sealed door in its basement that, if opened, could answer this unsolved mystery of the tunnel. For once and for all.

No assassination attempt was ever made on Doc Ames, although in real life he'd made comments in interviews that document his fear of an assassin's bullet. Anarchy was, indeed, a widespread movement amongst western countries at the turn of the century. In America, the gilded-age excesses of industrialists like Rockefeller and Carnegie enraged many in the working classes. In fact, in the fall of 1901, U.S. President William McKinley would be gunned down by a self-proclaimed anarchist. So the threats, while probably far-fetched for the Ames camp, still had a sound basis in that period's history. And to be clear, the 1901 University of Minnesota graduation went off without a hitch. Doc Ames wasn't actually invited to give the commencement speech. That was made by President Andrew Sloan Draper of the University of Illinois. The words I had Ames utter in his address in fact were taken directly from President Draper's speech.

One of the most entertaining parts of writing a historical novel is discovering unique period locations that in many cases have been forgotten completely. The cave saloon, known in its day as the *"Felsenkeller,"* must have been an incredible place, with a bowling alley and staircase hand-cut from soft sandstone some of the interior highlights. The only known evidence of its existence comes from an 1891 fire insurance map and a couple of sketches in an 1880s travel magazine. The Saint Paul Public Baths on Harriet Island opened every July to help Saint Paulites beat the summer heat. They were built not only to give relief, but to combat filth and disease, especially for those living in cramped, unsanitary downtown quarters. In Minneapolis, the Theater Comique was the site of some of the most lewd and provocative shows in the city. Among others, the scandalous "can-can" debuted there to scathing criticism by God-fearing civic and church leaders in the 1880s. Nina Clifford's brothel, and the surrounding brothels and saloons in the Italian district on the lower levee added their own special character to Saint Paul. Minnesota historian Jim Sazevich helped me tremendously in filling out some of the detail of the red light district on Washington Avenue, and is a local expert on the history of Nina Clifford.

My sister Alison, as always, is my loyal beta-reader, and read each first-draft chapter with enthusiasm and speed. My other sister, Jen acts as my research assistant when required; on call to visit the bowels of the Minnesota Historical Society for documents I can't get online.

It's been great fun writing this second book in the Harm Queen series, and I look forward to revisiting Detective Queen, Maisy Anderson and the Ames brothers in the next.

If you haven't had a chance to read the first novel in the series, "The Big Mitt", it is available at Amazon, Barnes and Noble online, and many local bookstores.

Also, if you have the time or inclination, visit my author website at www.ErikRivenes.com. For more historical crime stories, go to www.MostNotorious.com. You can also check out and "like" www.facebook.com/TheBigMitt for the latest in series information.

www.ingramcontent.com/pod-product-compliance
Lightning Source LLC
Chambersburg PA
CBHW022157260626
47155CB00019B/3069